Lovesick

KATIE CROSS

KCW

Contents

To the OG's: Sam, Kristen, and McKenna.
Thanks for the late-night dates.
Having my back.
And always making me laugh.

You light up my life.

This book takes place five years after the previous book, *Coffee Shop Girl*.

For those of you who have read my book *I Am Girl Power* from the *Health and Happiness Society* series (not something that needs to be read before this book), then you'll recognize Lizbeth as the barista from the Frolicking Moose.

You'll also recognize JJ as Megan Bailey's brother.

Lizbeth's story takes place a couple months after *I Am Girl Power* ends.

Now, that's not confusing at all, is it?!

Chapter One

LIZBETH

My knuckles turned white as I gripped the steering wheel of my 1992 Honda, a silent mantra playing on repeat in my head.

I won't slide off the canyon road. I won't plunge into the icy river below. I won't die tonight. I won't slide off the canyon road . . .

"Don't be so dramatic, Lizbeth," I muttered to myself. "This is fine. Everything is fine. I'm not panicked. Nope." My voice broke as a gust of wind slammed snow flurries into my window. "Not at all!"

No consolation in sight.

Snow pelted my windshield like a vortex of flying white icicles. Only my headlights illuminated the darkness of this mountain canyon. I'd never felt so alone or so tired.

The soft scent of baby powder lingered in the car as a sublime reminder of the reason for my fatigue. My older sister, Bethany, had just been in labor for forty-eight hours before she gave birth to my nephew, Shane. The most adorable, squishy, wrinkled, funny-looking baby that had ever existed. He was exquisite.

Despite the arrival of my first nephew, every muscle in my body remained tense. I shouldn't have left the hospital. Shouldn't have brushed off the storm. Shouldn't have arrogantly claimed that I'd driven the mountain pass from Jackson City to Pineville a dozen times in *far worse snow than this.*

I crept along toward home in Pineville at twenty miles an hour, but felt like I wasn't moving. Maverick would kill me when he found out I hadn't put winter tires on my car yet. But really, who'd expected a late-November blizzard?

Maybe I should have.

The subzero temperature left a delicate swirl of frost along the windows' edges, despite the heat blasting on maximum. All happy vibes from the hospital vanished when my front tire skidded on a patch of black ice. The car jerked to the right, then back. My heart dropped into my stomach as I let off the gas.

The car whipped right again. By sheer willpower, I managed not to scream as I pumped the brakes and counter-turned.

The Honda headed right for a break in the trees anyway.

The forest was the only barrier between me and a frothing river at the bottom of a rocky canyon a hundred yards below. The snow had frozen over like a field of pearlescent lacquer. In one second, I comprehended that, if kept on this trajectory, I would plunge right into the canyon.

A burst of cold terror shot through my body when my car vaulted past the trees.

"No!" I screamed. "Stop!"

As if possessed, the car lurched downhill between gaps in the forest. I stomped on my brakes, but the tires skidded on the frozen snow.

With a sickening *crunch*, my front bumper collided with a rock. A *pop* rang in my ears as the airbag deployed. The car flipped onto its side, and the seat belt strained against my chest. I pitched upside down, seized by a stomach-turning sensation.

Half in a daze, I barely registered the car swinging onto its hood, then rocking back onto the passenger side. It remained there for a moment, then two. A burning scent filled my nostrils as I risked a look down at the snowy ground beneath the passenger door.

"Oh no," I whimpered.

One move and my body weight would tip us back onto the hood. Would that squish me? Could I wiggle out? What if the seat belt was jammed? I'd freeze here in less than an hour.

Or the car could tip back onto the tires and head right for the river.

How far away was the canyon wall? Couldn't be far. The general downward slant meant I was near the edge of a slippery shale slope. Thousands of gallons of freezing whitewater rapids streamed onward a couple hundred feet below.

The odds were precarious either way. The seat belt ground into my shoulder as I drew in a deep breath.

"I'm calm," I whispered. "I'm calm. I'm fine. This is fine. Everything is fine."

The car engine had stopped. My headlights illuminated the underside of the snow-laden trees. I tried to shove the gear into park, but the shift had jammed. My emergency brake had broken a year ago.

A gust of wind shook the car. I blinked through the haze from the airbag, barely able to make out a murky darkness ahead. Fractured glass marred the windshield in a spiderweb pattern. My thoughts settled onto one point of focus: I could not fall with the car. And if it rocked onto its tires, this car was *going* to fall.

Snow pelted the cracked windshield. A burst of cold brushed across my face. I realized the whistle I was hearing wasn't the wind, but my own frantic breaths.

"Okay," I whispered. "I have to remain calm."

Maybe someone would come help. Could anyone have noticed from the road? Not likely, but I flashed the brights just in case. There was a small chance someone would see my brake lights.

But the chance was very, very small. Almost nonexistent. I hadn't seen any other cars in the canyon. Nope, help wasn't an option, then.

Had to get out of this myself.

Panic filled me like a hot teakettle. How long would it take them to find me? What if the car washed downriver and took my body with it? Bethany might never know what happened. Ellie would always wonder.

The car moaned.

I froze.

The snow continued to fall, thick and gauzy, while I fingered the seat belt. Maybe I could get free, then jump out once the car landed back on the wheels. But how to undo the seat belt now without falling toward the passenger side?

Well, I had to try.

Moving an inch at a time, I reached for the door. Thankfully, the window rolled down. An icy chill snaked into the car. I froze as the car groaned, tires inching closer to the ground.

It didn't matter anymore. Whether or not I moved, this car was going down. If I wanted to live, I had to get myself out. With a sharp breath, I threw my weight against my door and jammed my hand into the seat belt. The car shivered. The seat belt stuck.

I did it again.

The car shrieked this time. With a guttural cry, I slammed my hand into the seat belt again. It loosened, hissing as it retracted. The movement tipped the car to the side until it landed back on the tires.

Blood pulsed through my body. It thundered in my ears. A

scream built in my throat, rushing out in a wild shriek even though no one could hear.

"Help! Please!"

Frantic, I threw myself out the window just as the wheels started to roll. The edge of the window cut into my torso as I tried to scramble free. My left leg didn't follow the rest of my body. Something hugged my ankle.

The seat belt.

Ice cut into my palms as I grabbed at snow in a poor attempt to extricate myself. The car inched forward. Grunting, I yanked at my left foot. Rocks skidded beneath the front tires as the car crested the edge of the cliff face. It slipped, then shuddered.

"No!" I shouted. "No!"

My body slid forward with the car. Ice raked against my fingers as I uselessly grasped for purchase. The movement only seemed to encourage the car forward. Just as the front tires tipped off the edge, a hand gripped my arm.

With a cry, someone yanked me free.

My leg pulled away from the seat belt, and I slammed into my rescuer. A pair of strong arms dragged me to safety. We landed on the ground together.

"Oof."

The sound of the Honda crashing down the mountainside ended with a splash and a sickening *crunch*. I blinked, suspended in time as I stared at the snow swirling in the spot where the car had disappeared. My mind raced, unable to comprehend any of it.

How was I not in that car?

A voice called over the gusting wind. "You all right?"

I spotted a pair of bright olive eyes tucked into the hood of a parka. Broad shoulders and a strong hand held onto me.

My breath caught—this time, I wasn't sure I'd get it back. I knew those eyes. The sprinkling of stubble on a chiseled face. My stomach dropped all the way to the river.

"JJ?" I whispered.

He grabbed my shoulders. "Lizbeth, are you okay?"

What were the odds that JJ Bailey, of all people, would have saved me? I put a hand on my swimming head as my fingers tingled.

Then everything went black.

Chapter Two

JJ

Lizbeth shivered on the seat next to me.

This old truck—aptly named the Zombie Mobile—issued only a desperate gasp of heat. It drove like a tanker, weighed as much as a mountain, and plowed through snowdrifts with joy, but it kicked out heat like an arctic breeze. The perfect truck for a night like this, unless you wanted to be warm.

She blinked awake slowly, half-dazed. She looked so frightened with her wide emerald eyes, ghost-white skin, and limp hair.

I fiddled with the knobs on the dash to give myself something to do. "Are you cold?"

She stared at me, blinking.

"Did you hit your head?" I asked.

Her fingers brushed her forehead. She shook her head. "No."

I reached into a bag behind her seat. An assortment of clothes were stashed in a small duffel there. I grabbed a hoodie and handed it to her.

"Put this on. Then you can put on my parka. They'll help."

She wasn't wearing a coat, although there had likely been one in the car. Her thinness probably meant a whiff of wind could chill her. There weren't many lights in the Zombie Mobile, but her dazed expression and dusky lips were unmistakable. She slipped her arms into the hoodie and pulled it as far down her body as she could. I slid out of my parka and handed it to her.

"My parka too."

She hesitated. "W-what a-a-bout you?"

"I'll be fine. We're only a few miles away from the turnoff to Adventura. Once we get over the bridge, it'll be much safer."

She nodded. The parka nearly swallowed her, but her shivers had already slowed. I set a hand on her shoulder.

"Are you all right? That was . . . that was nasty business back there."

She nodded again, the muscles in her neck tight. How had she survived such a fast-moving event? How easy it would have been for me to miss her. If I hadn't glanced to the left at the exact right moment, I never would have seen her brake lights. The flashing brights. If the Zombie Mobile didn't amble so slowly, I couldn't have stopped in time to help.

To arrive seconds before she plunged into the river.

Unable to contemplate that thought further, I set it aside. Right now, I had to make sure we both remained intact.

"I'll get us to Adventura safely." I put the old truck into drive again. "I promise."

My muddled brain turned back to the road, which looked like a white cloud. By now, the canyon would be closed. I doubt we'd see any other cars, which made it all the more miraculous that I'd found her.

"Okay," I muttered. "Here we go."

Striking off into the white set my hair on edge. Definitely the worst storm I'd seen since moving back to Pineville late last winter. Lizbeth's recent scrape with death didn't help my nerves. Still, I forced my mind to focus on the path ahead.

The road rumbled if I drifted toward the edge, which helped

me stay in the middle. We crawled along at twenty miles an hour. Lizbeth clutched her seat belt, nostrils flared. She held her breath when we crossed the river over the bridge that would take us to my home, a camp named Adventura on the other side of the canyon from Pineville.

Seconds later, the Zombie Mobile roared through eight inches of fresh powder without a problem. That's when my mind opened again. Under the canopy of trees and the comforting rock faces on either side of the valley, I let out my first metaphorical breath.

The universe had been kind to Lizbeth, but Lizbeth could also be a gift for me. With Lizbeth at my side when I returned, I wouldn't have to explain to Mark why I'd been in Jackson City on a random Friday night.

Everything happened for a reason.

I wasn't a full-on hippie, but I was zen enough to believe that.

Chapter Three

LIZBETH

JJ's intent concentration on the road helped me stop my mental sobbing and get a hold of myself again. If I had to speak, I'd lose it.

Absolutely *lose* it.

Despite the horrifying conditions, he appeared as laid back as ever. JJ had always been easygoing. Quick to smile. He was calm water compared to his boundlessly energetic twin, Mark. I couldn't have picked anyone better to be my saving grace.

Or so I hoped.

The fact that I was plunging into the snowy mountains with a man I didn't really know—despite my raging crush on him—didn't escape my notice.

Snow fell in buckets as JJ smoothly navigated a pristine lane. The mountains loomed overhead, dark specters behind the snow. The wind slowed slightly. Frigid air crept in from the windows and the bottom of the truck, which I strongly suspected had a hole beneath a wooden board at my feet. The old thing smelled like rust and hot dogs.

"Adventura is just around the corner," he murmured a few minutes later. "We'll get you all warmed up, Lizbeth."

JJ and Mark Bailey were enigmas. People spoken of constantly in our small mountain town, but rarely seen. Mark and JJ had returned to Pineville around the same time I did. They came late last winter to open Adventura, a summer camp. I came back after graduating college in May. The summer with them in town had set my world on an awkward axis.

Every time JJ came into the Frolicking Moose for a green tea, my heart somersaulted. Maybe it was his olive eyes, subdued but bright. Or his corded, muscular arms or equally strong legs. His climbing expertise was legendary. His affinity for hiding in the rocks made him even more popular.

The Zombie Mobile, the name Mark had given his truck, sputtered to a stop next to a bank of snow, then died. JJ chuckled. Through a thick blanket of snow, I could barely make out a building in the dim headlights. Relief coursed through me so profoundly I sagged.

Safe.

The wintry world gave only a few clues to the building that seemed to lurk in the storm. A flash of warm light appeared, then vanished. JJ looked at me. For what felt like the first time that night, I really saw him.

My heart almost seized again.

Gentle hazel eyes. Long hair pulled into a sloppy man bun at the back of his head. With his wiry, strong shoulders, quick smile, and tight jaw, he was the picture of masculine grace. He regarded me with concern and compassion.

"You okay?" he asked.

A thousand replies surfaced on my tongue, but I forced them back. "Yeah," I croaked. "Getting there. Th-thank you."

"Your car just plunged into an icy river in the middle of a snowstorm, and you almost went with it. It's okay if you're not really feeling great."

He slapped on a panty-melting smile that would have reduced a lesser woman to goo.

"Let's get inside," he said. "Both of us could use something very warm."

Snow blasted the back of my neck as I stumbled out of the truck. I couldn't feel my toes. The storm swirled in eddies of ice as I attempted to wade forward. JJ reached out, clamped a hand on the parka, and guided me to him. Once he was at my side, he hooked an arm around my shoulder and all but held me up as we trudged through two feet of snow. He wore a long-sleeved gray shirt that fit him a little *too* well.

Only a few feet away stood a wooden door. We hurried inside and were greeted by a blast of blessed heat.

"You're alive, J-man."

A man with black hair and meaty shoulders stood up from a chair near a cluttered desk. Mark, JJ's twin. Despite being twins, they only had their face structure in common. All three of the Bailey kids, their sister Megan included, seemed to have the same face but with vastly different expressions. Where JJ was more thoughtful, Mark reminded me of an enigmatic quarterback: in love with the spotlight and adored by all.

JJ shut the door behind us with a shiver. "Definitely alive."

"And you brought a friend!" Mark cried. "Tell me you also have coffee, Lizbeth. I could really do with a cappuccino right now."

I felt, more than saw, JJ shake his head.

Mark's face fell. He appraised me with open curiosity. Mark and I had never really spoken. Although he came to the coffee shop I managed, he was always on his phone. JJ and I sometimes spoke, but it was rare that I could summon words in the face of my soul-deep crush.

"She's going to hang out with us for the night," JJ said. "She's . . . had some car troubles."

Suddenly, the warm fire was especially warm, and the smell of man-cave especially pungent. My trembling had ceased, but I still felt sick to my stomach. When the *crunch* of the falling car replayed in my head, I forced back a wave of nausea.

JJ rested a warm hand on my shoulder. It grounded me against the rush of hysteria. My eternal gratitude for his perceptiveness deepened another notch. I just wanted Bethany to wrap me in her arms while I cried.

"She needs a hot shower," JJ said with a gentle squeeze. "Storytime later."

"No problem, Liz," Mark said as I peeled off the parka. "Get warmed up. JJ's on deck for dinner tonight, so you know it's going to be good. You're shaking. I'll build up the fire."

Mark grabbed a coat and disappeared through a back door at the end of a hallway. The area was sparsely decorated. What *was* there looked accidental. A giant desk with a computer and phone filled the far wall, near the fireplace. Papers, file folders, unwashed coffee mugs, fast-food wrappers, and a ridiculous number of pens littered the desk's surface. A rolling chair burdened with winter coats, pants, and a pair of wool socks sat behind it.

A few old couches occupied most of the floor. Behind the front door, a ladder led to what appeared to be an attic. Posters cluttered the walls, displaying snowboards, mountains, and treacherous climbs.

"Mark and I sleep upstairs," JJ said. His hand fell away from my shoulder. A physical pang jolted through me at the loss of his touch. "We have a spare bedroom down here you can sleep in."

"That's perfect. Thank you."

On reflex, I reached for my phone, then realized too late that I didn't have one anymore. This situation would be far more terrifying if I didn't know the Bailey boys.

"Can I borrow a phone?"

"Oh, yes. Of course." He reached into his back pocket. "Here."

With numb fingers, I typed a quick text to Maverick.

Lizbeth: Hey, it's Lizbeth texting from JJ Bailey's phone. Had some car trouble in the canyon. Everything is fine. JJ stopped and helped me out. I'm staying with them at Adventura until the storm passes. Can you let Ellie know?

A reply came moments later.

Maverick: Glad to hear you're all right. I'll let Bethany know in the morning. Texting Ellie now. Be safe, Liz.

The simple connection with Maverick eased my heart. Tears thickened my throat. He wouldn't be dealing with a birth and a death in the same day, at least.

Lizbeth: Baby boy okay?

Maverick: Stealing my breath every minute, just like his mama. :)

I released a relieved sigh. I'd tell them the full truth later. In ten years. Or maybe never. Except for the part about the missing car . . .

With a weak smile, I passed the phone back to JJ. "Thanks."

He held out a hand, and I accepted it, trusting myself into his care for a few moments. Right then, I needed it.

"C'mon." He gently steered me toward the hallway. "You need a hot shower first, dinner second. It's been a helluva day."

* * *

Standing in a square shower with cobwebs in the upper corners, I bit into a clean washcloth and silently cried. Letting go of my tears felt as cleansing as the hot spray that prickled my skin. I'd put up my hair in a bun so I didn't have to worry about drying it.

With shaky legs, I leaned against the wall and let my thoughts roll out. The air grew humid, sharpening the scent of pine and curling the stray hairs at my neck. Eventually, JJ knocked and said, "Leaving some clean clothes on the counter for you, Lizbeth."

The door whispered open, then shut.

Steam clogged the room when I grabbed a towel, wrapped it around me, and stepped out of the shower. The heat had restored life and humanity to my frozen limbs. I stumbled into a pair of ridiculously big workout pants and one of JJ's sister's shirts. The top fit me better than one of his would have, but it still hung loose. JJ's heady, masculine smell lingered in my nose.

Rallying my courage again, I wiped steam off the mirror. My cheeks had pinked from the heat, which at least distracted from my bloodshot eyes. I removed my residual mascara, folded my clothes, made sure the bathroom was clean, and slipped out the door.

The hallway was empty, so I ditched my other clothes in the guest bedroom JJ had pointed out, then wandered back toward the living room/office. JJ stood on the far side of a room divided by a half wall. It appeared to be a makeshift kitchen. He'd changed into a pair of sweats and a long-sleeved T-shirt that hugged the contours of his shoulders.

His expression brightened when he saw me. "Feel better?"

"Much, thank you."

"Have a seat." He nodded to the couch. "The hot chocolate is almost ready."

"Thanks."

Instead of sitting, I perused a bookshelf against the far wall.

Death on the Mountain and *A Climber's Guide to Everything* drew my attention. I pulled them down, my thoughts wandering. Surely these were JJ's. Likely *all* these books were JJ's. Mark didn't strike me as a reader.

By the time I finished my brief perusal, JJ had returned, a mug of hot chocolate in hand. He passed it to me, then sat on a nearby chair to nurse what appeared to be tea.

"Thank you," I said.

The sweet warmth calmed my stomach. I took another eager sip, suddenly ravenous. It seemed to expand in the hollow part of my body. I peered at him over the top of the cup.

"And thank you for . . . you know."

He shrugged. "Don't mention it."

"But you could have—"

"And didn't." He finished firmly. "I'm grateful I was there to help. You would have done the same. You just came back to Pineville this summer, didn't you?"

Grateful for the change in subject, I let out a long breath. "Yes. Around the same time as you. I graduated college in May. Since Bethany was pregnant all summer, and very sick, I've been running the coffee shop. I just came from the hospital, actually. She had a little boy."

His eyes lit up. "Wow. Quite the day for you."

"Yes. I'm a proud auntie—who's alive, thanks to you." I lifted my mug. "Here's to several new beginnings."

He clinked his mug against mine with a witty smile.

"What did you graduate in?" he asked.

"Bachelor's in Computer Science."

"Impressive."

"Thanks."

"You should fix Adventura's website," he said. "Mark attempted it last winter. It's absolutely hideous."

"I'd love to look at it."

Website makeovers were a fun part of what I could do, but

the idea of working with the Bailey boys was too unreal to think about. Besides, the warm purl of heat in my stomach surely had nothing to do with the curious expression on his face. I curled deeper into the couch, feeling drowsy after the shower.

"What are you going to do next?" he asked.

Great question. "Um . . . there are job options."

"Ah. I know that hesitation."

He sat halfway on the couch, elbows resting on his knees. There was something sexy about the way he held the cup of tea in his whole hand, the palm cupping the bottom. Although tempted to drop my gaze, I didn't.

"I just needed a break for a year," I said. "College was hard-core for me. Nonstop. So when I finished, I just . . . I needed some time to figure out what I wanted to do. Running the Frolicking Moose and paying down some debt was ideal."

A grimace crossed his face. "Adulting stuff."

"Unfortunately. There's also this job I *really* want."

"Oh?"

I nodded.

JJ regarded me curiously for a moment, then turned back to his tea. "I remember that transition. As if it wasn't hard enough just to graduate, now you have to figure your life out. There's a lot of pressure."

Several things startled me there. First of all, I didn't know college had been part of his world. Second, he was at least nine years older than me. Word around town pegged the Bailey boys at thirty.

"You graduated college?" I asked.

He nodded. "Bachelor's in Environmental Science." Then he laughed, presumably at my expression. "I take it you're surprised?"

"A little." I gave him a sheepish smile. "I guess I assumed you've just always been climbing and living in a van."

He shrugged and leaned back, leaving the tea to cool. His arms looped behind his head, and it was a struggle not to stare.

"I've always climbed. Just like you, after I graduated, I took a step back to see what I wanted to do. Then I just . . . never did it. We did live in a van," he tacked on with a roguish grin. "For about a year."

The last words came out quieter, but I couldn't tell if it was regret in his voice, or something else. A loud bark of laughter came from the attic.

"What about Mark?" I asked, taking another sip of hot chocolate. It was over halfway gone by now, and I almost was too. The snap of the fire had lulled me. Being alert and on guard for so long had worn me out. Not to mention sleeping on and off in a ball on the hospital bed for forty-eight hours.

"Mark went too. Graduated with a degree in business. Eventually did his MBA online while we traveled."

"And then?"

"We bummed around together for a long time. Neither of us wanted to grow up, so we just kept playing. Traveling. Getting into trouble. My poor mother has too much gray hair because of us."

I smiled. His mother, a flight nurse in Jackson City where Bethany had just birthed my adorable nephew, was lovely.

"We messed around for almost a decade, living off climbing sponsorships, odd jobs, and sometimes Mark's rampant charm. We did that right up until he bought Adventura and 'settled in.'" JJ's air quotes looked ironic, at best. "Mark will never really stop. He's started one business and he's already on to another one. He's a moving target."

Sensing something beneath the surface, I asked, "And what about you? Are you a moving target also?"

"Dunno yet."

The last sip of hot chocolate slid down my throat. Although curiosity tugged at me, I stood with the empty mug.

"Thank you, JJ. This helped calm me down. But I think I'll go to bed, if you don't mind."

My body had relaxed into a state of near-sleep. This seemed as good a time as any to hide away. To avoid the beautiful way the fire warmed his skin to golden tones. No reason for me to study the angle of his jaw and replay the way his arms had kept me from death.

He took the mug from me. "Good. I'm sure some rest will help. I'll take care of the cup."

"Thank you."

"Oh, Lizbeth?" he called as I headed for the bedroom.

I glanced over my shoulder. He stood there, holding my mug, looking gorgeous in the firelight.

"If you get too cold, we keep the fire running all night. Feel free to add more logs to it, or sleep on the couch. Mark and I are upstairs if you need anything."

"Okay."

"We can report the accident in the morning, but there isn't much they can do now, anyway. It'll eventually have to get towed. If they can even reach it down there."

My mind spun. I hadn't even thought of getting the car out. "Thanks."

I closed the door behind me, bathed in a sudden chill. This little cabin clearly didn't have central heating, and the window didn't keep out the cold. JJ had set a few more blankets and a pillow on the bed. I fluffed the pillows and climbed in. When I tugged the blankets all the way to my chin, I realized that the pillow smelled like JJ. Was it his?

My body molded to it like mush.

Chapter Four

JJ

Mark appeared from the attic thirty minutes after Lizbeth went to bed. He tilted his head toward the spare bedroom. "Bed?" he mouthed.

I nodded.

Once she'd left, I'd sunk into food preparation. The smell of marinara and pasta filled the room. Mark gravitated to the food naturally.

"She okay?" Mark asked in a quiet voice as he approached. "She didn't look so great when you arrived."

"Fine, I think." I rubbed a hand over my face, suddenly exhausted. I recounted the story, with the scariest parts emphasized appropriately. While I told it, Mark grabbed dishes for dinner.

"Seriously?" he whispered and clapped a hand on my shoulder. "JJ, you're a freaking hero. It's all those climbing muscles. I always knew you had a knight in shining armor buried underneath all those layers of hippie."

"I couldn't have done anything if she hadn't gotten herself halfway out already."

"You look shaken up."

He leaned back in his chair, spaghetti piled high in a bowl. I *felt* shaken up. Reality had set in. Tonight could have been a tragedy. I loosed my hair and let it fall to my shoulders, relieved to ease the pressure from the hair tie.

"I *am* shaken. I almost didn't get her."

"Well done, brother. You saved her."

He decked me lightly in the arm as he dove into his food. My mind wandered to Lizbeth. She still seemed to be in shock. Her overall mien was a bit too calm. I wasn't the one who'd dangled over a white-capped river, seconds away from death, and even I felt it all the way to my gut.

"I made you some hot chocolate," I said. "It's in the microwave staying warm."

"But not because you made it in there."

"Don't insult me."

"You're the best brother ever. Real, made-from-scratch hot chocolate on a blizzard night? You'll always be my fave, JJ. What would I ever do without you? Fortunately, we never have to know. Hey, I had an idea tonight and started putting out some feelers. You want in on it?"

His voice faded into the background as I turned my attention back to my food. Mark rarely wanted me to respond—he just wanted a listening ear—so I let my mind drift.

Thoughts of a certain terrorized redhead circled my brain in an endless loop for the rest of the night.

Chapter Five

LIZBETH

When I woke up, my neck felt as tight as the spine of a new book.

I straightened carefully. My collarbone protested each millimeter where it had pressed against the seat belt. My stomach felt a bit sore from lying on the windowsill before the car fell. A quick inventory confirmed I was fine. Alive.

A wooden ceiling loomed overhead. Behind me, the warm crackle of a dying fire filled the air. I blinked away a dream of tangled steel, grating metal, and deep ravines.

Yet here I sat in . . . Adventura.

Memory returned quickly. With a groan, I rubbed a hand over my face. At some point in the night, I'd slipped out to the living room, too cold to sleep. The Bailey brothers had already gone to bed, so I'd made a little nest on the couch closest to the fire and slept there.

Nightmares had replayed every second of the crash in excruciating detail all night long. As if my brain wanted to process it in slow motion. In the dream, my car hadn't just been sliding. No, I'd dangled on the edge, one finger on a rock. I screamed and screamed and screamed, stuck in the awful sensation of *almost* dying.

It left me feeling cold.

I blinked and forced my thoughts back to the present moment. The clock said 7:34, but the room lay in shadows. Little light made it past the ongoing storm outside. But the wind seemed to have lessened. A quick look at the windowpanes confirmed that snow had frozen to the glass.

What a perfect setting for a romance novel.

I'd read my fair share of mountain romances. Handsome stranger fetches feisty woman from inevitable death in a whirling snowstorm. Forced to stay in the same cabin, they secretly connect and realize they've never been so disarmed by someone else before.

I stared at the ceiling and blinked.

Odd.

I'd read almost every romance novel in existence. Dreamt of the day I'd live my own because, frankly, I'd dated almost no one in college. Now I sat in a literal storyline for a perfect romance. And all I could think about was my pale eyelashes. Or the awkward fact that, when I read romance books, I often pictured JJ as the love interest.

Which just made all of this totally surreal and weird.

A quick review confirmed it: I was definitely stuck in a cabin, in a storm, having been saved by the one man I couldn't have but always wanted. Last night should have been far sexier. Really, it had just been terrifying.

So . . . when would the ultra-giddy romance vibes hit me?

Soon.

Maybe after the crushing reality that I'd almost lost my life—and definitely lost my car—faded. Not only the car, but my phone with pictures of little baby Shane. The keys to the coffee shop. Some newly purchased winter clothes. My laptop.

The surge of panic that swelled in my chest ebbed quickly

this time. All of that didn't matter. The pictures were backed up to the cloud. I could replace my car and laptop . . . eventually. There was car insurance, even if it wasn't the best because I'd limped by as a college student.

At least I hadn't died.

Regardless, the romance books never covered braless nights and invisible eyebrows. They sped right to the sparks and fireworks. But this? This was crusty reality. My car and accoutrements had just plunged into an icy abyss.

Besides, the idea of anything between me and JJ was a literal dream. Not only was he nine years older, but a declared *perpetual bachelor*. He wouldn't fit anywhere in my ultra-specific, very-much-happening-soon plans.

After landing my dream job at my favorite social media company, Pinnable, I would have a storybook romance, get married, and have babies. That's when I'd settle into the sort of magical romance that Bethany and Maverick had.

The one I craved all the way to my bones.

I would have marriage and babies while armed with a college degree—because Mama never did care about education, and I'd die before I ended up like her.

But first, I'd make breakfast.

* * *

For the next ten minutes, I shuffled through cupboards and the mini fridge, tiptoeing around so I didn't wake the Bailey boys. The open floorplan transmitted sound like an empty cave.

Finally, I settled on pancake mix made with water instead of milk and the last of a dozen eggs. No bacon, sausage, or OJ in the fridge. Some old, frostbitten breakfast sandwiches lingered at the back of a tiny freezer, but I wasn't putting my hand back there. Only bachelors would run out of food in advance of a blizzard. I bet they only had one roll of toilet paper, too.

Pancakes were easy enough, although I really wasn't into the food scene. But making them on a hot plate in the middle of what should have been a camp office?

Not my kind of party.

Still, I endured. Because JJ deserved a light, happy breakfast to counter the intensity of last night.

The hot plate smelled like burnt iron as it warmed, and I wafted away a few initial fumes while I stirred batter with a plastic spoon. The first two pancakes were a total flop, so I set those aside. The third came out half-decent. Just then, someone appeared from the attic.

"Lizbeth?"

JJ languorously stretched his arms above his head, eyelashes heavy against the morning light. My heart gave a little *whomp* at the adorable, sleepy way he smiled. Why did men always have the biggest eye fans? Mine were so light they were almost translucent. Putting on mascara changed me incalculably.

"Smells good down here."

There it was—the rush of giddiness at the sound of his still-sleepy voice didn't disappoint. The way his muscled arms reached overhead in taut perfection gave my heart a second reason to race. Romance books had something perfect, all right: there was definite beauty in the male form.

"Good morning," I said, gaze averted.

He paused. His gaze dropped to the semi-chaos around me. I prayed there wasn't batter on my face.

"Are you . . ."

"Making you breakfast. I guarantee nothing. But I . . . I wanted to do something nice for you. It's poor thanks but . . ."

"It's amazing."

He blinked several times. His mouth parted as if he were about to say something, but then he stopped.

"I'm not great with a hot plate." I grimaced. "But I think they're edible."

"I bet they're the best I've tasted. Thank you. I can't remember the last time someone else cooked around here. Did you sleep okay?"

"Better than in a freezing river."

Mark's barking laugh broke the still morning. "Good one," he called from the attic. Footsteps thundered down the ladder.

He appeared, hand shoved through his shaggy hair, with a growl of frustration. His eyes were bright, face darkly stubbled. The usual intensity of his bright, ever-changing expression wasn't dimmed by the early hour. Mark was quite handsome . . . if you could get him to stop moving.

"Morning," he sang in a grating operetta.

"You look like a bear," JJ said.

Mark threw something at him as he walked past, clad in flannel pajama pants and an old race T-shirt that said, *Tough Mudder*. His broad shoulders filled it out. He disappeared into the bathroom.

Concern filled JJ's expression. "You sleep all right?" he asked me.

"Yeah. Yes. I mean, in the light of day, it's not all quite so overwhelming. And I'm alive, right? So I'm definitely okay."

JJ glanced outside and grimaced. "The sort-of light of day."

He pulled back repurposed pillowcases that doubled as drapes to reveal another foot of snow. I could just make out the Zombie Mobile coated so thick with white that it almost blended into the forest. Flurries whirled around it.

"Pretty cool storm, isn't it?" he asked.

I had other opinions about extreme winter weather. "It's something," I muttered.

JJ laughed and stepped behind me, setting a hand on my shoulder as he pulled a cup out of a high cupboard. Was he always so touchy? I'd take it seven days a week. My heart woke up again at the heavy heat of his hand.

"It's supposed to last through the day," he said, "but

without as much wind. I think it'll taper off in the night. I bet the canyon opens back up in the morning if there aren't any avalanches. Coffee?"

"Already going." I pointed to the Keurig across the way. "Now *that* is one food I can make."

"You're a godsend."

He squeezed my shoulder, then turned to the machine. There was no frisson of electricity that slid between us. No unreadable frown on his face as his skin touched mine. No small gasp that I tried to hide at the unexpected fireworks of his touch. But his firm hand on a cold winter day was comfort without words.

Mark hurried upstairs to the attic, phone already to his ear, while I finished the pancakes. JJ set out some faded plates and camping utensils. When we finally settled at the table with my almost-pancakes-mostly-crepe-looking-concoctions, Mark slid back down the ladder again and into the kitchenette with a whoop.

"I am the literal master of the universe. I figured it out, JJ. I did it!" Mark punched the air once, his expression taut with energy. "I know what I'm going to build on that lot I bought in Pineville last year."

"What?"

"A spa."

Mark stopped for a second to take in JJ's reaction. When JJ's face scrunched, Mark started to pace.

"A spa?" JJ asked.

"A full-service day spa. Mani. Pedi. Hair. Fingers. Meditation. Whatever it is people do in places like that, I want in."

"Mark, that's . . . insane."

Mark rolled his eyes in the most dramatic fashion I'd seen since Ellie turned eight. "It's not insane, JJ! It's good business. Crazy people are hated all the time for their progressive ideas."

"A spa? In Pineville? Population 100?"

"It's a business idea, not a cultural revolution." Mark threw himself into a chair. "The people in Pineville are way too wound up. They could use a few massages. Pineville is adorable, right? A cozy little mountain town. What better advertising is there for a place to relax? This could create more traffic, which would boost the economy. It's so close to Jackson City that we have a guaranteed funnel from . . ."

Mark trailed off as he jogged to his desk in the other room and grabbed a piece of paper. Then he came back to the table to frantically scribble on it. There was more space to be agitated behind his desk, but he seemed glued to JJ. I tilted my head to the side, a syrupy piece of pancake on the end of my fork.

How interesting.

"Is he always like this?" I whispered to JJ.

JJ nodded with a sigh. "It's worse when he's cooped up like this in the winter, though. Mark very spontaneously bought a lot on his own last year. Normally we've done our business ventures together, but this time he used his own cash. He's trying to figure out what to do next."

"Obviously any good spa has a salon—" Mark continued, this time slashing lines across the piece of paper. A few scrawled numbers came next, then something that wasn't legible. Perhaps a list.

"It won't turn a profit for years, Mark," JJ said. "You'll have a steep build-out."

"True. Good point. Heavy build-out."

"You sound like you've done this before," I murmured.

JJ nodded. "He always has ideas."

"Okay, fine," Mark muttered. He scribbled something on the next page. "What if I start it as a hair salon and eventually grow the offerings? Reduces the build-out and decreases time to profit. Millie Blaine has been looking for a new space since the previous salon owner shut down and left town."

"You're going to build a three thousand square foot building for a salon?" JJ asked as he peered at Mark's scribbles.

"No, a spa!"

JJ muttered something unintelligible in response while he scooped a few pancakes onto his plate. The smell of butter and syrup lay thick on the air now. The banter bounced back and forth between them like a ping-pong ball.

Fascinating. So *this* was the Bailey brothers in their natural habitat. I chewed on a piece of pancake as I watched. For having been made on a hot plate, these were delicious.

"Opening a spa would seriously cut into your plans for next year," JJ said.

"I won't run the spa," Mark mumbled, deep in thought. "Someone else will. I'm just funding and giving the initial push. I'll need a manager."

"He wants to go full mountain man," JJ said to me as an aside. "Beard, attitude, flannel, everything. He said it was his goal next year to finally realize it. He just needs a little more guaranteed income to make it happen."

"A man can only dream," I said wryly.

JJ waved Mark back to his seat. "Mark, eat breakfast. Keep thinking on it. You'll have to round up some investors, anyway, so let the idea simmer."

Mark rubbed a hand over his scruffy face. He tossed the pen away and shoved the papers under a plate JJ had set out for him. "Fine. You're right. But keep thinking on it. I'm willing to bet the idea grows on you. You survived the night, Lizzy?"

"Thanks to your hospitality, yes."

"You can stay with us anytime you drive your car off a cliff."

I snorted into my coffee.

Mark winked. Several minutes passed in companionable, hungry silence. Mark flipped through his phone, muttering under his breath, spitting out details on the weather. JJ seemed lost in thought as he stared at the top of the table. The pancakes disappeared quickly to their wolfish appetite.

Mark swore at his phone when the internet failed, then stood up. "Thanks, Lizbeth. Breakfast was delicious. We'll see how the weather does later today. I might be able to take you home. More likely I'll take you tomorrow when I leave for a business meeting."

"Thanks, Mark."

He stalked out of the room, cursing the *gods of mountain internet*. I watched JJ slowly unwind in the aftermath.

"When did you guys get internet, anyway?" I asked.

"A couple months ago," said JJ, still shaking his head. "It's actually not too bad. Faster than I expected it to be when Netcast announced they were expanding out here in the canyon. Does seem to be hit-or-miss in bad weather. But it's really letting Mark go full steam ahead with his expansion plans."

"Oh, is that why you guys haven't been in the Frolicking Moose as much lately?" I teased with a grin. "I was afraid you'd found a new favorite coffee shop."

He shot me a quizzical look, like he was surprised I'd noticed, and I scrambled to change the subject.

"What do you do while Mark does . . . all this?" I asked casually. My coffee mug half-covered my face. Not only was I hesitant to ask, but I didn't have a book to hide behind. Coffee was the next best thing.

JJ froze. I held my breath.

His jaw tightened, but he didn't look back at me. "Ah . . . stuff here and there."

"Oh. Prep for summer campers?"

"Sort of."

Silence fell around us, which gave me ample time to study him. His hair was tied out of his face. He wore a pair of workout pants and a T-shirt with a picture of a climber on the back. Sleep lingered in his eyes.

Why was he so weird about such a simple question?

What *did* a man like JJ do to stay busy in the wilds of Adventura? Maybe nothing. Maybe he was bored out of his mind. But something in his response told me there was a hidden layer here. This seemed like the perfect world for him. He and Mark fit together like twin puzzle pieces that fed off one another.

JJ took a deep breath. Just as he opened his mouth to say something, Mark breezed back through the room like a hurricane.

"Internet is gone-zo, bro. Hate these storms. Had a text from Justin last night, though. He got snowed in after his date with Meg. Said he'll be back when the roads open. He took Atticus with him."

"Glad he's safe."

Mark grabbed something from his desk, then returned to the attic.

"Climbing is my world," JJ said to me then. "But it's not easy to live off money from climbing."

"So you and Mark came up with Adventura?"

"Yeah."

"But in the winter?"

He shrugged. "I have a . . . few things in the works. For the most part, I make a lot of food, do a lot of hiking, and help Justin with maintenance if it's needed."

Sounded . . . like not much.

"Oh," I said, because what else was there to say?

JJ leaned back in his chair. "Mark and I have only ever known life together. Born together. Grew up together. Graduated high school together. Moved to college together. We've traveled the world . . . together. Started several other stupid companies that failed. Eventually, we bought Adventura together. We've pushed through our parents' bad marriage and nasty divorce. Ex-girlfriends, broken bones, you name it. We've experienced it. Together. We've never been apart for more than a few weeks at a time."

The picture slowly became clearer. "You want a chance to be on your own, don't you?"

"Maybe." He hesitated. "But maybe not. I know I want to climb, but that doesn't pay the bills."

"Mark seems to have endless ideas."

He grinned. "Yes, he has that. But I don't want to keep investing in businesses. That's his thing, which is why he's doing this . . . *spa* . . . without me. He's a brilliant man. Energetic. Full of ideas. He's not really afraid of anything. Since our parents' divorce, he's sort of been the glue that's kept me, Megan, and him together. But that's not who I am or what I want."

"Then what *do* you want?"

He hesitated, gaze on me. "Not sure yet. Still working that out."

I could sense that JJ had opened up as much as he ever would. He yanked his hair out of its bun and ran his hands through it. I jerked my gaze back to the pancakes to avoid an awkward open-mouthed-drooling encounter.

"Anytime you need to talk about it," I said, "I'm here."

His mouth cracked a half smile as he grabbed the empty plates from the small table. "You mean you didn't expect to do therapy while you were here?"

"Naturally, I did. It's being Mark's therapist that scares me the most."

His laugh rang through the snowy cabin, warming me all the way to my bones.

Chapter Six

JJ

Lizbeth had curled up like a cat on the couch. Unexpectedly, having someone else in this house had been . . . nice. Despite being a contented bachelor who loved the quiet, I didn't want her to stop talking. I only knew her as the barista at the Frolicking Moose. Mark and I bummed Wi-Fi off there all the time. She had a green tea ready whenever she saw me coming and seemed happy enough, if occasionally quiet. But I'd never really noticed her.

Now I couldn't stop.

"Liz," I called, "you up for Scrabble?"

Snow was still collecting rapidly outside, but the wind had calmed. Within the hour, I'd start unburying the truck and shoveling the worst of it away from the door.

Lizbeth set aside *Robinson Crusoe* with a cheery expression. "Anything but this, please."

"You don't like the classics?"

"Not *those* classics."

"Ooh, do tell."

"Truthfully, I mostly read romance, but for every five

romance books I read, I venture into a different genre. It's a rule. It keeps me from getting too jaded."

"What are your favorites?"

"Right now? *The Lais of Marie de France*." She brightened. "They're poems about love, written in 1170, or something like that. I adore them. They're all courtly love, illicit affairs, and romantic tragedy."

"Ah, you love a little drama?"

"I love a little love," she quipped, then murmured, "*I saw this lady; now a dart of agony has struck my heart. It makes my body shake and shiver. I think I really have to love her.*"

"One of the poems?"

She smiled and tossed me the bag of tiles, her own already neatly arrayed on her tray. "Since you're the hero, you go first."

The fire crackled as I regarded my options. *L, P, F, U, H, M,* and *Q* didn't give me many. I laid out a rather pathetic *L-U-M-P.*

"You just finished college, and now you're taking a break for a year, but you have a job application in somewhere, right?" I ventured.

"Mmm-hmm."

"Where is it?"

"Pinnable."

"Pinnable? What's that?"

Her eyes widened. "Don't tell me you've never heard of it."

"Never."

"JJ!" Shock threaded her voice. "Are you so removed from the world that you don't know what Pinnable is? It's one of the biggest social media platforms ever. You can organize things by corkboards and notes and images and . . ."

I shrugged.

She laughed. "I'm not sure if I'm impressed by the fact that you've never heard of it, or frightened by it."

"You should be impressed."

Her smile broadened. "Then I am. It's a social media app

that I use all the time, and have for years. Working there would be . . . a dream. At least, I hope it would. I think it would. I could use my expertise in computer programming to help them improve basic layouts, functionality, etc. I'd hopefully work more on the back end. The layers of complexity in that kind of coding have me intrigued."

Another stretch of calm fell between us as she rearranged a few letters. Her thoughts seemed far from the game, however.

"Is it a job that would make you happy?" I asked.

She frowned. "I don't know. I think so. I mean . . . I'm concerned that it's based out of Florida because I missed my sisters so much when I was away for college, but I guess I'll have to deal with that."

"What *does* make you happy?"

Why I asked, I had no idea, but a hint of color appeared in her cheeks, so I didn't regret it. For a moment, I thought she'd change the subject, but then she laid down her letters. *L-O-V-E.* Her eyes slammed into mine like a wall of bricks.

"What makes me happy? Well, that's easy. My wall of romance books at home in the Frolicking Moose."

"You have a wall of books?"

"Last count was 956."

"What?" I leaned back. "That's incredible!"

"They're all romance."

I almost laughed, then realized she was serious. Instead, I managed to only lift my eyebrows. "Wait, what?"

"I have almost a thousand romance novels." She grinned. "They make me so happy."

"Romance makes you happy?"

"Deeply."

Stunned, I could only blink for a moment. "Do tell."

"Romance is a lifesaver."

If I hadn't been curious before, I was utterly transfixed now. Instead of considering my tiles, I just stared at her. Living with

Mark for the last thirty years meant I'd heard a lot of crazy things, but not that.

Never that.

"Please," I said, "explain."

She grinned. "Gladly. That cheesy saying that *love makes the world go round?* I actually believe that. I think romance saves lives. It enhances. We crave it all the way to the marrow of our bones. Look at Hollywood. At the top music charts. Everyone talks, acts, and sings about love."

"Well, it sells, right?"

"Yes! You prove my point."

"That proves nothing except people want it and they pay for it."

"Love and romance are built inside us." She pressed a hand to her heart. "They're instincts."

I scoffed. "Love and romance are totally different."

She raised an eyebrow. "Are they?"

My response faltered before I decided to sidestep that and focus on something else. Because I honestly didn't know. Romance and I were not friends. Not since my ex-girlfriend Stacey pulled my heart out with her bare hands and stomped on it. Love?

Even worse.

"Have you ever been in love?" I asked.

The expression on her face dimmed. "No."

"In a relationship?"

She shook her head.

Interesting that someone of her intelligence would buy into such a . . . naive scheme. Doubly interesting that she'd never been in a relationship. What kind of idiots at her college had let *her* go? Then again, if she'd never been heartbroken, maybe it was easy to hold on to the hope that storybook romance was real.

"Can you tell me why you think it saves lives?" I asked.

"In the same way that anything *good* saves lives. Maybe it inspires hope. Stops people from doing something stupid. Helps someone feel like they belong. Creates safety." Her angled jaw highlighted the challenge in her stare. I wondered if she was upset by my questions. She seemed nothing but determined.

"Inspiring hope doesn't save lives."

"What if you're on the verge of suicide but you find hope again through love?"

My mouth opened, then closed. She stared hard at me now. Did she want me to protest, or something? Because I would, once I found my voice again. This was the most ridiculous thing I'd ever heard.

"Romance also destroys," I said.

She tilted her head. "In what way?"

"Romance is just as destructive as it is hopeful. What about hearts that get crushed? Relationships that don't make it? Love that's one-sided? Romance is the kind of thing people never recover from in the worst way."

Lizbeth regarded me for a second. The question seemed to hover on the tip of her tongue. *Who broke your heart, JJ?* I imagined her asking.

But I wouldn't tell.

Not yet, anyway. And she didn't ask, which earned her a point of respect in my mind.

"But that's not romance," she replied. "That's manipulation. *True* romance is two-sided."

"Disagree."

She smiled. "That's fine. I'm not trying to convert you to a religion, JJ."

Then why did I feel like a spotlight was shining on me and holy water awaited? I licked my lips. "I've never thought of love or romance the way you've talked about it," I admitted to soften my next blow. "And I think it sounds totally . . ."

"Insane?" she supplied.

"Unrealistic."

"You think because I haven't been in a relationship before, nor been in love, that I couldn't know what I'm talking about."

My silence spoke for me. Her grin broadened, clearly unbothered.

"I'm not surprised you think so. It's a little too traditional for most people these days. But it's . . . I choose to believe in this. I choose to believe that love and romance are real. One day I could be proven wrong, but I don't think so."

"Do you go full traditional?" I asked. "Barefoot and pregnant? White picket fence? Babies on babies?"

"Yes. Do you?"

The thought of marriage and babies used to make my throat close. Inhibition of my freedom? No thanks. Lately, it didn't seem so bad. Maybe it was age. Life experience. Maybe desperation. Her comment didn't frighten me the way it would have five years ago.

But it sure didn't feel comfortable now.

I shuffled the tiles around the bag. "Ah . . . not sure on that."

She made a sound in her throat, then motioned to my tiles. "It's your turn."

I set down another pathetic word—*S-C-A-R-E-D*. My palms started to sweat. Stacey had worked a real number on me eight years ago. Since she'd crushed my heart, I hadn't tried again. Sometimes I felt pathetic, like she'd won. She'd been a post-college love affair. My feelings for her had spiraled deep and fast. I'd thrown almost everything away to be with her, thinking it had been real.

My throat thickened in the few moments it took Lizbeth to consider her tiles and lay down another word. *H-E-A-R-T*.

With a mental whip, I forced myself back to focus. Lizbeth rearranged her new tiles. She hummed so softly that I wondered if she even realized she was doing it.

"Why?"

The word came out of me as a croak.

Her lips twitched, but she didn't smile. "Why have such loyalty to romance?" she asked.

"I mean . . . it's a concept."

Why did my voice sound so defensive?

"Like love?" she countered.

"I have no idea."

She held two fingers apart from each other. "Romance and love aren't the same thing. Romance is what paves the way for love. It aligns the situation so love happens." She brought the fingers together. "When love and romance are paired? I believe anything can happen. Romance is . . . proof that you do love. That you know that person deeply enough you'll *do* something to show it. Romance must come first."

"Romance meaning chocolates and flowers and . . ."

My mind went blank.

She shrugged. "Maybe."

"What's *your* definition of romance?"

Her hands paused over her tiles as I arranged *C-U-S-P* on the board. She licked her lips and let out a long breath.

"That," she murmured, "is a very personal question indeed."

My desire to know her answer unnerved me. I let it ebb away. The very act of withholding the information only made me want it more, but I didn't think Lizbeth insincere enough to do that on purpose.

We didn't say another word for a long time, and in the silence, I finally found my breath again.

Lizbeth won.

Chapter Seven

LIZBETH

The day unfurled in a whirl of games, laughter, and reading from the safety of their couch in front of the fire. At noon I called Maverick and told him the sordid details of what had happened, but only after I secured his agreement not to tell Bethany yet. With every word, I felt a little better. More firmly rooted in reality.

For me, the quiet day was almost perfect. Mark paced the attic and popped in and out. JJ inventoried his climbing gear and muttered to himself.

Time with the Bailey brothers hadn't been what I'd expected. JJ had a restless energy of his own, different from Mark's. He seemed . . . bored. Uncertain. Mark was exactly like I thought he'd be, but kinder.

In the depths of my heart, I couldn't believe I'd spent the day with them. My mind couldn't seem to wrap around it.

It was too distracted by JJ's sincere smile.

Part of me never wanted to leave. Another part couldn't wait to go. Real life awaited. The more I lingered here, the closer I felt to JJ.

Sweet baby pineapple, but this whole living-a-romance-plot

was not what I'd hoped. The books made this all so romantic. So simple. Instead, I felt stressed out by the fact that I'd almost died and annoyed that I couldn't stop looking at JJ.

At 9:00 the next morning, my breath puffed out in front of me as JJ led me to the Zombie Mobile. The truck rumbled to life with Mark in the driver's seat, and the tailpipe belched black smoke. Three feet of snow ringed us on either side of the pathway Mark had cleared. The banks glittered in the bitter-cold sunshine.

JJ wore no coat, just a simple jacket that zipped all the way up. A hat covered his head and pushed his long hair onto his neck. I wanted to run my fingers through it. Although I was eager to prepare Bethany's house for their return, I wished I could stay and observe more.

What was JJ hiding?

What had *really* made him look so cornered during our conversation yesterday?

Someone had broken his heart, and I wanted to know how. Likely he thought me a romantic fool for believing in love like I did. He wasn't the only one. Others had certainly told me as much. I always ignored them easily, but something about the wariness in his gaze wouldn't leave me.

JJ faced me with a smile. "Thanks for the company, Lizbeth. It'd be great if you could be here every time we were snowed in."

"Thank you," I said with a laugh, and cleared my throat. "I mean . . . for everything."

The first hint of a rueful smile crossed his lips. "Anytime."

"Listen, I—"

"I'll see you in town?" he said at the same time.

"Yeah." I nodded. "Yeah, of course."

"Did you have something else you were about to say?"

Just don't stop being my friend? I thought. *Never cut your hair? Sweep me off my feet?*

"No." I shook my head and cursed my awkwardness. "Nothing."

Mark banged a hand on the roof of the Zombie Mobile. "Regulators!" he shouted. "Mount up."

JJ grinned. "You'll win bonus points with Mark if you rap the rest of that song on the way into town."

My lips twitched. "I happen to know it. Come in for free green tea anytime. On the house."

His half grin broke into a true smile that melted my heart. If he looked at me like that every day, I'd never get anything done. Pinnable would be forgotten. My romance books would burn to ash in my hands. The world would fall apart. I could stare into those warm eyes for the rest of eternity.

So *that* feeling in the books wasn't a lie.

My parting words failed halfway out of my mouth, landing in my lap in a garbled heap. His brow lifted in silent question as I stood there, half-gaping at him. A thousand words whipped through my mind, but I couldn't bring myself to say any of them.

Will I see you again soon?

Do you think I'm crazy because I love romance?

"Bye, JJ."

My insides turned to mush when he yanked open the ancient truck door. Although I could have stared at his jawline all day, I felt a modicum of relief that I could leave the pressure of being around him. It had been years since I'd crushed on anyone this hard.

An almost-romance was exhausting.

As I turned to go, I hoped for a classic romantic ending to this highly romantic situation. A hand on my wrist, maybe. He'd stop me. Nervously lick his lips, then ask me to stay. Maybe laugh about his brashness and say it's just not like him to ask that. Or tell me he'd never opened up like that before, and he felt something. Wanted to see what would happen if we indulged in it.

But no touch on my wrist followed.

Instead, I climbed into the ancient truck that groaned under even my paltry weight. Out of sheer pride, I refused to look back. He called out a cheery farewell. I thought I saw him wave from the corner of my eye as I managed a blind wave back.

I didn't want to see him standing there in the winter brilliance, as far from me as any person had ever been.

* * *

"Don't let him scare you off. He's a total teddy bear."

Mark made that announcement as he plowed a narrow path down the road. Snow scraped the side with an intense grating sound. I held onto a bar above my head as we bounced along, and thanked the goddess of winter storms that JJ, rather than Mark, had found me.

"Wh-what do you mean?" I called.

"JJ." Mark glanced at me for a second. "He's like a freaking acorn. Hard as hell on the outside, but the goodness is really inside."

Awful metaphor aside, he couldn't be more wrong.

"JJ is the sweetest guy I've ever met. He's not hard on the outside."

"Sure. Unless you're interested in him, like you are. Then he's a nightmare."

Mark chuckled when my eyes widened, then he downshifted and shaved off a healthy chunk of snow as we turned a sharp corner. The back wheels slid into a snowbank, and the entire truck shuddered. Although I braced myself for the inevitable *crunch* of whipping into the bank, it never came. The reliable old monster just kept eating up the snowy road.

"Who said I'm interested?" I managed to choke out.

Mark scoffed. "Right, Lizbeth. As if your entire heart isn't written on your face. You've always crushed on him. You light up like a Christmas tree when he walks into the Frolicking Moose."

I scowled. He laughed. I folded my arms over my chest, and my cheeks flared with heat. This situation had always been way funnier in the books. Novels never emphasized the pure mortification of being read so easily.

Of course, I could deny it, but what was the point? Mark already knew. And if he'd seen it, JJ might know. That explained his very normal goodbye. Maybe he'd intentionally interrupted me earlier and made it look like an accident.

Friend-zoned.

"Well," Mark called over the rumble of the truck. "At least you aren't denying it."

"No. I'm not going to deny it. JJ is . . . special."

"You're in good company. Women flock to him. It's the most aggravating thing. He's got those great eyelashes, the sexy hair. Then women talk to him and he's gentle, cares about animals and people's emotions, then, *bam*! Walks away, leaving broken hearts in his wake."

"Why?" I asked, shivering and pulling my sweater tighter around me. The Zombie Mobile wasn't any better at producing heat today.

Mark shrugged. "To be fair, he doesn't do it on purpose."

"Doesn't he want a relationship?"

"Nope."

"Who broke his heart?"

Mark chuckled as he downshifted. The bridge loomed ahead. Flashbacks of two nights ago raced through my mind. I dug my fingers into the seat.

"He broke his own heart. Kind of. JJ used to be a wild romantic. Flowers. True love. Sparkle lights, or whatever that crap is."

My heart thudded as we rattled over the old bridge, but it had nothing to do with the river frothing below. *Sparkle lights?* I wanted to say. *Are you five? It's twinkle.*

"You're lying," I said.

"I swear it."

"What happened?"

"Not my story to tell. Romance? Dating? That stuff just doesn't reach him anymore."

"Then what does?"

"Climbing."

Mark's enthusiasm for the topic would be borderline comical if my heart wasn't the punchline. My nose wrinkled as I comprehended his subtext. Mark was warning me.

"Thanks," I said.

I startled him by meaning it. He glanced at me twice for only quick flashes, keeping his attention on the road.

"Sure."

"Think he noticed?" I looked out the window as he pulled onto the canyon road.

"No." He blew a bubble with his gum. "Your secret is safe with me."

I groaned. A satisfied grin overtook his face.

Well, what a great plot twist that made.

Didn't matter, anyway. JJ wasn't the picket-fence type. He was almost a decade older than me and wanted to branch out to grasp at the unlimited freedom of untethered bachelorhood. Live life on his own terms. At least, that's how it had sounded.

We fell into silence for the rest of the trip back to the Frolicking Moose.

Chapter Eight

JJ

After Lizbeth left, I shuffled through my gear half-heartedly, my mind far away. A yellow notepad lay next to me. Quiet reigned over the office, but it wasn't as deeply refreshing as usual. Normally, I yearned for some distance from Mark's prattle. He was always making some kind of noise, as if he couldn't stand the quiet.

I pulled a pen out of my hair and scribbled a few notes. Thoughts of Lizbeth and her deep loyalty to romance kept intruding on my thoughts.

Who *seriously* believed that?

And owned it?

Maybe she just equated safety with romance. I'd bet half my ropes that the moment she had any experience with heartbreak, her mind would change. Anyone with real-world know-how would be far more jaded. Or at least less . . .

Idealistic.

With a growl, I pitched the pen to the floor. It landed on the notepad with a *thud*. I leaned back, let out a long breath, and rubbed my hands over my eyes. This shouldn't bother me so much, but it did. The thought of her figuring out the dark side of romance—like I had—set my teeth on edge. I didn't even know her, not really, but I still didn't want that for her. She deserved better.

Crimson hair, soft as silk, flashed through my mind.

Why couldn't I just focus?

Daylight waned outside. My stomach growled, reminding me that I'd forgotten to eat lunch. There were a lot of things I hadn't done yet. Boredom had a way of doing that. The utter lack of direction in my life used to be thrilling. When we had ten different countries to hike through and no return ticket.

But now?

Now, I couldn't peg it. Something restless had awoken inside me. Like a slow gnaw from the inside out.

My brain wandered back to Lizbeth's declaration. A thousand romance books. Who had the time for that?

Or the space?

"Bro!" Mark barked up the ladder. "I stopped by the bank. I think we could make this spa idea happen."

A deep sigh rippled through me. That didn't feel any more exciting, of course. Another business. Another tangled mess. Another volley of ideas. Even that was better than staring at the ceiling, trying not to catalogue all the ways Lizbeth was wrong about romance. Why did I have to prove it to her, anyway?

Why couldn't I just let her believe it?

"Coming!" I stood up. Because it was time to forget Lizbeth and let her live her life. Maybe she would find her romance and live happily ever after.

I wished her luck.

Chapter Nine

LIZBETH

The Frolicking Moose had never looked more like home.

The moment Mark pulled into the parking lot, I wanted to throw myself into the arms of a latte, a new romance novel, and fresh pastries. Once inside, I closed my eyes and inhaled the aroma of vanilla and coffee beans.

"Devin, if you squirt that Cool Whip in your mouth straight from the container, and I have to go buy another one *again*, I will have your head," Ellie threatened.

Ah, home.

While the winter wonderland with JJ had been idyllic, returning to the shop and my sisters filled me with a happy buzz. Also, a new phone awaited very soon in my future. Couldn't deny myself that joy.

The door closed at my back, and Ellie's emerald eyes shot to me in relief. No customers in the shop, only Ellie and Devin behind the counter. The gleam in Devin's eyes faded when he saw me.

"Hey, Lizbeth!" He rushed around the counter and crushed me in a hug with his thick football arms. "I'm so glad you're okay."

Ellie ran up behind him, and they wrapped me in their not-so-casual love. I melted into them. Devin had thickened up and grown taller in the last couple of years. Right into the beloved star of the town as high school quarterback.

"Dev," Ellie finally gasped. "Lay off."

He released us enough to allow a quick gasp for breath, gave one last vise-grip squeeze, then stepped back.

Ellie grabbed my arm. "Mav told us everything. That scared me," she whispered. "Please never do that again. You're okay, right?"

"Yes, I'm okay. And it scared me too."

"You're good?" Devin asked.

"Good."

Ellie didn't look convinced. She leaned back against a table, the essence of casualness in her leggings and knockoff Uggs. An oversized sweatshirt of Maverick's, rolled to her elbows, completed the relaxed ensemble. Like usual, she'd thrown her black hair into a loose knot at the top of her head.

"The fate of the car is . . ." she drawled.

"An icy grave?" Nonchalance came more easily now that I wasn't dangling precariously over the edge. "I have no idea. Maverick texted me that we'd deal with it later. JJ isn't sure they can tow it from that far down."

"May it rest in peace," Devin said through a half bite of what appeared to be an egg sandwich.

Ellie rolled her eyes. "*Stop* eating! That's your fourth one this shift."

He said something unintelligible through his last bite, pushing a hand toward her face. She deftly dodged. The buttery, warm smell of croissants caught me by surprise.

"Croissants?" I asked.

Ellie gestured toward the display. "Le Grand Boulangerie sent them with the order this weekend. Said they had some extras. They've been selling like crazy so far."

My absence for even a few days left me feeling disoriented. The Frolicking Moose had been under my sole care for so many months it felt like mine. Would I feel like this when I left for the Pinnable job? If I got it, of course.

My stomach growled, so I dismissed those thoughts. JJ's breakfast seemed ages ago. I stepped behind the counter, already reaching for a coffee mug.

"Talked to Bethie a bit ago," Ellie said. "Mav said they'll come home tonight. The canyon was mostly plowed, so it should be safe. Dev and I cleaned the house yesterday. It's all ready to go."

"Thank you."

Unlike Ellie, I'd never been able to bluff my way through things. She trained her piercing glare on me.

"Are you really okay, Lizbeth?"

I nodded, but I was so far from it. Being home made it all seem so much scarier. *Almost died. Saved by the man I've adored for months. Saw a new side of him. Fell even harder. Don't have a chance.*

As sweet as JJ had been, I felt like a tightly wound braid ready to loosen. Coffee warmed my cup with radiant heat. I grabbed creamer and syrup. Coffee was just a vehicle for all the other delicious stuff.

"Oh, Dev and I are touring State University next weekend," Ellie said. "Can we swap shifts?"

"Sure."

"Thanks. I'll put it on the calendar."

"You excited?" I asked.

Ellie nodded emphatically. Devin's expression dimmed for half a second but then recovered. Had I imagined it?

Probably.

"Oh, and some mail came for you." Ellie motioned upstairs with a flick of her wrist. "I tossed it on your bed."

The blood in my body froze all at once. "Anything interesting?" I asked.

She sent me a look that suggested I'd failed at seeming casual. "Not a big white envelope from Pinnable, if that's what you mean."

"Dang."

The bell on the door rang, admitting a group of brawny high schoolers. A scowl leapt to Ellie's face, and a grin to Devin's. She was a year younger in school and decidedly less extroverted, particularly with his football friends.

Or with anyone but Devin, in fact.

Fortunately, his rampant extroversion had no fear of her extreme dislike of people and crowds. Somehow, those two oddballs made their strange friendship work.

I cast a knowing smirk at Ellie. "Have fun," I mouthed, slipping past Devin with my coffee. By the time I disappeared around the counter, she'd already made herself scarce in her catlike way.

* * *

The attic room where I lived above the Frolicking Moose had a steep, sloping roof. My bed—a four-poster wrought iron beast swathed with gauzy fabric—took up most of the space. On the other side of the attic was a small bathroom with a shower, toilet, and sink so closely packed together I could barely spin around.

The most important part of all greeted me: my books.

Maverick had built in an entire wall of bookshelves. He'd even trimmed them around the windows. I'd crammed all 957 novels into every spare spot and then some. The cacophony of titles, colors, and paper gave me a physical thrill every time I saw it.

Today was no exception.

Right now, all I wanted was to dive into one of those

romance-affirming books and prove JJ wrong. Romance was *real*. More importantly, it was a force for good in this world.

I snuggled into a pair of bright-red flannel pants, a long white snowman T-shirt that said *Frosty is my jam*, and a pair of monster slippers. Sunshine trickled into the room through the frozen windowpanes. A pair of soft, glowing lights wrapped around my canopy bed. The gentle smell of evergreen mingled with coffee felt like a warm embrace.

With my thoughts churning like a winter storm, I set my coffee down on a small table and reached for my laptop. It wasn't there. That, too, had been lost in the crash. I let out a frustrated breath.

A nap would work wonders. With a shake of my head, I closed my curtains, crawled under my covers, and lay on my cool pillow. JJ lingered in the back of my mind like he'd taken up residence, even though I tried to evict him countless times. Thoughts of him intruded until I sighed in frustration.

Did he really *not* believe in romance?

Or know about Pinnable?

The man had been hiding for far too long. From what, though? Did it matter to me? No. Not necessarily. Except I hadn't exactly gotten the most romantic ending to our time together. It was clear what *should* have happened.

The lovely, grief-stricken woman would be in dire circumstances that the love interest selflessly battled out with her, despite his own problems. After waiting out the storm and sparking undeniable chemistry with literal zips of electricity that skated through their blood, they just couldn't *bear* to part, even if they didn't understand it.

Even if it had only been five hours since they first met.

Obviously.

And that was *so* far from what had happened.

JJ had some serious lessons to learn about romance, and I intended to teach him. In fact, I knew exactly how to do it. JJ was a man invested in logic, facts, and science. There was no woman who straddled those lines as well as me. Computer programmer obsessed with romance?

Oh, I would *so* give him all the data on romance.

With that promise ringing in my head, I shoved JJ far from my mind and dropped into a welcome sleep.

* * *

My eyelids drooped from exhaustion all the next day. After my nap, I'd spent time with Shane until midnight while Bethany slept. I just couldn't let go of his downy skin and perfect little breaths. Totally worth it.

Thick piles of snow boxed in Main Street after the massive storm. Rafi, the middle-aged man who plowed every winter, had just scraped out our parking lot. Cars drove by every now and then, tires hissing on the icy street.

The temptation to turn on Christmas music nearly overwhelmed me, but Ellie and Devin would relieve me soon. Ellie, the perpetual scrooge, would glare me to pieces, then put on something dramatic like polka just to make a point.

My third cup of coffee steamed into my face as I peered over it at my friend, Leslie. She had frizzy blonde hair with dark roots, and a pair of wide-brim glasses. With her sophisticated, long black coat, she cut an impressive figure in the quaint little shop. Four kids and a husband kept her busy. We'd first connected when Bethany and I started the Frolicking Moose Book Club years ago.

"What genre is book club this month?" she asked, nose wrinkled.

I waggled my eyebrows. "Romance."

She fake-gagged.

"Sounds like you need to get a little pizzazz back into your marriage, Les," I said. "You always hate romance month."

She stared at me as if I'd grown another head. One dark brow quirked. "You're kidding."

"What?" I cried. "Romance spices up everything. You've been down in the dumps for a while."

"I'd rather buy a new garbage disposal."

I laughed.

"I'm serious," she deadpanned. "My sink keeps clogging. It's driving me crazy. Have you ever had to plunge your sink with the same plunger you use in your bathroom because it's the middle of the night? It's not pretty."

"Why were you doing dishes in the middle of the night?"

"Because that's when I have *time*."

"C'mon. Romance helps you remember why you got married in the first place. No?"

"Not true."

"Really?" I drawled. My hand fell on top of an unmarked binder. "Please, tell me more."

Her eyes tapered at my tone. "What are you up to, Lizbeth?"

"Nothing."

"A lie. You have a new binder, which is scary in itself. And it's a pink binder with glitter hearts. Oh, heavens, you aren't writing a romance novel about me, are you?"

My eyes flew open. "No, but that's the best idea ever!" I grabbed a pen, flipped the binder open to the first page, and scribbled a note.

"Most boring romance ever."

"You just need to spice things up."

"What *is* that, Lizbeth?"

"It's . . . a social experiment."

"From the computer coder?"

"Don't stereotype me." I nudged my coffee cup so I had room to sprawl the binder out. "I love people, and I love to code."

"Fair enough. So, spill."

"It's a love binder."

She blinked at me.

I rolled my eyes. "It's not weird, so don't even say it. And it's not *that* kind of love binder. I'm trying to define romance and love and prove they're real through scientific data. So, I've written down quasi-romantic experiences, created a rubric by which to grade them, and put it on graph paper so I can score it in different capacities. Part of my research involves hearing from other people—not just women—on what they think is romantic."

She shook her head. "Your brain makes mine shrivel every time we interact. Why are you doing this?"

"Let's just say I'm trying to turn a skeptic."

"Oookay."

"The first step is to define romance, and then define love."

"That's easy."

"Oh, really?" I drawled. "Go for it. Give me a one-line definition of romance, right now."

She opened her mouth to speak, paused, then closed it again. The skin between her brows wrinkled. "Well . . . maybe it's not easy."

"Ha!"

"Romance is . . . you know . . . it makes you feel special, I guess?"

"That was a question, not a statement."

She shrugged. "I honestly haven't thought of romance in like eight years. I have four children. Romance just doesn't rank."

"So?" I cried. "All the more reason to get some more of it in your life."

Leslie tilted her head, a comical expression on her face that basically screamed, *You have no idea what you're talking about.*

I leaned forward. "Look, I get it. I've never had kids. I don't know what it's like to be up all night and all day with screaming children. Or to share that much of yourself. So much of yourself that you aren't sure there's enough left over for your husband."

Her gaze slowly softened. This was too easy. I'd read enough second-chance romances to be a professional at this.

Leslie looked down at her hands. "Yeah. I guess it does feel like that sometimes. But that doesn't mean I'm *dying* for romance. I'd really just rather he run the vacuum without me having to ask him to do it. Can the man just do a *chore* without me initiating it?"

"So, let's break this down." I straightened, pen at the ready. Ink spilled frantically across the page titled *Leslie* while I wrote. "Your idea of romance is doing chores?"

"I didn't say that."

"You didn't *not* say it."

"Don't double-negative me."

"Then tell me what you think is romantic."

She threw her hands in the air. "I have no idea, Lizbeth!"

"How do chocolates sound?"

Her nose wrinkled.

I crossed that off. "Okay, not that. How about flowers?"

She rolled her eyes. "It's just something else to keep alive and feed."

"Definitely not that." Crossed it off. "How about dinner and dancing?"

"He'd trip and fall on top of me, and we'd both break an ankle. Then my mother-in-law would have to live with us and we'd get divorced. No thanks."

"Do you watch rom-coms?"

"No." She scoffed. "They're too unrealistic. Like a good mother of four, I watch animated animals through a streaming service. At the end of the day, I try to pretend like I'm a single woman and go to bed at seven thirty after a glass of wine."

"Sweet baby pineapple, Leslie. Give me something here."

She spread her arms. "I *am*, Lizbeth. This is the most

romantic my brain gets. This is the most I've thought about romance in . . . years. My life is not like yours. I don't have the mental space to prioritize it."

My shoulders slumped. While not ideal, it still all helped. I couldn't let JJ ever talk to her, though. They'd agree on far too much.

"Well," she sighed as she stood. "Good talk. I need to go root through my laundry and find where I misplaced my life."

"Best of luck."

She snorted. "I need it. Also." She pointed dramatically to the porch. "I almost died on that ice."

"I'll fix it."

After she left, I stared down at the paper with a frown. I wasn't naive. I knew romance wasn't a priority for some people, and I knew a lot of people thought it was frippery. Silly. A way to escape troubles. Which it was.

But it was also more.

How do I get JJ to see that? And, of course, there was a deeper question: *Why does he need to?*

That was the question I didn't want to answer.

I straightened with a sigh. A slightly acrid smell filled my nose, then disappeared. I glanced around, saw nothing, and sniffed again. Must have imagined it.

My morning had consisted of making coffee and creating this binder. Using my brain to reduce romance to a ledger had been a fun challenge. Programming required far more creativity than most people realized. Organization was important, but so was flexibility when it came to data. Today felt good.

Hopefully, work at Pinnable would feel equally good.

I took my binder upstairs, set it lovingly on my bookshelf, and studied the titles. Sometimes, I just liked to look at them. When I lived with Mama and Dad, we never had money for books. I'd grasped onto them at the library like they'd save my life.

And they had.

I wound down the stairs and headed out the back door and into the storage shed, where I searched for the bag of ice salt. After almost ten minutes, I located the bag, plus a trowel and shovel, and headed carefully to the front with Leslie's words ringing in my mind. In the breeze, snow had drifted back onto the porch and stairs in front of the store.

The strange smell came again, like . . . burning tires.

"What *is* that?" I murmured.

A quick glance around Main Street revealed nothing. I set the salt down and reached for the shovel. The snow on the stairs thawed quickly, so I stepped up onto the porch. My eyes caught a flicker inside. When I turned to peer through the window, my heart dropped to my stomach.

Flames consumed the far wall of the shop.

Chapter Ten

JJ

The scent of snow and fresh apples lingered in the air as I wheeled around the grocery store in Pineville, trying to *not* think about Lizbeth. Her quick-to-smile lips. The light that carried her around. She had alabaster skin with freckles I found a step beyond charming.

And distracting.

I stood in the middle of the vegetables and frowned at a rutabaga for who knew how long. A quick glance confirmed no one seemed to have noticed. I shoved it into the cart and moved toward the dairy section. Maybe it was time for Mark to try out a new chocolate mousse recipe. Still, I needed some cheesecloth and cake flour.

Ten minutes later, I wheeled my squeaky cart out of the store, stopped at the Zombie Mobile, and shoved all the groceries inside. Then I spared myself a glance across the street.

Then another one.

Was that smoke billowing out of the back of the Frolicking Moose?

The bright flicker of orange flames was visible through the windows. With a sinking feeling in my chest, I abandoned the

Zombie Mobile and dashed through the parking lot and across the slushy road. The smell of burning wood filled the air as I approached, running past an old woman who had stopped on the sidewalk to stare.

"Call 911!" I barked. "Now!"

She fumbled in her pocket, eyes wide. Heat rushed out of the shop as I leapt up the stairs and slipped inside.

"Lizbeth!" I called. "Get out!"

"No!"

She stood behind the counter, a fire extinguisher in her hands. Several white patches already coated the far wall, but the crackling flames had ascended to the ceiling. I grabbed her by the coat and yanked her back. Heat blazed over us.

"It's too late!"

"It's not! Grab the hose at the sink. We can still put it out!"

"We can't. It's already on the ceiling. It might even be on the next floor."

She stumbled back with a cry, fighting me at every step. The fire extinguisher still spurted at random as she flailed, attempting to hit any part of the flame.

"It's not worth your life!"

"This *is* my life, JJ!"

Thankfully, she was small. I hooked an arm around her and carted her outside without an issue. Choking smoke burned my eyes. I coughed. She gasped, dropping to her knees when I released her into the snow a safe distance away. When she looked back at the burning building, her mouth opened wordlessly. Not far away, the old woman spoke frantically into her phone.

"Fire at the coffee shop," she stammered. "It's a bad blaze!"

Flames consumed the back roof, vaulting over the top in a terrifying dance. How could it move so quickly? Then again . . . in a building so old, with planked wood on the outside and a non-metal roof, how could it not?

Lizbeth let out a cry. "My books!"

With a quick hand, I grabbed her shoulder before she could move again. There was no real fight in her. She collapsed back to the ground with an unintelligible whisper.

A few things lay in the snow, and I realized she'd had the presence of mind to gather the money out of the register and a few binders. Probably pitched them outside before attacking with the extinguisher.

For several shocked moments, I waited to hear sirens. Pineville was too small for a full-time fire department. The 911 dispatch would have to page volunteers, who would have to leave their lives, get to the station, and then come here.

It could be too late by then.

It almost was.

The three of us stood there in a silence interrupted only by the crackle of flames and the hum of cars creeping by. All of Pineville's Main Street seemed to spill outside to watch. A warm body appeared at my side. Mark.

"What happened?" he asked, breathless. "I saw the flames and ran over from the bank."

I shrugged helplessly. "Don't know."

Mark glanced at my hold on Lizbeth, then back to the coffee shop.

"Everyone out?" he asked.

"Yeah."

What felt like an eternity later, sirens broke the weird quiet. The fire truck approached, lights blazing. I pulled Lizbeth off the ground and kept her propped up by an arm around her shoulders. A hose appeared. Then came the sound of gushing water and organized shouts. Smoke lay acrid in the air.

"Call Maverick," I said to Mark as I handed him my phone. "His number is in my texts from when Lizbeth messaged him. He needs to be here. If Bethany answers, don't say anything to her."

Mark nodded. "Of course."

He stepped away as I grabbed Lizbeth's arms and forced her to look at me. Her gaze was surprisingly clear. Emotion-free. She stared at me with wide eyes glazed by shock.

"Everything is going to be all right, Lizbeth. You're alive. That's all that matters."

"Everything is gone," she whimpered.

"But you aren't."

She crashed into me with a little sob.

LIZBETH

How did fire move so fast?

This was my fault.

No, they said it was likely old wiring.

What if I'd been asleep?

Hours later, my thoughts whirled in a frenzy. A warm blanket wrapped around my shoulders and jerked me out of the spiral. Ellie stood behind me. Her dog, a gentle but massive Rhodesian Ridgeback named Thor, trailed on her heels.

Ellie sank down on the nearest chair, studying me with a concerned look while Thor settled at her feet. Nursing pads and a breast pump littered the table. I scooted them aside, propped my elbows on the flat surface, and leaned my face into my palms.

"Are you sure you're okay?" she asked.

"Fine. I promise."

"Can you stop almost dying, please?"

Her plea wasn't humorous at all. I looked at her helplessly.

Bethany slipped into the room in a pair of obnoxiously pink slippers. "Shane finally fell asleep." She yawned. "My arm is numb and both my nipples almost cracked, but that child is quiet, so I'll take it."

Tears filled my eyes. "Bethie, do you—"

"No, I don't hate you." She sat down next to me. Her gaze softened. "I could never hate you, Lizbeth."

"But it's your dad's shop. I was there. It—"

"Wasn't your fault."

She reached across the table and laid a hand on mine. Her touch instantly soothed me. I relaxed beneath the warm weight of the blanket. The world had turned upside down in the space of a breath again, and the realization startled me.

Ellie let out a long, slow sigh and slumped back against the chair. Her gaze darted outside. Devin must be on his way over.

"I can't say I'm all that surprised," Bethany murmured with a little shake of her head. As if she, too, couldn't believe it. "Actually, I feel terrible. If it's old, faulty wiring, how could I let you live there?"

"You didn't know."

"Maybe we should have had it checked before now. Cause is not confirmed, of course, but I have little doubt it's the wiring. That shop is so old . . ." She trailed off, then shook her head again. Her bloodshot eyes met mine. "I'm just glad you're okay. If this had happened while you were sleeping, or if you hadn't been able to get away, I wouldn't have been able to live with myself."

The minutes before I'd noticed the fire replayed through my head again. "I smelled something but couldn't figure it out. It . . . smelled sharp. I was only outside like ten minutes, but . . ."

"Long enough for it to get going. They think the fire began in the back and then moved up the back wall. Everything there was so old, the wood so dry, that it burned fast."

"Everything is gone from the attic, isn't it?" I asked.

She hesitated.

"That's what they reported to Maverick," Ellie said softly, casting a pained look my way.

Car. Home. Job. Computer. Clothes. Phone. All wiped out

within days. All my books, most likely. How could they have survived? The fire climbed that wall.

Tears filled my eyes. What next?

Where next?

I literally had the clothes on my back. That was it. It seemed so ridiculous, I couldn't even fathom that it was real. Of course I could stay with Bethany and Maverick. Would have to. But for how long?

They had a new baby, plus Ellie and her dog, chickens, and a goat. Could I move back here after living on my own?

Did I have a choice?

In the background, Maverick spoke to the insurance agency on the phone. Bethany wore a pair of his sweatpants and an old T-shirt. Her silky black hair was pulled away from her face in a messy knot. I'd never seen her this tired. Despite the humming chaos of a baby-filled house, she still wore a light swipe of lipstick. Her power shade.

We sat in the silence for several minutes more before Maverick joined us. He ran a hand over his bleary face and muttered, "Stupid insurance companies," as he sat down next to Bethany. He put a hand on her shoulder with a questioning glance. She nodded as if to say she was fine. He didn't move his hand.

This was the second call in the space of forty-eight hours he'd made that involved some major accident and me.

"Sorry, Mav," I said, "I don't know what to say. I swear, none of this was intentional. The car, the store. I'm a walking disaster."

He sent me a sharp look. "Don't apologize. This wasn't your fault."

"Still . . ."

"Are you okay?" he asked me pointedly. "I haven't gotten a chance to check on you in all this. JJ said you were fighting it with a fire extinguisher until he pulled you out."

I nodded reluctantly.

"That shop doesn't matter at all," he said. "Only you and Ellie, got it?"

Unable to speak for fear of sobbing again, I simply nodded. Bethany leaned toward him, bags under her eyes as she yawned. He scooted closer to let her rest against his chest.

"What did the insurance people say?" she asked sleepily.

"They're sending an adjuster out next week."

She murmured something, eyes at half-mast. "'Kay."

Maverick squeezed her shoulder. "Go lie down, Bethany. Lizbeth, Ellie, and I will take care of the rest."

"I need to make dinner."

"I already started it," Ellie said.

"I didn't do the laundry."

"I'll fold it," I said.

"Lizbeth needs to talk this out. I—"

A mega yawn cut off the rest of her response. Before she could refuse again, Maverick picked her up off the chair and carried her out of the room, his prosthetic leg thumping on the floor as he moved. I stood, arms filled with dirty baby bottles. After shoving the bottles in soapy water, I gathered up the rest of the dishes and pushed them in too.

A gentle growl came from Thor seconds before Ellie said, "Heads up."

A knock sounded at the door. I glanced out the windows to see Mark and JJ standing on the porch. Even after all that had just happened, my stomach flipped.

They were the last people I wanted to see right now.

I motioned for Ellie to stay put and answered the door myself. Relief crossed JJ's face the moment our eyes met.

"Hey," he said.

"Hey." A cold brush of air accompanied them, so I immediately pulled the door open wider. "Come on in."

They stomped their heavy boots off before trekking inside. Mark waved toward Ellie. She didn't reciprocate.

"We came to check on our new damsel in distress," Mark said with a wink.

"Thanks," I said wryly. "She's fine."

I motioned them farther into the room, closer to the roaring fire in the hearth that Maverick had installed himself a few years ago. He'd inherited this house from his grandfather and had been doing renovations ever since he moved in. Before they could settle onto a couch, Maverick returned.

"Greetings, gentlemen," he said in his rolling baritone. The three of them shook hands in a gruff, manly way. Then Maverick turned the full power of his gaze on JJ. "Thank you for rescuing my daughter twice, JJ."

Maverick ignored my dramatic eye roll.

"I didn't rescue her this time," JJ said. "Just helped her out."

"How much of the shop is gone?" Mark asked.

"Over half, I think." Mav ran a hand over his head. "The main area is fine except for smoke damage and some floor that got eaten up, but the area behind the counter is scorched."

"Adjuster coming soon?"

"Yeah."

JJ studied me while Mark and Mav fell into business talk about the fallout.

"Sure you're all right?" JJ asked quietly. Concern filled his gaze.

I nodded. "Thank you again."

He smiled in a gentle way that made my heart catch, like someone had just pulled a string through it.

He shook his head. "Rough week, right?"

"Yeah." I managed a wobbly smile. "Very."

The loss hit me again. Not only my car, which was mostly inconvenient, but everything else. My job. My ability to pay my student loans. The people who came in for coffee every day and had become my friends.

My *books*.

Tears clogged my throat every time I thought about it.

Maverick motioned us onto the couch once their chatter died, and I realized I'd frowned at the floor for an awkward amount of time. JJ and Mark sat together, across from us.

Mark leaned forward and looked right at me. "Lizbeth, I'm glad you're all right. But that's not the only reason we came."

"Oh?"

Mark's gaze flickered to Maverick before returning to me. "I know everything is crazy right now, but once it settles down, I want to offer you a job."

"A job?"

"I need help in the worst way."

After a moment of astonished silence, I asked, "What kind of help?"

"Today I pitched my spa idea to some local investors, and they're excited about it. But I need a little more backing. The bank may be willing to make up the leftovers if I can't pull enough support, but I want to try a different route first. I need to be able to focus on that while . . . other things are taken care of."

It didn't take a degree in computer programming to know what he needed. "You need websites."

And a live-in maid. A hairdresser would be welcome, and so would an interior designer, but I'd tack that on later.

"Among other things," he said.

"What other things?"

"I need everything I have now organized online. Up until today, I've lived and breathed paper because I like to feel and see it. My mind remembers contracts and information better when it's tactile." He put a hand to his head. "If I can see something and touch it, I never forget it. But . . . well, let's say the fire at the

Frolicking Moose made me realize that our own building isn't so young and I have nothing backed up."

He shrugged as if to say, *What do you do?*

The disaster that was his desk flitted to mind. If all his business records were there, only on paper, he absolutely could lose everything.

"Okay."

"For all the paperwork you saw while you were at our place, there's more. A few boxes in the spare bedroom. Then, of course, we need help moving to a digital presence as much as possible. Website redesign for Adventura. A new website for the spa, if it happens. Some online processes, that kind of thing. While you're waiting to hear back from your other job, this could be something you put on your résumé. Right?"

JJ shifted uneasily. He must have told Mark about Pinnable and felt awkward about it now, but I didn't mind. Mark's offer wasn't half-bad.

"How much?" Maverick asked.

I fought not to roll my eyes.

Guess what? I wanted to say. *I got this. I even went to college on my own.* Maverick stepping into a fatherly role had probably saved Ellie and me from becoming our mama. But at moments like this, I just wanted him to back off. The prospect of living here again seemed suddenly suffocating.

"Forty dollars an hour," Mark said.

Mav said nothing, but his poker face nearly broke. His lack of rebuttal was silent approval. My own astonishment gave me pause. Did Mark *have* that kind of money? Mark, who aspired to be a mountain man?

They must have more going on than I thought.

"This is easy work, Mark," I said. "Website design is more specialized, of course, but the cataloguing and uploading of your records is assistant-level stuff. Why would you pay me that much when you could get people to do it for fifteen dollars an hour?"

"For your flexibility and . . . you'd probably need to stay at Adventura. Rent-free, of course. There are so many papers, files, folders, and more that you'd need to ask me about in order to categorize them correctly. I don't want to send that away, because things could get lost. I need more control over this project than that. Plus, I want to be part of the website development. Trying to do this remotely would only be frustrating. I can't get anyone who would be willing to move to Adventura in the winter and work for fifteen dollars an hour, even with housing thrown in."

Ah, the clincher. I silently agreed that being in person was ideal if he truly had that much paperwork, but the idea of living in the wilderness, cut off from civilization, my sisters, and my brand-new nephew, was far from appealing. The Baileys used pillowcases for drapes.

Plus, the chances of befriending mice was too high for comfort.

"How many hours a week?" Mav asked.

I glared at him. He held up two hands as if to say he'd back off. I turned to Mark.

"What sort of schedule?" I asked.

He shrugged. "Until it's done. Work fourteen hours a day if you want. My only deadline for it is the end of the year. Oh, I also promised investors an online dashboard. I'd like to create one, then link it to the website."

Could be complicated, depending on how many layers he wanted, but intriguing all the same. That kind of complexity might work in my favor.

Assuming full-time work, self-employment taxes, and a few other considerations . . . I quickly calculated the math. It would help offset the cost of today. Laptop, phone, clothes. Those would have to be replaced, not to mention the debt that had followed me home from college.

"And you think I'm going to be okay with her staying with

two thirty-year-old men?" Maverick asked, his voice deepening an octave.

I ground my teeth.

Did he remember that I spent four years at college without him?

"Three," JJ said. "Justin lives there too. He's our full-time maintenance man and pops in and out."

Maverick glowered. I could have sworn Mark shoved his heel into JJ's toes, but neither of their expressions changed.

"You deserve to know," JJ said to me.

"Snow White would live in her own cabin in the woods." Mark's charming grin covered the sudden tension in the room. "I will vouch for Justin, and I think the whole town would vouch for both of us. Plus, Justin's dating our sister, so he's not a problem. Lizbeth's cabin wouldn't be far from the office—just behind it, in fact. We have walkie-talkies, and if she needed anything, we'd be about fifteen steps away. It has a lock," Mark added before Maverick could ask, "that we wouldn't have access to. She'd have all the keys."

Maverick's tense shoulders relaxed slightly.

For several moments, no one said a word. The fire popped and hissed in the background. I didn't dare look at JJ. If Mark didn't put a weekly cap on my hours, I could potentially speed through this while the Frolicking Moose got sorted out. Not to mention earn some money to get my life back together. It would give me something besides Pinnable—and all my lost books—to focus on for a while.

Right now, my grieving mind desperately needed a focus.

"I want weekly pay," I said.

"You got it."

"Since my car is currently swimming with fishes, can I bum rides to come into town?"

"Of course."

"At least twice a week? I want to come see Shane and help Bethany."

"I'll bring you," JJ said immediately.

Some intensity hadn't burned off of him yet, and I wished it wasn't from the fire. But of course it was from the fire, because JJ had sworn himself to bachelorhood—he wasn't feeling anything toward me.

Filled with even more surreal disbelief, I kept my gaze on Mark. Was this happening? Was I about to agree to this?

Yes. Yes, I was.

Not only would I be working for Mark Bailey, I'd basically live with JJ. The man of my most sacred, secret dreams. The person who tangled my heart into knots but still convinced it to beat. Who had no idea about my wild crush.

The man who didn't believe in romance.

Now *that* I was still determined to change. And if this wasn't a worthy opportunity to convince him of the error of his ways, I didn't know what was.

All the breath rushed out of me at once. I nodded.

"Then I'll take it. Thank you, Mark."

Mark grinned and stuck a hand out. "Welcome to Adventura, Lizbeth. We're happy to have you."

JJ

"You were right."

Mark said it as the Zombie Mobile ambled around a tight corner away from Lizbeth's house. The headlights illuminated a snow-packed dirt road with dark trees on either side. A knot had taken up residence in my stomach. Surely, the unease I felt had more to do with inviting a new person into our world, not with that new person being Lizbeth.

"About what?" I asked.

"Lizbeth. She'll be good for this."

"You didn't seem convinced at first that hiring her would be a good idea," I said.

"I wasn't. But then I thought about the way she presented herself after almost dying. Her general disposition. The fact that she has a really intense degree and a few weeks to spare. It fit. Also, I think you have the hots for her."

He looked at me as he said it, but I kept my expression unchanged and pretended to ignore him. Of course Mark had noticed.

Whether he'd keep it to himself or not was the real question.

"I don't have the hots for her. I'm . . . intrigued by her opinions on romance."

"Right," he drawled.

I punched him.

He laughed. "She'll be good," he said in the tone that meant he'd already convinced himself. "This is smart. I feel good about this direction. I thought you were insane about offering forty dollars an hour, but now I see your point. Website design is specialized. Mav would never have let her come for less, I bet. The fact that he didn't counter meant something. I mean, did you see the looks he gave us? That guy would *destroy* us if we ever laid a finger on her."

"But that would never be a problem," I said in a controlled tone.

Mark grinned. "You *do* have the hots for her, bro. Niiiice."

My suggestion of forty dollars an hour had been legitimate —Mark needed to get all of that paperwork out of the office. He needed an online presence to satisfy antsy investors. Finding someone else to come all the way to Adventura wasn't likely. Nor was I at all interested, nor the person for the job.

But planting the idea of Mark hiring Lizbeth had been *somewhat* selfish on my part. Adventura had been bleak in the days following her visit. Now she'd lost everything and needed a job.

There had to be arithmetic here that led to this being a good idea, but I couldn't find it.

Silently, I cursed that deep part of me that wanted to protect Lizbeth. Because why? Of all the people on this planet, we would likely be the worst suited. Her unusual, bright innocence. My jaded logic. A relationship with such a polar opposite could slowly shave away all that made her who she was.

"You're still good getting her cabin squared away?" Mark asked, drawing me from my thoughts. "I bet Mav drops her off right on time in the afternoon after she goes shopping for clothes in Jackson City. She seems like the punctual type."

"Of course."

"Better get some mousetraps." He flashed a grin as he pulled onto the highway that led to the canyon. "She doesn't seem like the rodent-tolerant kind."

"Can do."

Maybe this was just *utter* selfishness on my part because I wanted to be around her more. See if I could gently let her down and help her realize that romance wasn't worth the heartbreak that followed. Because my path had been dark, and maybe hers didn't have to be.

Regardless, a part of me couldn't help but look forward to tomorrow.

Chapter Thirteen

LIZBETH

My first day at Adventura started like a fireworks show.

In a cabin.

In the middle of the forest.

With leaky gas tanks.

And three feet of snow piled outside.

I arrived loaded down with bags of clothes charged to Maverick's credit card as a gracious I'm-sorry-your-life-burned-down gift. He'd thrown in a couple of new books for good measure, even though I'd stopped at the library and borrowed ten. Ellie loaned me a backpack, and Bethany a laptop. With what I had left in savings, I managed to get a new phone.

But when I walked into Adventura, all my certainty faded.

An explosion seemed to have detonated since my visit, because Mark's desk was absolutely piled with papers. His computer screen—an ancient PC that wheezed every few minutes—had practically disappeared amid the stacks.

"Glad you're here!" Mark cried as he shook the snow off his coat. He'd helped Mav take all my stuff to my new cabin. "Have a seat."

He waved across the desk to a folding chair that spewed

stuffing from a rip across the top. Thankfully, JJ was nowhere in sight, but the vague scent of outdoors lingered in the air. He must be somewhere close.

Mark wore a pair of workout pants, an old T-shirt, and ratty tennis shoes. But his eyes were bright, and he seemed eager. I let out a long breath.

I could do this.

First, I just had to get out my spreadsheet. I'd created a matrix where I could note all his expectations, the final list of desired projects, and a timeline for each. Then I'd easily be able to map out some sort of schedule and figure out what kind of time it would take.

"Ready to get started?" he asked.

"Yes, of course. Do you mind if I ask a few questions first?"

He shrugged. "Sure." He tipped his head to the buried computer. "Need access to it?"

"Ah, no."

I lifted my backpack, where I'd stuffed Bethany's laptop and headphones. "Where do you want me to work? Then I'll start asking."

His neck straightened. "Ah. Workspace. Right. Comes at a premium here." He hummed to himself for a second as he scanned the area. "Good question."

Although I'd been here before, it seemed so different without JJ in the room. The haphazard elements—clothes hanging off a nail on the wall, a spare roll of toilet paper—were out in bulk this morning. A single, dangling lightbulb had burned out over his desk, casting this side of the room in shadows. The whole place smelled like dust.

It needed a good offensive attack.

Pinnable board, here I come.

Mark tsked under his breath. "I'll need access to my desk, so I can't put you here for now. How about the table?"

The *table* was a foldout that stood on three rickety legs, with books jammed under two of them. It was half behind his desk, half in the hallway that led to the bathroom. But it was that or the floor.

I shuddered thinking of what had crawled across those wooden planks.

By some miracle, I could potentially move this work to my own cabin where I could control the environment a bit more. I hadn't seen said cabin yet, for obvious reasons. Because I was secretly terrified of what I'd find.

"This table is good for now," I said. While I set up my laptop, plugged it in, and booted it, Mark stood behind his desk and stared at the mess with a furrowed brow. He nudged a towering pile of papers with his toe and a hearty dose of what appeared to be fear.

"Ah, my questions shouldn't take long," I said. "I'd love to nail down your expectations for my work."

"Right. Sure." He gestured to the mess. "This is a good chunk of the paperwork that we need organized and put in the cloud, or whatever."

I eyed it warily. "A good chunk?"

"The rest of it is boxed in the spare bedroom. Probably under the cot you slept on."

"And how many boxes are there to go through?"

"Dunno."

"How will I know which ones?"

"Just look through them. If there's paperwork, go through it."

"Okay."

My brain almost malfunctioned. Knowing the Bailey boys as I did now, anything could be in those boxes. I'd have to deal with that later. What if it was personal in nature? What if it was alive —or had been once? I shook my head to clear my thoughts.

"Is this your first priority?" I asked.

"I mean . . . you could start the website whenever you want."

He shrugged. "We'll probably need that completed before we can build the investor dashboard. However, we could really use some space around here."

"Website. Right. I almost forgot. What's the URL again?"

"For which one?"

Which one? He hadn't mentioned multiple existing ones. "Adventura?"

"Oh, that's just a page on a social media site. We'll need to amp that up. Actually, we may have a Wordpass domain."

"Self-hosted?"

He blinked. "Uh . . ."

I waved a hand. "Never mind that. What's the URL?"

"I can't remember off the top of my head. Should be in the paperwork."

He couldn't remember his own website?

"What paperwork?" I asked.

He gestured at the desk with two hands. "That paperwork."

My fingers stiffened on the keyboard. He wanted websites created, I had no idea if he even had a domain, and I was facing years' worth of paperwork shoved into haphazard piles. Somewhere in said paperwork lurked the most basic answers. Answers that he didn't keep in his supposedly brilliant mind.

"Oh."

His phone rang, startling me. "Oh, gotta take this." He clapped me on the shoulder. "Good luck, Lizbeth. Wi-Fi is pretty solid unless there's a storm. Not sure where the password is, but it's on the desk."

"Wait!" I called after him. "What's your priority? Where do you want me to start?"

"Don't care!" he called. Then he answered the phone with a quick, "This is Mark," and disappeared up the attic ladder with the light pounce of a cat. I swallowed hard and stared at the explosion of papers on the table.

Sweet baby pineapple, but what had I gotten myself into?

* * *

An hour later, I stood knee-deep in a mess of paperwork that didn't make any sense, attempting for the tenth time to connect to the internet with a different password because Mark couldn't remember which one was current, all while trying to note on a new spreadsheet just how many categories of paperwork I'd unearthed from one stack.

One of which included a midterm exam from eighth grade.

The list stopped at ninety-seven categories so far, only five of which were business.

When JJ breezed into the cabin, smelling like sunshine and snow, with flushed cheeks and a radiant smile, I wanted to throw said paperwork at his head and tell him to leave me alone or give me coffee. The last thing I needed was the equivalent of a Greek god watching me fail.

"Hey." His smile widened. "You made it."

He closed the door behind him, darkening the room again. Then he tilted his head back and frowned. "Did the bulb burn out over there?"

I set down a folder full of receipts. "Please tell me you can change it. I need the light and can't find the light bulbs."

"Of course."

He slipped past me and into the back, rummaging in a closet near the bathroom. Less than a minute later, light flooded my disastrous workspace.

"Thank you!"

JJ rolled his eyes. "That's Mark. Bet you a hundred bucks he didn't even notice it'd burned out."

"I think you are a hundred percent correct."

He propped his hands on his hips. Breath failed me when he pulled his hair down and ran his fingers through it. This was going to be harder than I'd thought. *Way* harder than I'd thought.

And that had nothing to do with Mark's disorganization.

"So," JJ said. "He got the paperwork out for you, eh?"

"This is only some of it." I ran a hand over my face, already weary. "I haven't even attempted the boxes in the guest bedroom. I'm a little afraid a mouse will jump out at me when I open them."

"Oh, I can help with that."

"Really?" There was entirely too much hope in my voice.

Five minutes later, as I swept an unholy amount of unused lined paper into another pile, he'd stacked four more boxes in front of me.

"That should be the last of it."

My heart sank to the floor. "This is going to take forever," I whispered.

JJ rested a sympathetic hand on my shoulder. "I think you're brave, for what it's worth. And probably not paid enough even at forty an hour, so go for a raise."

He moved into the kitchen with a wink.

I used the reprieve to slow my traitorous heart. Eventually, I worked up the moxie to ask, "Where have you been?"

"Climbing."

"I'm sorry, you were what?"

"Climbing."

"There's three feet of snow outside."

He reached for a coffee mug, his hair still wild on his shoulders. "Well, more mountaineering. Trying to see if I can maneuver back to ice-climb the waterfall at the end of the canyon. I think it was probably too low before the cold hit, but I want to see. The snow is four feet deep in some places, so I think I'll need a snowmobile."

Naturally.

Because who didn't do that during their free time?

While he filled a coffee mug with water and shoved it into

the microwave, I tried to recover my senses and not swallow my tongue. Ice-climb a waterfall?

Was that a *thing?*

I take my adventure indoors, thanks, I thought of saying. *With a side of cream and sugar. Like the adventure of trying a new kind of espresso bean.*

The life he led couldn't be farther from mine. I resisted the urge to slip onto Pinnable and create a corkboard for him. Mountains, grasses, and for some reason, I pictured sage. That would be perfect for him. Wild man, wild places.

No, that would only distract me from the mess I had surely stepped into. Two minutes later he stood in front of me with a fresh mug of coffee.

"Cream and sugar," he said. "I made assumptions on amounts."

"How did you know?"

"Your withdrawal is obvious."

The first sip—perfectly warm—slid all the way into my stomach like we were meant to be. I closed my eyes, savored the smell, and waited for the caffeine to recharge me.

"Thank you."

"Anytime."

JJ plunked a tea bag into his mug, then wrapped his hands around it and leaned back against the couch. I purposefully turned away from him, feigning interest in a stack near an old printer. Time to sort papers that were far away, facing a direction in which I couldn't possibly sneak a glance at him.

"I finished setting up your cabin this morning," he said after several minutes. "Took me a while to dig it out and get the power restored, but now I think you're good."

"Oh, thank you."

"Do you want me to take you to it?"

"Only if I never have to come back to this mess," I muttered.

He laughed, set aside his tea, and motioned with a wave. "C'mon. Time for a break."

"Hold on. I have to note it on my spreadsheet."

"For what?"

I cleared off the top of my laptop and pulled up another spreadsheet. "For time. I have a feeling Mark hasn't even thought of my time card, so I just created something."

"Oh. That's very . . . honest of you."

I shrugged.

Once I noted the time—it had only been two hours and felt like twenty years—I popped up, slipped on my coat, and followed him outside. A walking path had been cut into the three-foot bank of snow outside. Impressive at any rate, even if it was entirely too cold. I shivered in my jacket and hurried to keep up.

The cabin was a quaint little thing from the outside. A single window and door, with round logs stacked into a perfect square that might be barely big enough for a bed and a small table. Snow, thick and white as a wedding cake, was piled on the roof. Perfect insulation for a chill like this. Weather aside, I predicted it would be warm in there. Lazy smoke drifted upward from a chimney on the left.

JJ opened the door and motioned for me to go in first. Snow flaked off my boots as I stepped inside.

"Oh, it's so cute!"

The warmth of a homey cabin embraced me. A fire crackled in a small hearth piled high with wood on the side. A narrow bed on a cot filled the space behind the door. The hardwood floor appeared recently swept. Thankfully, no cobwebs lingered in the corners. No trails of mouse poop on the floor, either, or obvious spiders scuttling the walls. Relief swept over me.

In fact, the place was pristine. It even smelled like pine. All of my shopping bags and pillows from Bethany's were piled on the small bed, which had what appeared to be a newish quilt on top.

"This is much nicer than I expected."

He grinned ruefully. "It's still not the greatest, but it is warm and private. There's no bathroom, but you can get to ours from the back door. I've tamped down a path for you. I'm in charge of meals, so you won't have to worry about that."

"Full service." I grinned. "How nice."

A small table, just large enough for my laptop, a notebook, and a pen, stood off to the side. Beneath it lay a surge protector. The walls were the same wood as the exterior, but chinks in between the logs had been filled in with something like glue.

"Are you comfortable maintaining the fire for warmth?" he asked. "I plan to come out at the end of your work day and start it to get things warm for you. There's an extinguisher behind the bed if you need it." He cracked a smile. "We both know you can use that."

I managed a laugh but felt pained at the reminder. "Thanks. That's very thoughtful."

Scratching sounded at the door. JJ pulled it open, and a black dog bounded inside, floppy pink tongue flying wild. I laughed as he swept up to me, nudging my hand.

"Hello."

"This is Atticus." JJ pounded him affectionately on the back. "Justin's dog. He's our resident mountain lion watcher."

I swallowed hard. Mountain lions. Hadn't thought of that. I crouched down, laughing when a wet tongue got the best of my ear. Another pair of shoulders appeared in the doorway.

"Hey, man."

I glanced into the striking blue eyes of a man with short brown hair. JJ motioned to me with a tilt of his head.

"Justin, this is Lizbeth."

"Ah." Understanding flooded his features. "The brave soul who's taking on Mark's paper project. I'm Justin. I'm their resident maintenance guy and the one who's dating their sister. Atticus, down."

"Nice to meet you," I said with a little laugh as I straightened away from the dog.

Justin tilted his head back to study the rafters. "Thanks for getting in here today, JJ. Sorry I didn't make it. Place looks the best I've ever seen it. Roof is holding okay, looks like. Lizbeth, let me know if you need anything. We're all on the same radio channel, so you just need to speak. I take the radio with me everywhere, and it works up to a half mile away in this part of the canyon."

He gestured to a black thing sitting on the floor in the corner. A small light blinked an intermittent green.

"Thanks."

JJ answered a few more questions about some quick repairs he'd done this morning in the kitchen. I ran a finger along a dustless shelf next to the bed, just right for my collection of library books.

So all the cleanliness was thanks to JJ. How very thoughtful and detailed of him. My fingers itched to note it in the love binder—which I'd managed to save with the cash—that waited in my backpack. A clean place to sleep? Now *that* was romantic.

Maybe it wouldn't be so bad here after all.

Chapter Fourteen

JJ

Lizbeth hummed while she worked.

As she sorted through paperwork and muttered curses to Mark under her breath, she intermittently slipped into different tunes. Most of them I didn't recognize, but some were clear classics. Vivaldi's *Les Quatre Saisons* among them. She tended to prefer spring, like she was humming a wedding march.

Knowing her, she probably was.

Her second day was far less frazzled than her first. She'd eased into the paperwork, found a way to categorize most of it, and waded through the first half of what Mark had ready for her. I watched her out of the corner of my eye as I sipped my morning coffee, utterly intrigued by the way she pushed her lips to one side of her face when she was deep in thought.

Overall, no rampant fatigue showed on her face. She hadn't used the radio last night, so she must not have needed anything. Hopefully she'd slept okay. It had taken me an hour and a half to dig the best cot and mattress out of a storage cabin nearly buried by snow.

"Lizbeth, I need my desk," Mark said as he descended the ladder minutes before lunch was ready.

"Too bad," she replied.

He stopped, then blinked. "What?"

"I said too bad."

"But I need to work."

"Then work in the attic." She shuffled through a few more papers without looking up. "I have been working nonstop on this ridiculous pile of papers all day, and am about to finish. I will not stop."

I cracked a grin. Mark stumped by a beautiful woman —delightful.

"But I need to work," he said.

She finally looked at him. "Why?"

"Because my computer is there."

She used a folder to gesture to the folding table. "You can work there."

His eyes almost bugged out. "You're kidding."

Her less-than-amused stare suggested otherwise. I bit my bottom lip to keep from laughing. Maybe love *was* real. Watching her defeat Mark in a verbal battle—this was positively twitterpation.

"But . . ."

"You contracted me to do a job, and you initiated that job by putting *all this paperwork* right here. If you didn't want me to work here, you shouldn't have put it here. Because you gave me no other expectations, timelines, or milestones, I took over the job, created the rubric, and am proceeding as I see fit. That means you will defer to me. If you need your computer, I will happily reassemble it for you." She jabbed a finger at the folding desk. "Over there."

Mark blinked. I snorted burning-hot coffee, then hacked as it scalded my throat. Neither of them looked at me. Finally, Mark held up two hands.

"Right. Got it. I can probably figure it out later in the attic."

Her megawatt smile returned in a flash. "Great! I should be finished with this part by Friday."

"Lunch!" I called.

Mark waved me off as he shoved his wallet into his pocket and grabbed the Zombie Mobile keys. "Have a meeting in town, but thanks, JJ. Save it for me, and I'll eat it for dinner."

"Thought he had to work on his computer," Lizbeth muttered.

It was a struggle to contain my utter validation and amusement. "Buckwheat waffles with real maple syrup, a berry reduction, and fresh butter await you."

Lizbeth's head popped up. She appeared in the kitchenette seconds later, eyes closed, taking a deep inhale.

"That smells . . ."

"Amazing?"

"Yes."

"Have a seat, and it's yours."

It didn't escape me that Mark had left us alone in the office at least until lunchtime, and I felt relief. Lizbeth was far tenser when Mark was flittering around, throwing ideas left and right. She'd get used to it, eventually, but in the meantime, less Mark meant a smoother ride.

"So." I reached for the pure maple syrup I'd bought in Vermont. "How are you feeling?"

"Overwhelmed, but okay. Mark saves everything."

"I meant after the fire, but that too."

Surprise registered on her face. "Oh, that." Her expression fell. "Yeah . . . I haven't been thinking about it, to be honest."

"Don't want to talk about it?"

"Not really."

"No problem. I've also been thinking about what you said about romance. Care to spar on that?"

One fine eyebrow lifted in her porcelain, freckled face. "Oh? Do tell."

"Do you think romance is a cover for something else?"

Her forehead furrowed in silent question.

"Like security," I clarified as I grabbed my fork. "A relationship with romance is likely a more certain bet, right? Romance equates with effort and security. Maybe you look forward to the security romance brings."

"So, are we talking about security, certainty, or effort?"

"Security."

She chewed a bite of waffle, deep in thought. "You say it like they're two different things. Can you separate security from romance?"

"Can you?"

Her eyes tapered. "No. I don't think so. Security is an aspect of romance. As you pointed out yourself, there are other facets too. Certainty. Security. Effort. Romance is like a diamond."

I had pointed that out, hadn't I? Which wasn't at all what I expected to do.

"Back to my original point," I said as she dug into her waffle, then closed her eyes and moaned at the first bite. "Maybe it's security you want more than romance."

"If I wanted security, I'd buy a home security system."

I cracked a smile. "Good try, but it's different."

"How?"

She was baiting me—I could feel it in the languid drawl of the question. But I had to rise to the occasion now, because I'd put the question out there.

"Romance comes from a person," I said, "not a thing."

"Disagree."

"Really?"

"Romance comes from a book. From a movie. From someone cleaning a cabin really, really well and making sure there aren't any spiders or mice. *Things* can be just as romantic as people. It's like religion." She sent me a vague look that I swore hid a smile as she forked another bite into her mouth.

My jaw dropped. "You have to be kidding. Cleaning your cabin and setting it up for you is not romantic."

"Was to me."

"But I didn't mean it that way."

She shrugged. "Still seemed romantic."

My head whirled in a thousand directions. The greatest of which revolved around the question: *Is Lizbeth looking for romance with me?*

No, that was too ridiculous. We hardly knew each other. Regardless, somehow, I'd thoroughly flummoxed myself here. I'd have to come better prepared next time.

"But if you assign romance to any random gesture, then what *is* it?" I asked in exasperation.

Why did it feel like we were talking in circles?

"Romance?"

"Yes."

"Good question." She blinked several times. "Not sure how to define it yet, honestly. But I'm working on that."

"If you can't define it, it's not real."

She snorted and leaned forward. "Maybe romance isn't real to you, JJ, but it is to me. Maybe it's like . . . God. Some people acknowledge God exists and others don't. But that doesn't make God any less real to those who *do* believe, right?"

"Your comparison is based on the assumption that God is real. Both romance and God are beliefs, regardless of what someone else perceives as truth. Therefore, your beliefs and expectations are pushed onto others when you hold a standard of romance onto them."

The fire that had built in her eyes ebbed into confusion.

"We weren't talking about me pushing my beliefs or expectations of romance onto anybody. We were talking about it being real to me, but not you. And that's okay."

I gulped. Right. I had introduced that out of nowhere. *Why* had I said that?

"Right," I said.

An awkward silence filled the space for a couple of heartbeats. How to backpedal out of this? She spared me the pain of salvaging my pride by putting a hand on my arm.

"It's not that I'd want to push my expectations onto anyone," she said quietly. "If a man I dated didn't believe in romance, that'd be fine. But I expect my belief to be respected. If that person wanted to keep me, I would expect certain romantic gestures. Is that fair?"

Unable to speak with her warm hand sending fire up my arm, I nodded. She smiled, dissolving the strangeness between us.

"What are they?" I asked in a poor attempt to recover some ground. "Your expectations, I mean."

The rogue question slipped out of me before I could stop it. I cleared my throat. She grinned like a Cheshire cat, gathered her empty plate and fork, and stood up.

"Wouldn't you love to know?"

I *would* love to know.

That was precisely the problem.

Thankfully, my phone rang. I grabbed it out of my pocket, saw the name on the screen, and quickly picked it up. Lizbeth waved me off before I could apologize, and I gratefully slipped outside without a jacket.

No need for her to overhear this.

Not yet, anyway.

Chapter Fifteen

LIZBETH

"Please tell me that it's safe and fun and you're warm. Then proceed to tell me everything that's happened."

Bethany's pixelated image peered at me through the phone. The Wi-Fi wasn't too bad for this far from civilization, but it certainly took a while sometimes. She didn't look as tired today. The rocking chair framed her shoulders, and I could just see the pink tip of an ear as Shane nursed. My heart squeezed.

"Not as fun as it would be if I were there with Shane," I said with a little melancholy. "I wish I could help you more. Though, arguably, there may not be a person on this planet who needs more help than Mark Bailey."

She chuckled. "You'd get wildly bored. Beyond burping, diapers, and cleaning up messes, I mostly just nurse him and bounce on that stupid exercise ball to help him fall asleep. It's not thrilling. But it has lovely moments."

"Any news on the shop?"

"Just waiting for the insurance adjuster."

"Any mail?"

The question fell like a thousand-pound rock.

Bethany shook her head. "Sorry, no word from Pinnable yet."

My hope plummeted. Asking about news from the regular mail only made my desperation obvious—they'd probably email or call if they wanted an interview. Bethany leaned her head back and studied me through the phone.

"So? How is living around the Bailey boys? I'm dying of curiosity."

"Things are fine." I shrugged. "Mark is . . . interesting. He's kind of a pack rat, honestly. Some of the papers he's kept? Random."

She grinned. "So I've heard. I don't know them that well. Their dad came by for coffee pretty often, but that's the extent of it for me."

"I don't think many people know them well anymore. Part of me thinks they like being hermits."

"What does JJ do for a living?"

"Great question. I can't figure it out. If he's not out on the mountain or helping Justin, he's buying groceries or cooking in the big camp kitchen."

"Huh."

"Something is going on with him," I said. "I'm sure I'll figure it out. But everything he cooks is delicious, so I'll take it."

"Does it stink like man-cave?"

I laughed. "Not anymore. I brought your old wax warmer and hid it behind a stack of papers. Now it smells like vanilla. But frankly, I'm not sure I can live here much longer in this state, so I made a Pinnable corkboard. That office is a man-disaster. Mark uses socks to warm his hands because he can't find his gloves. Which are on the floor by the fire, but he couldn't see them because of his boots."

She snorted.

"Don't laugh." I angled my phone to show her my computer screen, propped up on my bed next to me. "See? I've already started a corkboard that will help me rearrange the office with a new aesthetic."

"What?"

"I know." I panned the camera back to me. "Outside my job description. But it's needed. They're a hot mess."

"How are you going to do that?" she asked, subtly readjusting Shane with a little grimace.

"Slowly. And quietly. I have a plan."

Bethany laughed again. "I'm sure you do. They probably won't even notice until you do something drastic."

"I could probably shave Mark's head and he wouldn't notice."

"Stop." She giggled. "I think I'm squirting Shane in the face."

My mind wandered to the bizarre discussion I'd had with JJ yesterday morning about romance. As soon as the idea of telling Bethany about it surfaced, I shoved it back down. There wasn't much to say.

In fact, I'd left as confused as him.

For how much I loved romance, I *still* didn't know how to define it in an appropriate and all-encompassing way. Not without an entire paragraph and an army of adjectives at my beck and call. My binder was mostly empty.

Plus, the moment I'd called out his gesture as romantic, I'd felt a jolt all the way to my spine. Why had I done that? It had taken us both by surprise. He probably thought I looked for romance in *everything*.

Which wasn't actually wrong.

Of course, this sort of thing happened all the time in romance novels. The heroine, fighting her startling attraction, would study the love interest for any sign of affection. He'd give only a few hints—obvious though they were to me, the reader— that seemed to pass by the heroine. But still, I'd know his feelings for her.

Even better if the book had a dual point-of-view.

It always felt better when I actually knew what was happening. In real life, there was no dual point-of-view. My utter lack of insight into JJ's mind left me swimming in uncertainty, engulfed in the desire to hole up in my room.

Besides, he had a few points, I had to reluctantly admit. Why had his cleaning and mice removal been a romantic gesture? I had no idea, but it *was*. Surely, it had roots in something. I'd have to psychoanalyze it later.

Despite all my best efforts to stay strong, I couldn't stop a niggling doubt: What if he was right? What if romance wasn't real and I was in for a world of hurt?

Before that grew steam, Bethany turned the conversation. "When are you coming home next?"

"Not sure. Maybe this weekend? I told Mark I wanted Saturday and Sunday off."

"Great."

"Why?"

"Because I have a huge favor to ask."

"Anything."

She grimaced. "Don't say that yet, because you may not be on board. There's a couple I've been working with for a month now. They found a house they want, and an offer is about to come through. But the buyers want to check out the Jackson City area to make sure they like it. They're city people."

"Okay."

She bit her bottom lip. "I think their son might buy it for them."

"Well, that's nice."

"He told them he wants to *get a feel for the place* before he gives his blessing on buying it. They said something about him possibly moving out to be near them? I'm not really sure. It's their we're-going-to-buy-it-and-live-there-till-we-die house."

"Don't tell me you want me to show him around."

"No. They're exploring on their own, but the son would like to talk to a local about Jackson City. I want you to go to dinner with him and talk to him about what it's like living in the mountains."

"What?" I cried. "Why?"

"Because it will make him feel more comfortable! They're a really cute family with money to burn, and closing this sale would be huge. If their son is on board, they'll go for it. Plus, it's just one dinner. I'll tell him that you'll meet him in Jackson City and give him some insight."

"I don't live in Jackson City. I live in Pineville."

She rolled her eyes. "It's all mountain living, right? Plus, he's filthy rich. I bet he takes you somewhere really nice for dinner. His mom happened to drop several hints that he's single and looking. You know, if he sees how cute the girls are here . . ."

Thankfully, she let that trail away.

Of course I'd do it—I'd do anything for Bethie—but that didn't mean I liked it. Setups like this were the worst. I felt awkward and judged and like I had to be peppy and bright and show off my best side when all I wanted to do was talk books. Or better yet, text the person instead and hole up at home *with* said books.

"Fine. I'll do it."

Relief melted her features. "Thank you," she whisper-cried after a quick peek at Shane, who I guessed had fallen asleep. "I'll give you a bonus based on the final price. That should help with that whole-buying-a-new-car predicament you're in. It's a sixteen million dollar house."

"Done!" I cried.

"All right. I'll check with them, then email you the details."

After a few more parting coos at Shane, we ended the call. I leaned back against the wall with a heavy sigh. Maybe this unexpected date would work to my advantage in several ways. Besides, wasn't this a *classic* romance novel plot twist?

Go on a date with someone else to test the actual love interest?

Nah, JJ wouldn't care.

But while out there, I would refine some romantic theories. Resume my progress on proving in a data-driven way that romance existed. My wobbling certainty could benefit from a boost. If nothing else, the date would give me a control sample to record.

Then JJ would eat the romantic leftovers for breakfast.

Chapter Sixteen

JJ

Lizbeth sat at the folding table near Mark's desk, red hair spilling onto her shoulders. She was mapping out a scanning system and organizational structure for Mark's paperwork now that it was all categorized and alphabetized.

I lounged on the couch and tried hard not to stare.

After separating Mark's disaster of papers—and freeing up a ridiculous amount of space—Lizbeth had stacked them all in alternating directions in three separate piles. They towered in the corner, where she hovered protectively over them and glared at anyone who came too close.

I glanced at the timer on my watch. Fifteen fresh loaves of miniature ciabatta had only a few minutes left to rise before I had to trek back to the main lodge and bake them. Meanwhile, Mark was spouting like a volcano, muttering in that maniacal way that meant a breakthrough was on the horizon.

"No." He shook his head back and forth. "That won't work, either."

With my hands threaded behind my head, I leaned back against the couch and waited. About seventeen seconds would produce the desired revelation, if his hair standing on end meant anything. His initial spa plan had been thwarted by a zoning issue on the land he wanted to use. Now he was pacing, determined to work through it.

Most humans drowned when overwhelmed with ideas, but Mark drew energy from the impossible. From the unlikely. Adversity fueled him.

In a poor attempt to escape Mark's impending outburst, I thought of Lizbeth. Again. Nine seconds later, Mark slammed a hand against the wall. I jumped, startled out of my thoughts. Lizbeth glowered at him with a precious fury beneath those light eyebrows.

"I'll buy the old pizza place!" he cried. "I thought of renting, but this is better."

My brow quirked. "What?"

"That'll get rid of my zoning issue while keeping the building tucked away from the main road. It has that fenced area, remember?"

"It'll still be loud when cars drive by. No one wants noise while they're getting a massage."

"We can reinforce the walls. Or put up some trees."

"That would take more capital up front, or years."

"True," he murmured.

"What about the lot?"

He shrugged. "I'll sell it or find something else."

"Buying the pizza place also means you'll still have a build-out." I yawned. "Maybe even worse because they have to tear down the existing interior. You know you're not patient enough for a build-out. And you don't have the cash flow."

He waved that off. "Funding isn't the problem."

"You barely saved Adventura."

He rolled his eyes. "Adventura is fine now. Meg is paying me back. It had the same rocky beginning as any venture."

Sensing a chance, I casually said, "Why not repurpose Adventura to do something else and bring in more cash?"

"I will." He stroked his cheeks. "Once I can go full mountain man."

This was where I had to stop. Mark's dependence on me to save him from himself had become a problem between us. I wasn't his mother. Granted, I was the person closest to him on this planet, but that didn't mean he was my responsibility.

"When are you going to start drawing up boards?" I asked, bending my knee.

He settled on the edge of the other couch, then sprang back up. "Tomorrow."

A strangled noise came from my throat. The question had been a joke, but his response wasn't. I sat up.

"What?"

His grin deepened. "Oh, yeah. I've already got this rolling. Approval for a new loan came through yesterday. I could meet with the real estate agent tomorrow about the pizza place if it works out. Gotta get my eyes on it first, of course."

"Damn, Mark," I muttered.

He slugged me in the shoulder, but it didn't move me. "JJ! This is it! We're doing our next big one. Adventura is coming along. We're successfully running four Airbnbs in three separate Colorado ski towns, and the car wash in Nebraska is holding its own."

"It's not profitable."

"It's . . . getting there. You can't expect a toddler to swim. Give it time. This is awesome. This spa could bring in the revenue I need for my final push to mountain-man status, or at least fuel our retirement funds."

"You did it, Mark."

He shrugged that off. "I'm nothing without you, bro. We just gotta figure out the interior restructuring now. Let's see if we can pull images off the internet."

The sound of Lizbeth clearing her throat startled both of us.

She stood near the couch. Her fingers fidgeted with the bottom of her shirt. Mark sat down next to me, laptop in hand.

"What's up?" he asked.

"Ah, quick question. Are either of you going into town tomorrow?"

Mark and I both shook our heads.

"Oh."

"Do you need a ride?" Mark asked.

"Yes, if possible. I, uh . . ." She cleared her throat and lifted her chin. "Have a dinner I need to go to in Jackson City."

"Oooh?" Mark drawled dramatically, eyebrows waggling. "Hot guy, Lizbeth?"

She refused to look at me, which was fine. Because something was burning in my throat, and if I had to speak, I'd croak. Like an utter imbecile.

"Ah, I don't know," she said. "It's just a dinner. I was supposed to borrow Mav's SUV, but he'll be using it. With my car in the river . . ."

"I'll take you."

The words came from me, but I'd had no intention of saying them. Or even realized that they were in my head.

She blinked. "Great. Thanks. I, um . . . you don't have to do that, though. Maybe I could just drive it? Then you don't have to wait around?"

I shrugged. "Not a big deal."

Her forehead wrinkled. "You're just going to wait in Jackson City while I'm on a date?"

So it wasn't just dinner.

"Sure. I have some errands I could run."

She pulled in a breath, opened her mouth, and paused. Mark looked at me with a grin I didn't care to acknowledge.

"I mean . . . do you not want me to drive the Zombie Mobile?" she asked.

"You could try," Mark offered, "but it doesn't have power steering, and the floor is about to fall out."

He wasn't kidding.

"Plus," Mark added, "if this guy ends up being a serial killer, the Zombie Mobile isn't your best option."

I punched him in the arm. He grimaced.

"Serial killer," Lizbeth muttered with deep annoyance. "Seriously?"

Mark shrugged.

She shook that off, then tucked a strand of hair behind her ears and pulled her shoulders back. "Got it. Okay. Well, thank you, JJ. I'm sorry if this is inconvenient."

"Not at all." I shook my head. "It's good."

"Thanks." She shuffled back a step. "I'm going to finish up some work in my cabin."

Like a flash, she disappeared out the back door with her laptop clutched to her chest. The heaviness in the air seemed to hover for several long moments before Mark broke it.

"You're a friggin' mess, JJ."

"Shut up."

"What? Tell me you don't see it in her eyes when she's looking at you all day long and tries to pretend she isn't."

"I don't see it in her eyes."

"Then you're choosing to be blind."

I frowned. "I'm practically her employer."

"Correction: *I* am her employer. Adventura is in my name, per your request. You are an investor and employee in the company that's contracted her to work for a very short amount of time."

"Mav would kill me."

"Nah. You've earned your way into his good graces with the fact that you've saved her life one and a half times."

"One and a half?"

"I don't count the fire." He smirked. "She would have left on her own."

I rolled my eyes, which only made him laugh. "You have no idea what you're talking about, Mark."

He sobered. "What has you so freaked out?"

"Who said I was freaked out?"

"The fact that confident JJ has suddenly gone all weird? The fact that you *won't* ask her out, which is a dead giveaway. Not every woman is Stacey, you know. That witch was something else. You lucked out, brother."

A thousand memories whirled through my mind. A beach. Candles. The strange feeling of nausea and anticipation in my stomach. Then Mom crying. Dad's stoic, pressed-together lips. A dusty day at Adventura when they announced the official demise of their marriage, then bickered like children.

The feeling of being rent in half when the family fell apart.

Of being the only one on the outside.

"Nothing," I said.

He stood up. "Okay, brother. Tell yourself you don't like her. Tell yourself you're not raving jealous. Tell yourself you're not scared. But it will only work for so long. And if you don't ask her out yourself, I might. And we both know she'll fall madly in love with my charms once I fully unleash them and you won't have a prayer."

He shuffled out the front door, likely to talk to the real estate agent. I simmered on the couch for a few minutes. My jealousy was new, and that bothered me. My annoyance wasn't entirely new, but it *really* bothered me.

The sudden sense of fear that cropped up at the idea of Lizbeth out with some other guy? Definitely new.

Definitely bothered me.

* * *

Friday night came a little too quickly.

Before I knew it, Lizbeth and I were ambling along the snowy path to the bridge that crossed the river. It was a thirty-minute drive to Jackson City from there. The way things were going, it would pass in total silence. I'd already been grumpy and concerned over this "dinner." Then I saw her sleek black pants, flowing white top, and the pop of her eyes in makeup.

After that, I was downright irascible in my head.

Lizbeth cleared her throat and said, "I had you bring me a little early. I hope that's okay. There are a few things I need to pick up."

"That's fine."

"Tyler's email said to meet at Belle Vie at five."

Tyler was his name. Interesting.

"Where do you want to go first?" I asked as we pulled onto the highway. Belle Vie was a fancy upscale restaurant with a hundred-dollar-per-plate average. Which all but firmly refuted my hope that this was a punk college kid. Also destroyed the idea of this being *just a dinner*. This Tyler guy was taking her on a date.

And damn if it didn't annoy me that it would probably be a romantic date.

"The Antique Barn, if you don't mind?"

For what felt like the first time in days, I cracked a smile. "The Antique Barn? What do you need from there?"

"Something very important," she replied mysteriously, but some of the uncertainty had left her voice. Which meant it was probably time for me to lose the annoyed vibe that I wasn't meaning to give off.

"Got it."

The silence was less burdened after that. When I pulled into the Antique Barn, she popped out, then held up a palm.

"Wait. Don't follow. I'll be five minutes."

My hand paused halfway to the seat belt.

"Okay."

Less than ten minutes later, she dashed back outside, clutching a bulky bag in her hands. Whatever lay inside was wrapped in a cardboard box.

"Very mysterious," I said.

Her wide smile returned. "I know. Now can you stop at Bed and Bath?"

"Can I come into this one?"

She shook her head, eyes bright.

With a dramatic sigh, I put the Zombie Mobile in reverse. "Sure."

I wanted to go in with her, see what she was like in a store like that. Did she light up? Probably. The girl was practically a living Christmas tree.

Four stops later—including a kitchen store, a home repair store, and an office supply store—she climbed back into the Zombie Mobile. Bags littered the floor at her feet. Our easy banter had returned while I unsuccessfully tried to guess her mission with all these tightly controlled packages. I couldn't even peek inside to see what she'd bought. Somehow, she'd had them all double-bagged or covered up.

Odd.

What could she possibly be hiding?

"Okay." She yanked the seat belt across her. "I think it's time to head to the restaurant."

The steering wheel was already pointing that way, so I hit the gas. The weight of her impending departure felt like my chest was a balloon someone was slowly letting air out of. She was bottled, red-haired sunshine. With resolve, I forced my mind back to the task at hand. I really *did* have an errand to run in Jackson City. An errand that mattered dramatically to the rest of my life and also involved the petit fours hidden behind my seat.

But that errand didn't feel as important as Lizbeth.

"Just text me when you're done," I said. "I'll be around. And if you need anything in the meantime."

"Thanks. I'm sure he'll be a perfect gentleman."

At that, I almost snorted.

"He better be," I muttered.

If she heard, she gave no indication. The Zombie Mobile ambled into the street. Cars whizzed past as we slowly built up speed.

"Do you know this Tyler guy?" I asked.

"No. Bethany set this up."

"She do this a lot?"

"Not really. He's a client of hers who's considering moving here. Just wanted to meet for dinner and ask about life in the mountains."

"At Belle Vie?" I asked. "That's extremely upscale."

She chewed on her bottom lip. "Maybe I'm not dressed right."

"You're perfect," I immediately replied. "Are you anticipating lots of romance?"

At that, she laughed. I wanted to laugh with her but couldn't even make a sound because a new wave of annoyance crested in my throat. Tyler would get to laugh with her tonight. She shook her head, her hair like strands of fire.

"No. Blind dates are not romantic."

"Are you sure?"

For the first time, her unwavering confidence seemed to falter. She covered it quickly, but I sensed a tension in her that was new.

"Well, I guess they could be."

"Probably would be weird if it was romantic too soon, right?"

She frowned. "Not necessarily. Lots of books have adorable, romantic meet-cutes with total strangers."

"Meet-cutes?"

"The moment the love interest and the heroine meet."

"There's a term for it?" I chuckled. "That's wild."

"It's smart. Authors need to know what readers expect. You can't recover from a bad meet-cute, if you ask me."

"Of *course* not."

She sent me a smarmy grin, and seconds later, we pulled up to Belle Vie. I let the truck slow to a stop.

"Seriously. If he's weird, I'm only a few minutes away," I said.

"It'll be fine."

"But if it's not—"

Lizbeth slipped the seat belt off and smiled as she reached for the doorknob. "Thanks. I anticipate a completely boring, awkward blind date and then a payout after."

"A payout?" I cried. "What the hell does that mean?"

She stopped, then laughed. "No, not like that! It's from my sister! If these clients close on the house, she'll give me a bonus."

Still didn't like this. I didn't have a great feeling about Tyler. Lizbeth hopped out of the car, a small purse slung over her left shoulder. Just before the door closed, she paused. "Oh, JJ? Don't open any of them."

"What?"

"The bags. Leave them closed, okay?"

I hesitated, shot her a grin, and finally agreed. "Fine."

For half a second, I saw hesitation in her gaze.

She opened her mouth, then closed it. "Thanks, JJ. Talk soon."

"Be safe, Lizbeth."

It was the best I could do. She shut the door and walked away, looking gorgeous in her sleek gray jacket. This Tyler guy would be an idiot if he didn't gobble her up. Which said nothing good about me.

Resigned, I turned the Zombie Mobile and headed downtown. I had a date of my own, but it wasn't with an adorable, perky redhead.

Chapter Seventeen

LIZBETH

Blind dates stressed me out.

Normally, I put too much pressure on a new guy. Mentally catalogued whether they fit my idea of a storybook romance. What kind of love interest would *they* make? Would they dance in the rain? Kiss me senseless in the kitchen? Would they be safe, gentle, and kind?

Tonight felt twenty times worse, and it was all because of JJ. His perfectly easy smile while I shopped for him without him even knowing it. The unaffected way he took me to the date. It had been a bit weird when I asked them for the ride, but now he seemed as unattached as ever. Like he'd friend-zoned me.

Again.

One could argue that all the romance books covered this, and he was secretly seething with jealousy, but I doubted it. He certainly wasn't coming off that way. At all.

Disappointing.

The Zombie Mobile let out a belch of black smoke and then pulled back into traffic. At the door, I stopped, pulling in a deep breath. My phone vibrated, so I stepped to the side.

From JJ, maybe?

Ellie: Good luck on the date and be safe. I slipped a handheld taser into your purse before you left for Adventura, just in case.

A quick inspection confirmed. I rolled my eyes.

Lizbeth: Thanks. You're worse than Mav, you know?

Ellie: I know. Devin and I are driving to Jackson City now to hit up a movie. If you need anything, we're literally up the road.

Lizbeth: How ironic is the fact that you're driving from little old Pineville to Jackson City right now?

Ellie: It's entirely on purpose. I wanted to make sure you're safe because blind dates can be weird. Dev talked me out of doing dinner at the same restaurant, so be grateful.

A little smile graced my face. Ellie's obsession with safety wasn't new—it had always been a bit extreme. A pang tugged at my heart. I already missed her, and it had only been a few days. Devin, even as a football player, wouldn't be half as scary as my sister if I found myself in a bad date situation.

Lizbeth: I'll be safe. JJ is in Jackson City too. He gave me a ride.

Ellie: On the date?!

Lizbeth: No, that would be totally weird.

Ellie: So are we if you need us. Seriously—we can be there in minutes. If he's some weird serial killer . . .

Lizbeth: What is it with everyone and the serial killer thing? We're in a very public restaurant! And I'm good, but thank you. I'm going to go in, enjoy that date, then go back to my cabin in Adventura alone, take off my bra, and enjoy a romance novel. Easy night!

Feeling better for some reason, I shoved my phone in my purse, drew in a deep breath, and banished JJ from my mind. I was fine. This was fine.

Everything was fine.

* * *

The smell of wine and grapefruit hit me with a gentle wave when I stepped inside Belle Vie. Grapevines curled around the pillars at the entrance. Live violin music sang from somewhere within the restaurant. In the background, a few waiters bustled past in white shirts with black ties and pocketed aprons. A couple in the foyer wore an evening gown and a tux.

Whoa.

This place was something else.

"Lizbeth?"

A broad-shouldered man strode toward me from near a potted palm in the corner. He smiled warmly, a hand extended, the other behind his back.

"Tyler?" I asked.

A bright smile greeted me as our fingers touched. He had a firm shake and kind, soulful green eyes in a face framed by dark hair. His curls glistened in the dim light, and I wanted to run my hands through them. Holy swooner, but I wanted to lean in and *smell* him. He smelled like *Acqua di Gio* and perfection.

I internally squealed.

"Nice to officially meet you," he purred.

"You as well."

"I appreciate you coming to help me map this world a little better. You see, I'm far more used to a city, and the mountains . . . they're different."

"I understand."

Tyler's other hand came out from behind his back, proffering a sprawling bouquet of red roses.

"For you," he said. "As a token of my gratitude."

He thrust them toward me. I accepted out of a sense of numb shock. Sprigs of baby's breath littered the thick greenery nestled around the roses. Crimson veins ran like rivers through the gentle petals. Sweet baby pineapple, but these were the real deal. These were no grocery store flowers. They must have cost at least a hundred dollars.

"Wow." I blinked, inhaling their gentle fragrance. "Uh . . . thank you."

"Bethany had nothing but praise for you. She mentioned that you're a romantic at heart." He straightened and held out one arm, elbow bent. "I am as well. I also believe in the power of first impressions. You can never recover from a bad one."

My heart almost seized. Hadn't I *just* said that to JJ?

"Besides"—Tyler waved a hand—"every woman deserves a gorgeous set of flowers. Especially on a first date. Ready? They already have our table set up. I picked the back corner. Hope that's okay."

With the flowers cradled in my right arm, I gave him my left. Not only was I possibly underdressed in black slacks and a silky white dolman-sleeve shirt from Banana's—I was *definitely* totally overwhelmed.

"Of course it's okay. And the flowers—they're . . . they're beautiful. I don't know what to say beyond *thank you*."

"They pale in comparison to you." He winked and started to walk.

Senseless, I followed.

Was this a little weird? Not at all. *This* was a man who knew how to impress a girl on their first date. Romance on every axis. Flowers. Offering his arm. Commanding the date. *He's a little bit alpha,* I thought. Which piqued my curiosity. Alpha-male romances had always been so exciting. Daring.

Wouldn't it be wonderful to be so taken care of? If anything, this was an ideal date for my research. So, this was fine.

Except my throat felt a little hot.

Tyler led us farther into the dim restaurant, which smelled like a delectable mixture of gardenia and melted butter. Flickering candles danced among the low murmur of couples in dark wooden booths. The ambiance was sanguine and mellow. A violinist slowly sashayed around the tables.

Storybook romance.

He led me to a quiet corner all the way in the back, with only one table. The intimacy felt like a cocoon.

"Oh."

The sound escaped my mouth before I could stop it. Pillar candles illuminated our closed-off space. Red rose petals scattered the tabletop and chairs. Half-full wine glasses graced both place settings, along with what appeared to be a wrapped box of chocolates in gold foil on top of one plate. Gossamer curtains could be drawn to give us more privacy.

Tyler practically vomited romance from the books and right onto the table. The meaning of the quick patter of my heart wasn't clear even to me. Was this amazing or . . .

Or something.

"Dinner for two, my lady," he murmured.

My lady?

That felt a little weird.

"Are those . . . Norbert Love Signature chocolates?" I squeaked and gestured to the distinctively green box on my plate.

"Yes." He brightened. "You know your confectionaries?"

"Something like that," I murmured weakly. They were a mere $125 a box. I only recognized them because my roommate Aiko had bought them for her fiancée Tanesha for Valentine's Day last year. Tanesha had eaten them so slowly they'd lasted into summer semester. She'd cut them in fourths after a bad day and shared them with both of us.

"I'm not just a romantic, but a hopeless romantic," he admitted with a wide, unapologetic smile as we sat down.

"It's . . . impressive. I mean, I thought we were here to talk about you moving to the mountains."

Somehow, I tacked on what I hoped was a charming smile. He returned it.

"We will definitely do that. Yes, it may seem like I've gone overboard, but as I said—you can't recover from a bad first impression. Plus, this is how I show up in the world."

He shrugged a little as he said it. His lack of apology impressed me, but I leaned back against the booth as far as I could. For some reason, I wanted a little extra space from the *Acqua di Gio*. It filled the booth in a choking way.

Tyler continued, "For some women, this kind of treatment is a bit too much. I understand that. I believe women should be pampered, protected, and taken care of. It so rarely happens anymore that I like to give it. As a sort of . . . gift, if you will. Any woman with me is always safe."

My internal critic immediately shrieked, *Serial killer! Serial killer!*

Should a man have to insist he was a safe person? Would he expect a *gift* in return? With a lick of my lips, I brushed it off. Ellie had clearly gotten to me with her own fears. Tyler didn't seem like a creep. He was just . . . intense.

Obviously wealthy, too, with all this extravagance for a blind date.

So, everything was fine.

But what did he mean by *protected* and *pampered*? His charming routine felt slightly . . . sinister. Something inside of me recoiled at this situation. It felt like I was standing in a box with the walls caving in. Pressure all around me.

Instead of screaming, I managed a smile. "That's a . . . lovely sentiment."

Tyler leaned back and spread his hands. "Lizbeth, tell me everything about you. I've so looked forward to getting to know you. I want to hear it all."

"Right! You want to hear about life in the mountains."

"Of course."

"Okay, well, life in the mountains is—"

"We'll get to that. What do you do for a living?"

"Oh. Okay. Well . . . I'm not that exciting. I—"

"I'll decide that."

My jaw tightened.

His eyebrows quirked in silent question.

"Will you give me a chance to finish a sentence," I asked, "or should I let you decide that too?"

Although my tone had cooled, a hint of something appeared in his gaze. I hated to call it respect, but it was too intense for amusement. With a flicker of his fingers, he indicated for me to continue.

"As I said . . ."

While I explained a few aspects of life in the mountains, his attention focused wholly on me. For a little courage, I sipped at a glass of Dom Pérignon. My mouth warmed as I swallowed the wine. It wasn't often that I drank. The scent reminded me of Mama, and any other liquor reminded me of Dad. He certainly drank them all, even mouthwash when he grew desperate while the bank account dwindled.

"Fascinating," Tyler said when I finished. He'd fallen into a contemplative expression, but the waiter saved me from the awkwardness of asking what such a face meant. Before I could reach for my menu, Tyler spoke up.

In French.

Two semesters living with a French Canadian foreign exchange student who'd quickly become one of my best friends had made me conversant in the language. I followed him with some difficulty. He ordered an elk chop with raspberry sauce, a plate of charcuterie, and sea bass with scallops in lemon butter, then dismissed the waiter with a twitch of his hand.

The melodic blur of his voice, like a string of velvet letters, left me stunned for a few seconds. Sexy. But kind of annoying. Fish? No thanks.

Had I missed how high-end this restaurant was on the Yelp reviews? Did he just assume the waiter would speak French? I mean . . . was speaking French *really* necessary? JJ flickered through my mind, but I couldn't place him in a restaurant like this, and he flitted back out.

Tyler turned his attention back to me with another deeply charming smile. "Forgive me," he said as he leaned forward. "I studied the menu beforehand, and I find the experience far more authentic in its original language. Do you trust my judgment?"

No.

The thought came so unexpectedly that I had to recover my thoughts and scramble to remember his question.

Did I trust him?

"As long as I get the elk chop."

His grin illuminated his handsome, dusky features. Another curl dropped onto his forehead. "You know French?" he asked, delighted.

"I'm conversational, yes."

"How lovely."

"Shall we talk about your transition to the mountains? Do you have any questions?"

"Yes, please, if you don't mind." A more sober expression came to his face. "My parents are getting old, and I don't want to lose what time we have left. If they move here, I may need to move my business here as well. I'm concerned things are just too small. A date may feel a bit . . . odd for such a conversation as this . . . but it helps me feel like I know someone in the area more than just in passing. Besides, I wanted to test the local flavor."

"I see."

He launched into an explanation of what he did for a living. Something with foreign trade, international business. Big dollars, I was sure. The details blurred together. One thing was abundantly clear: the man was ridiculously rich.

Basically, I was living a billionaire alpha romance novel meet-cute.

Something I'd read countless times and had always swooned over. Here was a strapping alpha-male character come to life right from the pages of my favorite contemporary romance novel, *His Burning Kiss.* Tyler was attentive to my needs, maybe overly so. He was confident, wealthy, firm, and decisive. He took control of the situation. I'd read this before and loved it.

Except now . . . I hated it.

Or maybe I just didn't like Tyler.

By the time he finished speaking, I'd mostly recovered from the shock of—yet again— a romantic experience not feeling the way it should.

"Well," I said, "there certainly is plenty of upscale local flavor here, as you said. We'll sample some tonight at this restaurant."

We spoke back and forth for several minutes. The arrival of the food interrupted my response to one of his questions— *What kinds of social events do you find most prominent here?* —and I grabbed my knife to dig into the elk chop.

Soft, but not my flavor.

"Sounds like a charming place overall," he declared. "I'm considering buying the house."

"For your parents?"

"Yes."

"How kind."

He shrugged. I helped myself to another bite of mashed potatoes so silky I could have worn them. My silence must have gone on a touch too long, because his eyebrows came together like a slinky. "Lizbeth? Did I say something wrong? You can absolutely trust me."

I cleared my throat as Mark's voice screamed in my mind, *Serial killer.* Just in case, I pulled my phone out of my purse and rested it on my lap.

"Just enjoying this delicious food," I said.

His gaze tapered. "You're lying."

I almost choked. "What?"

"Are you uncomfortable?"

We held a long, hard stare for a moment before I said, "Yes. I am uncomfortable."

He took that in without a change of expression. "I see."

"I just . . . this is a bit much for me. It's all so . . . perfect. On the nose. Like you walked out of a romance novel," I finished quietly.

Shiny coconuts, but what was I going to tell JJ about this? How would I possibly detail this for the love binder?

Tyler's gaze widened, though he didn't seem put out. Just startled. I'd taken him by surprise again. Shouldn't that feel more satisfying? When I read it, this sort of romance felt powerful. Instead, I just wanted to go.

"Really?" he asked.

"Well . . . yes."

"You're not a lover of romance?"

"It's not that. I'm actually very fond of romance."

The red roses filled the seat next to me with their delicate leaves and intricate veins. Alone, they would have been fine. A first date with a true romantic. But together with all of . . . this? This wasn't romance. This was . . . something else.

He grinned anyway, but it seemed tight. He was covering something with his easy amusement. Disappointment, perhaps.

"What a surprise," he murmured, his fork poised over his plate. "This usually wins over most women."

"You do this often?"

"Yes."

He replied with such confidence it took me a moment to respond. "That's not very promising for us, then," I said wryly.

He laughed. Nothing seemed to faze him, which disconcerted me more. How was he this smooth? How could I ever be my bookish self in front of someone so unruffled? Would he be upset if I wanted to curl up with a book instead of dress up for dinner?

"I'm picky," he admitted. "I know a good woman when I meet her. This sort of circumstance is my life. My everyday sort of life when I'm home and not traveling for work, anyway."

"And are you happy?"

He smiled. "Very. It suits me. It seems like it doesn't suit you?"

I shook my head, hair swaying.

"That's disappointing, because you're lovely, Lizbeth. To be honest, doing anything different for a date seems . . . dishonest. It doesn't seem fair to pretend otherwise. This may be overwhelming, but when I bring a woman into a situation like this, I want to see what happens. Romance and presentation and displays are important to me. I'm wealthy and plan to always climb that ladder. Any partner of mine will need to keep up with that."

"So, what if I wasn't well suited to that? Then what?"

He shrugged. "I decide at the end of the date whether we

would be compatible or not. If I decide we are, I move things forward at my own pace."

There was so much wrong there that I almost reached for the taser. *His* pace? *He* would decide?

But wasn't that the alpha male?

"What if you decided we *were* compatible?" I asked, reaching for the wine to give my hand something to do.

"Then I'd arrange our next date, pick you up, and sweep you off your feet again."

My mind spun with thoughts I couldn't fully articulate, but at least one was perfectly clear: *Why do you get to control everything?*

"When would I get to decide something?"

He smiled, but this time it failed to impress me. "Whenever you like, of course. But why make decisions when it feels so good to be taken care of?"

I decided not to answer that, too unnerved by how smoothly the words came out. The pad of my thumb ran over the edge of my phone. I thought of JJ, but kept my voice light when I asked, "And am I failing?"

"Of course not."

He said it so quickly that I doubted him. It would be easy to play the game I thought he wanted. Let him think he was in control. Or that I didn't care about these small touches, the aggressive gifts, just to make him want it more. Or antagonize him just to throw him off. In the books, that always impressed the hell out of men. It was delicious when I read about it.

But this just felt . . . like a game.

Beneath his easy elegance, I sensed there wasn't much I'd connect with. How did he feel about children? How would he feel about me running a coffee shop that he'd have no say in? I'd had my fill of controlling men when Dad grabbed me by the hair and threw me against the wall, thank you very much.

The flash of memory caught me by surprise.

The crumble of drywall beneath my head. Falling onto my shoulder, dazed. Utter disbelief had a way of stopping you in your tracks. The throb in my ears that gave way to his screams.

Everything had whirled around for a while after that, until it all just faded to black.

Then, in the morning light, Mama leaned over me. Stroked my cheek. Whispered softly while a tear dribbled from her black eye. In the background, red roses lay scattered on the table.

A solemn apology, years too late.

With difficulty, I extracted myself from the memory. My voice was hoarse when I asked, "What does your perfect day look like, Tyler?"

If he was startled by the turn in the conversation, he gave no hint of it.

"I'd be up early to make you breakfast in bed. We'd lounge for hours making love. Maybe pop into a hot tub with champagne and chocolate-covered strawberries. Enjoy a few movies at home, naked. Perhaps an elegant night out with you in an evening gown and me in a tux, finished off with dancing under the stars. Something along those lines. And yours?"

Confirmation.

"Books." I spread my hands out. "Piles of them. And myself, tucked into a chair, with food and drink at hand. At the end of the day, and after about four books so satisfying I couldn't stop reading long enough to eat lunch, I'd stop. I might get dinner with someone. Maybe they could even spend the day with me, but they'd have to be pretty special."

Tyler straightened, gaze tapered. He threaded his hands together and leaned his elbows on the table. "You're telling me something."

"I am."

He became solemn. "You're telling me this isn't a good fit?"

On some level, I wanted it to be. He was handsome and

confident and wealthy. But I wouldn't let him into my perfect day.

"Not in the slightest," I whispered back.

He hesitated only a breath. "After all this? That's . . . frustrating."

His nostrils flared. A new sense of tension appeared in his shoulders, and all my internal alarms began to peal. Though I couldn't identify why, a sense of panic pulsed through me. With it came the smell of alcohol. The distant sound of shouting, as if from a memory.

I stood unexpectedly. "I think it's best if I go."

Startled, he opened his mouth to say something, but I cut him off. "Thank you for this dinner, Tyler, and for meeting. Hopefully it was helpful."

Before he could respond, I strode away, breath held. Once in the foyer, I whirled around. He hadn't followed. Relieved, I sent JJ a text.

Lizbeth: Ready for you to come get me. Sooner than later would be preferable.

JJ: Almost there.

Chapter Eighteen

JJ

Lizbeth was quiet the whole ride home.

She didn't say a word except a warm, "Thank you for picking me up," and "It was okay." Once back at Adventura, I helped her carry her packages to her cabin, then she thanked me again and closed the door before I could offer to build up her fire.

I hovered there for a second, torn.

Had something happened?

Was she *really* okay?

The urge to knock on her door and ask again almost overwhelmed me, but I pushed it down. Finally, I reluctantly retreated. The sound of paws on snow joined me as I looped around the office to enter from the front. Justin and Atticus were there. Atty greeted me with a quick lick on the hand.

"Everything all right?" Justin asked, studying me.

"Fine."

But I wasn't fine. I was worried and pissed and annoyed that I was worried and pissed. Justin hesitated, then nodded. He and Atticus headed back toward his cabin while I trekked to the kitchen. If I couldn't climb, I could make and knead some dough for breakfast tomorrow. That would release some of this . . . tension.

* * *

The next day, Lizbeth started work before Mark and I woke up. When I made it down the ladder, she was sitting in Mark's desk chair, her hair in a single ponytail over her right shoulder. A coffee mug sat on the desk next to her. She wore no makeup today. The flicker of light on her pale lashes fascinated me.

"Morning, Lizbeth."

She waved distractedly but didn't take her gaze off the laptop. "Good morning."

A pile of papers sat next to her computer. Probably waiting to be scanned. How long had she been awake? The coffee was already lukewarm.

Once in the kitchenette, I paused. Something looked different. Before I could figure it out, Mark slipped down the ladder.

"I think we'll be able to close on the pizza shop today," he said as he yanked a jacket on and stepped into a pair of boots at the same time. "I'm late, see ya!"

He dashed out the door. Lizbeth glanced up, then back down. I turned back to the kitchen, completely confused. What was different? Wait, were our curtains a different color? At one point they'd been Mark's old Teenage Mutant Ninja Turtle pillowcases, but we'd swapped them out for the far classier old beige.

As I poured my coffee, stumped, Lizbeth broke the strained silence. Words flew out of her like they'd been stuffed inside waiting to get out.

"It totally sucked."

My head popped up.

She stood behind Mark's desk, hands planted on the papers in front of her, glaring at me.

"What?"

"The date."

She straightened, arms folded across her middle. Her eyebrows knitted together as she swallowed hard.

"He . . . Tyler . . . might as well have walked out of a romance novel. Everything was perfect. His hair. His voice. He even *smelled* the way I'd imagined an alpha billionaire—or maybe just a millionaire—would smell."

To give myself something to do, I had a sip of hot coffee. An *alpha billionaire?* What was she talking about? The scalding feeling in the back of my throat felt better than the one inside my chest. Lizbeth, on a roll, kept going. Except now she was pacing behind the desk and making almost no sense at all.

"He gave me roses. There were candles on the table. Curtains. Can you believe that? Curtains, JJ. And rose petals. The violinist?"

My brow lifted.

"Oh yeah," she said before I could utter a sound. "Rose. Petals."

Another hot sip that burned, burned, burned.

"Then he was so intense and . . . he ordered for me in French . . . and he insisted I was safe. I mean, elk chop? C'mon! I'm clearly a pasta girl! But, of course, I probably wasn't safe. Or maybe I was and we just weren't suited? I don't know, he was angry at the end."

"He what?"

She waved a hand. "He didn't touch me. But . . . that freaking walking violin was distracting me and . . . it was . . . so *weird*. I've read that date a hundred times. I used to *love* alpha-billionaire novels—"

What was she talking about?

"But now?"

She threw her hands in the air.

I paused, my mug halfway to my lips. The silence told me she wanted me to say something, but I could barely keep up with her fragmented thoughts.

"Can I get this straight?" I asked.

She gestured with a wave of her hand again.

"So he was handsome?"

Emphatic nod.

"He gave you flowers."

Another nod.

"He picked a romantic setting. There was a violin playing in the background?"

Another nod, this one more tentative. She chewed on her bottom lip.

"And you hated it?" I asked.

"Yes."

This didn't add up. If a guy like that couldn't pull off romance, the rest of us lowly suckers were clearly doomed.

"Why?" I asked.

"I don't know."

She said it with such desperation, such soulful despair, that I couldn't stop myself from setting aside my coffee and closing the distance between us. She stood there, bottom lip between her teeth, and watched me approach.

I stopped a foot away. "Why are you so sad?" I whispered.

"Because *that* should have been the most romantic date of my life. It was classic, storybook romance. Straight out of one of my favorite novels."

"And you didn't like it."

She nodded, then ran a hand over her eyes and collapsed into the chair behind her. "It's . . . frustrating. I've had two very romantic experiences recently, and neither of them felt the way they were supposed to." She faltered for a moment before adding quietly, "They were just too *real* to be romantic at the time. It's disorienting."

"Please tell me that one of them wasn't seeing your cabin free of mice for the first time?"

Her lips twitched. "That wasn't it."

"Good."

A hint of her usual lightness reassured me. Somehow, I suppressed the urge to ask what her other romantic experience was. Instead, I crouched in front of her. The feeling of her skin on mine when I put a hand under her chin sent a little shiver through me.

"It was just one date, Lizbeth. You don't have to give up on romance because of one date."

"Says you?"

"Says me."

A half smile teased her lips. "I'm not giving up on romance. I'm just frustrated that it hasn't felt the way I wanted it to. But maybe that's just reality."

"That's fair."

"When I lived with my dad, romance books were the only things that felt safe. He'd be drunk. I'd hear him breaking things. Threatening to hurt Ellie. Screaming Mama's name. Sometimes he'd come after us. Sometimes he'd go after Ellie, but I'd get in his way. The only thing that really took me away from him was my books."

"Where you felt safe," I whispered.

She nodded.

Well, that totally sucked. Love wasn't just some breezy distraction for her. Romance *had* actually saved her life. The revelation of life with her father was new to me. It explained so much.

When I imagined a bruise coloring her porcelain cheeks, I forced myself to take a deep breath. I needed to climb. Rise above this rage and get it out in a safe way so she didn't see it in me.

This was about her.

A hint of color pinked her cheeks, and she chuckled self-consciously. "Sorry. This is . . . I'm sorry. I just couldn't stop thinking about it and . . . had to let you know that maybe you're right." She drew in a deep breath and met my gaze. "I fully concede a point to you in our debate, JJ."

With that, she withdrew. Her warmth and smell drifted past me before the back door closed. I balled my hands into fists and let out a long, steady breath.

That was one point I'd give back all day long.

Chapter Nineteen

LIZBETH

A very pale version of myself peered back at me from my compact mirror. Did it mean something that I didn't try to hide my pale eyelashes in front of JJ? Normally, I stressed about wearing makeup. With the Bailey boys, it didn't seem to matter.

With a long breath, I shut the compact and slumped against my bed. Sleep had been elusive last night as I'd tangled with the idea that perhaps JJ *was* right. Maybe romance was a false protective wall. I didn't entertain the thought for long, but it lingered in the back of my mind.

Instead, I'd turned to two of my favorite romance books, slipped into their familiar words, and felt better for it after.

Now, I replayed the startled way he'd watched me. His gentle touch. There was no burn of his skin on mine when he'd taken my chin in his hands. Nothing but the burn of ugly reality. It was comforting, though. Just his olive eyes settled my prickling heart. He'd listened. Watched me with compassion and surprise.

He was the last person in the world I should have told about Dad, though no stress accompanied the thought that he knew part of my secret life.

Only part of it.

A flash of a memory skipped through my mind. Mama applying bright-red lipstick while she leaned over the sink, inspecting her pores in the mirror. She wore a skintight black dress and strappy heels, and her hair was still in curlers. She laughed while Ellie played on the floor at her feet.

"Don't settle, baby girl." Mama stared me right in the eye. "Hold onto those dreams of a great romance, because they're real. You give so much away when you love. If you settle like I did, you're in a world of hurt. Make him romance you, not bed you. There's a difference. That difference will change your life."

With a shudder, I snapped out of it.

Where had that come from? *Make him romance you.* Mama's voice rang in my head so clearly I couldn't dispute it. That day had ended in a bruised cheek for her. I'd spent the next day in my room alone.

The memory cleared as I thought back to Tyler. Then JJ.

It was just one date, JJ had said, and he was right. The date didn't mean anything about love. It simply meant that *that* wasn't actually my idea of romance. The alpha-billionaire thing didn't do much for me.

The plastic of my love binder was cold when I pulled it out from under the bed. I flipped past tabs and graph paper, and recorded the point I'd awarded to JJ. He'd won it. I scribbled a few observations, then shut the binder and shoved it back under the bed.

Time to pick myself up and keep going.

Filled with new resolve, I drew in a breath, pushed my hair out of my eyes, and marched back to the office. An empty room greeted me. JJ must have left, because I couldn't hear him shuffling around upstairs.

A note on my laptop drew me forward. A piece of paper sat on top of what appeared to be a homemade pastry. I picked up the note with a trembling hand.

Don't worry, you won't have to scan and file this paper.
I'm sorry about your date and formally reject that point.
You still have a lot to prove on behalf of romance, but this
experience doesn't count.
Have a homemade croissant. Carbs always make me
happy.
Also, that was his loss. You're amazing, Lizbeth.

—JJ

* * *

Later that afternoon, I pulled a few sticky hooks out of a shopping bag and crept over to the single sink. The hottest the water got was warm, and dishes were perennially piled at the bottom. I quickly peeled off the backs of the hooks and hung them in a zigzag pattern on the wall over the sink. Then I rooted through the cupboard and hung the Baileys' favorite coffee mugs. The tiny reorganization cleared up space and added a splash of much-needed color.

With a contented sigh, I appraised my work and then shuffled into the spare bedroom. Mark wanted to burn all these papers in a bonfire after they were confirmed as recorded, so I needed another box to hold the rest of the processed pages.

JJ hadn't returned since my outburst, so I'd enjoyed solitude and the music of Andrea and Matteo Bocelli. In the quiet, I'd dusted the fireplace and tucked a few functional pieces of decor from the Antique Barn on top of the mantel. Nothing too obvious. An old, rusted crampon from the early 1900s that reminded me of JJ, and an oil lamp that I used as a bookend for some of JJ's mountaineering books. Plus a drawer organizer in Mark's desk and a desktop organizer behind his computer. I'd cleaned out two drawers just by sorting his oddities.

The office door closed, breaking through my thoughts.

Someone shuffled inside and set down car keys with a light jangle. Not Mark. He made a lot more noise than that. JJ moved more like a cat.

"Whoa. Who's reading romance books?"

The astonished female voice carried into the spare bedroom. My hand froze on a box, and I lifted my head. A woman?

I stepped out of the room to find a thin but strong, dark-haired woman in the kitchenette. Crinkles lined her eyes. Kelly, the Bailey boys' mother. I could see Mark in her face, and JJ in her eyes.

On seeing me, her eyes widened. She tilted her head and held my favorite romance book up a little higher. I must have left it in the kitchen at lunch.

"Hi."

"Hi." I smiled and carted a box out. "I'm Lizbeth."

"I recognize you. You work at the coffee shop. Or . . . did." She grimaced. "Heard about that. So sorry. What a darling place that was."

"Thanks."

Her head cocked to the side. "Are JJ and Mark here?"

"Mark is in town closing a real estate deal, and I'm not sure where JJ went. He left hours ago."

She nodded, studying me. "And you are doing . . ."

"Work for Mark. Trying to get his paperwork under control." With a little shrug, I gestured to the box in my arms and then at the boxes of papers near the desk.

"Brave girl," she cried, chuckling. "Need some help?"

"Sure, thanks! I'm just carting these outside. Mark said he wanted all the boxes left by the woodpile so he could burn the paperwork when it's done."

She tilted her head back and laughed. "That's definitely my oldest son. Arsonist to the core. I'd love to help. Just show me which ones to move."

It took us ten minutes to lug the four boxes to the designated spot. Which left four more to scan and organize. Thankfully, the burn pile wasn't too far from the main lodge, and Justin had dug a path to it. Atticus trotted up to us, panting in the crisp air. The distant sound of a saw meant Justin was around somewhere.

Movement and sound came from the main kitchen, and I thought I glimpsed JJ inside. After my outburst this morning, I was grateful for some distance.

I dropped the last box and kicked it the final few feet through the snow. Supposedly, Justin would come burn it when Mark returned. Something about *a bonfire* and *s'mores* and *an offering to the snow gods.*

Kelly turned toward the kitchen, then beckoned me with a wave. "My nose detects something in there. Let's go check it out."

I had to admit I was hungry. I'd fended for myself for lunch, and I'd really only been able to find Froot Loops in the bachelor pad kitchenette.

I followed behind her, both eager and a little nervous. Curiosity pushed me forward. JJ's culinary creations seemed to just appear. What did it look like when he made them happen? Did he frown when he concentrated? Jabber nervously, like Mark? Somehow, I pictured him utterly quiet and focused.

Kelly knocked on a side door, but let us inside before JJ could respond. Warmth rushed out of the kitchen and over my skin. In the fading afternoon light, I welcomed it. A fierce chill had settled as the sun sank behind the mountain.

JJ looked up as we stepped inside. With his hair pulled away from his face and his shoulders broad beneath a long-sleeved T-shirt, he reminded me of a Nordic god. A Nordic god wearing a flour-covered apron. I almost swore under my breath. Sometimes it hurt to look at him.

Half a breath seemed to pass before he grinned at his mom. In that span, I saw hesitation. Maybe a flash of anger. It disappeared so quickly that I couldn't be sure.

Odd.

Kelly didn't seem to notice. She wrapped her arms around her son and squeezed him tight. Was it weird to feel jealous of a mom?

"Please tell me you're fixing something delicious," she said as she released him.

"Brioche."

He leaned against a counter, shoulders drawn tight against his shirt, and I almost swallowed my tongue. Instead, I focused on the mess of dough in the mixer. Only JJ could break hearts while wearing flour.

"Fancy," she sang. "What's the occasion?"

"Love a challenge."

He didn't quite meet her eyes as he said it. Instead, he gave me a smile that spoke worlds of reassurance. Did I imagine extra warmth in there?

Was I losing my mind?

"Hey, Liz."

My insides melted. "Hey."

He kept his gaze on me for a breath longer. It threw me off orbit, like he had his own gravity.

"Any chance we can try some?" Kelly asked as she clapped her hands together. He looked away from me and motioned to a counter behind him with a tilt of his head. A perfectly browned loaf of bread sitting there made my mouth water.

"Just finishing this final mix for this batch," he said. "Then we can try that one out while this one rises."

Minutes later, JJ finished his prep and set the lump of dough in the fridge to rise overnight. A ringing silence filled the kitchen. We sat on the floor with our backs to the counter while JJ split the loaf into three chunks and passed them around. The still-warm, buttery bread melted on my tongue. I fought a groan. Kelly didn't.

"You are my favorite son."

He laughed, but I heard an edge in it. "Thanks."

Snow fluttered past the window. I watched it, enjoying the delicious bread. Like everything with JJ, even the quiet felt easy and calm. He broke my concentration with a most unexpected question.

"Mom, do you read romance?"

My head snapped up. A twinkle filled JJ's eyes as he winked at me.

Kelly licked her thumb as she finished her bread. "Sure. It's been a few years, but I remember diving into it while you were in high school."

"What's your favorite kind?"

She frowned. "Are there different kinds?"

So. Many. I wanted to blurt out. In fear of listing every subcategory of romantic fiction out there, I shoved another bite of brioche into my mouth.

JJ's smile twitched. "Apparently there is," he said. "I'm partial to contemporary romance so far, myself."

I almost choked. Kelly reached over and slapped me on the back as I coughed. JJ rolled his lips together.

"Sorry," I wheezed. "I'm good."

"You're reading romance?" Kelly asked JJ.

"Had a friend suggest it as a life-changing experience. Thought I'd give it a try."

Kelly brushed a few crumbs off her legs. "I'm surprised."

"Why?" he asked.

She shrugged. "Wasn't Stacey big into the romance scene? Thought she turned you off from it."

He stiffened as flat as a board. I pretended there was a string on my knee to avoid staring as he floundered for a response.

Who was Stacey?

Kelly, seeming to realize she'd overstepped, said, "Well? What do you think of these romance books?"

Yes, I added silently. *What do you think, JJ?*

JJ acted like he didn't notice my intense interest as he recovered from his mom's question.

Had he actually been reading romance novels, or was he kidding? That would have required him to go into town and buy some. Or borrow from the library. I pictured him in the fiction aisle, perusing cheap romance novels, and almost choked again.

This time from laughter.

In the back of my mind, I silently congratulated him. *Well played.* He was likely reading them to get ammunition against me—but it might have the opposite effect.

Romance novels had pulled me through the hardest time of my life. I could turn my brain off and journey somewhere else. Could forget just how miserable reality had become. They were the reason I didn't give up. The idea of romance coming to even the most normal women made me hang on.

Stick it out.

Mama hadn't had a lick of romance in her life, and neither had Dad. But Maverick and Bethany? Spades of it. Every day I saw it in their weird glances, their poor attempts at hiding their affection, the constant excuses they invented to touch each other.

Romance for the win.

Maybe JJ would see that.

My attention landed on a stack of at least ten books tucked near the massive fridge. The spines were pointed toward me, and I skimmed the titles. Every single one was a romance. And I'd read all of them.

"Medieval is interesting," he said conversationally, as if the awkward moment hadn't happened. "Did romance exist back then?"

"Was there a God in the Middle Ages?" I quipped right back, unable to help myself.

Kelly's brow furrowed. "Does God have something to do with romance?"

JJ grinned so wide, and with such real delight, I almost couldn't be upset. "I don't think God would like being compared to romance," he said. "And yes, God definitely existed in the belief structure of the Middle Ages."

"To some it's the highest compliment," I said imperiously. Then I turned to Kelly. "He's teasing me, that's all. I'm the one who suggested he try reading romance."

"It's not teasing," he countered. "It's a debate on the benefits of romance. She made a few arguments I hadn't heard before. I countered. It's . . . an ongoing discussion."

"You're not trying to talk me out of it?" I asked.

"That's not my intent."

"Then what is?"

He spread his hands. "Discussion. If romance serves you, great. I'm happy for you. I'm just fascinated by your belief in it."

Kelly's eyes widened. She glanced between us and chewed slowly, nodding. Her eyes moved like a machine—I wished I knew what she was thinking.

"So, what is romantic about the medieval time period?" JJ asked. He pulled a muscular leg up and rested his arm on it. "They never married for love. They married out of necessity back then."

"*Never* is a strong word," I countered. "Can you prove that?"

He opened his mouth, then closed it. "I can prove that they married for practical reasons."

"Can you prove there was no romance or love between them?"

"Ah . . . no."

Smug, I folded my arms across my chest.

But he leaned forward, not ready to concede. "Can you prove it did exist as you understand it today?"

I scowled. He laughed. Kelly watched.

"You never answered my question," he pointed out. "How

can the Middle Ages be romantic? That time period was notoriously dark and brutal. I imagine most people spent their time eking out a life and trying to get enough to eat."

Like a dog with a bone, he'd never let this go. Better to just get it out and over with. Then I could just appreciate the delicious picture of him reading one of my favorite romances. My curious, traitorous mind *begged* me to ask him for a real summary of them.

I drew in a deep breath and said, "It's the dresses and the castles, thank you very much."

If possible, his expression grew more amused.

"What?"

"Castles! It's fun to read about a girl living in a stone castle and wearing . . . fun dresses we don't wear anymore. Plus, everything was more dangerous then." I paused, then mumbled, "Women needed to be saved."

Kelly, my modern saving grace, nodded. "I second that." She raised a hand. "It's fun to imagine the dresses and castles."

JJ held up two hands, as if conceding a point. "Fair enough. So it's really just about escapism. You want to picture yourself as someone else, doing something else."

"Yes."

His eyes met mine. "I get that. It's what climbing does for me."

With that, he stood. The intensity of his expression wouldn't leave me anytime soon. Nor would the fact that he didn't challenge me. He didn't use my heartbreak to prove his own point.

He really did just want to discuss it.

After I finished my pillowy, buttery brioche, I said a quick goodbye to give JJ and Kelly family time. But I felt a little empty as I left the warmth of the kitchen, and I desperately wished JJ was at my side.

It really was kind of fun talking romance with him.

Chapter Twenty

JJ

Darkness coated the world in shadows by the time Mom stopped talking about her new position at work. It would have felt cozy if my mind wasn't spinning so much.

Why was Mom here?

"Enough about me." She jumped onto the counter and plucked off another thin sliver of brioche. "You've got something new going on, don't you?"

I lifted one eyebrow. "What do you mean?"

She gestured around us. "Brioche bread. There was a tart in the fridge when I pulled it open. Half of a croissant left on Lizbeth's plate in the house. I happen to know none of that was purchased. So, what's going on?"

My plan wasn't really mine to reveal. I was a small cog in a greater machine, just the way I liked it.

"Baking is a fun challenge. I'm trying it out."

"You're a very intelligent man, JJ. You're calculated. You only take a risk if it's one you know you can tackle. It's why you're so good at climbing, and also why you keep Mark in check. So, what is it?"

I blew out a long breath. "I do have something in the works. I can't give details yet, but it would satisfy my . . . need to move on to something new without actually leaving."

Her expression softened. "You're trying to stay, aren't you?"

Stability wasn't a forte of Mark and me. We'd spent so many years bumming around because it felt good. The freedom of that life was exhilarating. But it was also wearying. Made it difficult to stay stable. I missed the mountains, Meg, and my parents deeply at times. At thirty years old, it was time to try something new.

"Yeah," I said. "I am."

Her smile seemed at once mysterious and wise. "It's hard, but there are some amazing advantages to staying in the same place for more than ten seconds. Well, I trust you to tell me in your time. But if not that, at least tell me what's going on with you and Lizbeth."

The explanation I'd rehearsed while Mom had been speaking turned to mere letters in my brain. I couldn't put them into sentences that made sense anymore. *She's working for Mark as a friend* was true but misleading. It was more than that, and I wanted to be wholly honest with her.

The way they hadn't been with me.

"I don't know."

Her brows rose. "That's not what I expected. You're one of the most self-aware and articulate people I've ever met. C'mon, JJ. You have to know you feel something for her. I can see it in the two of you. In the way you *look* at her."

"It's not . . . I just . . . I really *don't* know. We're friends. I . . . what do you want me to say?"

"That you'll fall in love, have babies, and not move away ever again."

I shot her a glare.

She shrugged. "You asked."

"It doesn't feel right to move on it."

"You mean ask her out."

"Yes."

"Well, why not?"

"That's what I don't know."

She frowned. "Something to do with me and your father, maybe? Afraid to fail like we did?"

That was Mom. Blunt to a fault. My hands rested on the counter because I didn't know how to respond. Maybe she was right, maybe she wasn't. It hadn't been my first thought. Mark popped into my head, but I didn't know why. Mark was pushing me to make a move on Lizbeth too.

"I don't know."

She put a hand on my shoulder. "Your father and I are different people, JJ. Our fate isn't entwined with yours."

"I know that."

"But do you really?"

No. Not really.

Which might have been why I asked the next question. The question that had been burning on my tongue for the last five months. My ribs expanded as I took a deep breath. I tried to force all my frustration out with it so it didn't leak into my voice. With everything going on at work, Mom didn't need more stress.

"You told Mark about the problems you and Dad were facing when your marriage was crumbling," I said. "He knew that divorce was a very strong possibility."

Her hand fell away from my shoulder. She drew back a little bit. "Yes."

I straightened to see her better. "There were big problems between the two of you when you separated. You confided in Mark and in Megan at different points. I had my suspicions that things had turned a corner, of course, but I had no idea just how much of a corner. Later I found out that they knew and I didn't. I was . . . boxed out. Why?"

It felt like something white-hot inside me had just been plucked. Now it vibrated, hissed, filled my chest with its ricochet.

"That's . . . that's not what we meant, JJ."

"I know."

"We love you."

"I know that too."

This was the first time I'd ever asked her. The first time I'd aired the words that had rubbed under my skin like salt for months. Her complexion had gone a little pale.

"Are you angry with us?" she whispered.

I took a moment to think the question through. "I'm hurt."

"JJ, I promise that wasn't the intent," she rushed to say. "At least, not mine. I can't speak for your father anymore."

An edge of bitterness cut through those last words. Also nothing new, but it still made me flinch.

Was this what relationships came to? It had certainly been true of Stacey and me. With a shake of my head to clear those thoughts, I asked, "How did you meet Dad?"

"How did I meet him?"

"Yeah."

Disoriented by the quick change of subject, she took a few seconds to respond. Her frown deepened. "Through a friend in high school. She introduced us at a football game after-party. He was quiet and calm and not like most of the other guys I'd dated. I liked that about him. At the time," she tacked on.

The same quiet and calm that eventually drove them apart, no doubt. Even I remembered that Dad had peeled farther and farther away from home life. A dozen memories swamped me. Their fights when I was in high school. Mom screaming. Dad ignoring her. The silence after.

Maybe Mark and I had been running away from home all those years.

"Was it romantic?" I asked.

"Romantic?"

"When you met."

"Incredibly. At the beginning, anyway. He stood up to some bullies for me. Cared for me. Bought me things. There was nothing we didn't do together. At the time, I was young and impressionable and thought that romance meant he was everything. And he was."

I studied her. The last year had aged her, leaving new lines near her eyes and on her forehead. Though she was noticeably brighter now that she wasn't living in the oppressive shadow of Dad's silence, she seemed like a different person. Lost. Wandering. Uncertain, though happy.

Was this the first time in my life I'd actually felt like Mom and I understood each other?

She'd always been closer to Mark. They had the same restless energy. The same burning desire to achieve, to be the center of attention. Only she had calmed over the years.

I took a page from Dad, the quiet brooder. Held my thoughts in until I couldn't. A flash of confusion—maybe regret—whispered through me. This felt like an ambush, only I was the one doing it.

"I'm sorry," I said. "I'm not angry with you, Mom. I'm confused. Trying to sort things out."

Tears filled her eyes. "You shouldn't be sorry. It's time Dad and I face the legacy of the choices we made. I didn't relish the divorce, but I should have done it years ago instead of putting all of you through this. Maybe it would have been easier. Although," she added in a soft voice, "I don't think this kind of thing is ever easy."

"You're doing great, Mom."

I reached over, pulled her into a warm hug, and rubbed her back as she cried.

* * *

JJ: Sorry if this wakes you up, but I wanted to let you know that I actually read some of those books that you saw in the kitchen tonight and am working through the rest.

Lizbeth: I'm not sure how to read that.

JJ: Factual.

Lizbeth: This is horrible over text because I can't see your body language.

JJ: You're always welcome inside.

Lizbeth: It's 11:00 at night! Too cold. Just tell it to me straight. Did you love the romance books or hate them?

JJ: I didn't hate them.

Lizbeth: Do you secretly love them but you don't know how to tell me without breaking your tough-guy exterior?

JJ: Not that. My tough-guy exterior is built on actual strength.

Lizbeth: Then what?

JJ: It was pretty much all unrealistic.

Lizbeth: And?

JJ: And I get the appeal. It's the same thing that drives people to binge Netflix or whatever. Or sends me climbing rocks. But that still doesn't make romantic love real.

Lizbeth: Romantic love is more than that. It isn't just an escape.

JJ: Then what is it?

Lizbeth: It's . . . hope.

JJ: That a Viking warrior is going to sweep you off your feet and to your own castle full of really fun dresses?

Lizbeth: Well, sort of. Yes. Obviously that probably won't happen in this day and age, right? Castles are at a premium. But books help me remember that that option isn't TOTALLY gone. Maybe it won't happen to me now, but I can pretend it will.

JJ: Do you want a Viking warrior to sweep you off your feet? They raped and pillaged and murdered like crazy people.

Lizbeth: Not the ones I like! There were gallant ones, I'm sure.

JJ: Gallant Vikings. Riiiiight. I mean, living in the Middle Ages?

Lizbeth: Yeah, I would have sucked at that.

JJ: Would not have been pretty.

Lizbeth: Maybe that's what romance does. It takes undesirable circumstances and makes them a little more . . . doable.

JJ: That's your best argument so far.

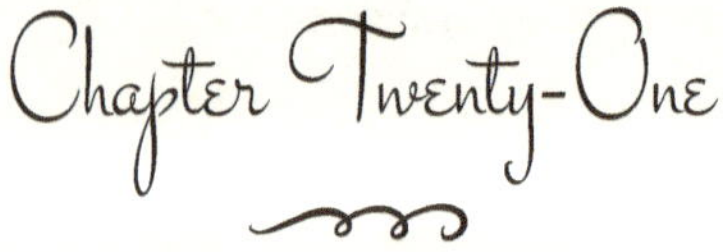

Chapter Twenty-One

LIZBETH

"Mark, I created some design boards for you to look at on Pinnable. They give some color schemes and a feel for what we can do with Adventura's website," I said the next day.

His head popped up from where he was sitting on the couch, pouring over some documents I'd eventually have to file. I leaned forward to put *push Mark into this century* on my list.

"Are you already working on the website?" he asked.

"Soon. I'm just prepping for it in between scanning these documents and losing all my brain cells. There's only two boxes left."

He grinned roguishly and stood up to skim through what was there. I angled my laptop to go through some of my ideas, but before I could explain, he nodded. "Looks good, Lizbeth."

"But you haven't even looked at it."

"I have. I read ahead of you. I can already tell you have a vision for it that aligns with mine. The colors are earth tones, I like the landing page on the left you have pinned there, and you already have the URL that reflects the company name. Looks good."

"You said part of the reason you wanted me to stay here was

so you could help design the website. This could easily be done remotely."

"Yeah, but that was before I implicitly trusted you."

"Oh."

"Looks good to me. Go for what you think is best." He turned back to his work without another word.

I sat there for a second, simultaneously flattered and stumped. Mark was a classic laissez-faire leader. He hated details and just wanted to guide the general direction, which made it easy for me to work with what I knew. But I hated the lack of guidance because it left more decisions for me. Still, this would help the résumé because I could create a stunning website. The back-end work was always fun.

And I really wanted to make him proud.

"Okay," I drawled slowly. "I can do that."

A few more hefty stacks of paper needed to be scanned and organized onto his new cloud storage. In between waiting for the internet to upload each file, I updated my spreadsheets and my to-do list and regarded the love binder, which I'd hidden underneath the desk.

Among my general theories on romance, I'd included the point that romance may have been defined differently in the medieval period, but surely it had existed. *The Lais of Marie de France* and all its courtly upheaval and romantic affairs proved it.

My task list outside of work included reading other historical texts that could prove romance had always existed, which would debunk any argument that romance was a modern construct created to sell products—a debate I'd certainly won with other people before.

But not with JJ.

Before my thoughts could spiral too far down that rabbit hole, JJ walked inside. The cold had pinked his cheeks in an adorable way. My pulse beat faster.

"Hey, Lizbeth, you busy this afternoon?" he asked as he peeled off his parka.

"Just working."

"Think you'd be interested in taking a few hours off?"

Something intriguing sparkled in his eyes when they met mine. If the afternoon involved him in any way, shape, or form, I was definitely interested. Unless it included strenuous physical activity—then I was out.

"What did you have in mind?" I asked.

"A movie. Maybe some lunch afterward."

My heart literally pitter-pattered. Was he asking me on a date? I forced myself to act casual. "Ooh," I said. "Which movie?"

"*The Heiress*."

An excited little squeal popped out of me before I could stop it. I'd been drooling over that movie—and the gorgeous, Victorian-esque wardrobe—for weeks now. "Really?" I cried. Then my enthusiasm died. "Wait, that's a romance."

"I know."

My gaze tapered. "Then why do you want to go?"

"Call it curiosity," he said. "It's been at least eight years since I've seen one. I'd like to try it again."

"And then debate with me?"

He grinned. "You got it."

Unfortunately, I couldn't resist those mossy eyes or that bright smile. Watching a romance movie with JJ? Heck yes. I'd always been a sucker for hearty banter, and we had it in spades.

Mark waved a hand. "Go for it if you want," he said before I could check with him. "I need a little peace and quiet around here."

JJ held out a hand with his usual smile. "Let's go. Next showing starts in an hour."

* * *

"Number one rule," I whispered as we sat down in the cool, dark theater. "You have to be honest. No softening it."

He made an *X* over his heart. "Promise."

"Great. I'll give you a summary."

"Doesn't that ruin the movie?"

"Not for a romance! When you start a romance, you always know how it ends. *The Heiress* is about a princess named Elody who inherits the crown unexpectedly. Her older brother was always slated for the position, but he dies, along with her parents, in a plane crash. Not only is Elody devastated, but she now has to lead her country."

"Naturally."

I shot him a glare that made him grin. He gestured for me to continue. On the towering screen, the opening credits began to roll, with a little splash of violin in the background.

"Her parents' adviser, a severe man named D'artagnan, is tasked with helping her transition into the position. Foibles ensue as she attempts to ascend to a role that was never supposed to be hers to begin with."

"Did you just say *foibles*?" he asked.

"My vocabulary is extensive."

"I can see that," he said seriously. "It sounds like you memorized the trailer pitch."

"*D'artagnan,*" I said, stressing the word to draw his attention back to what was most important—imminent romance, "is the only guide who really helps her through all the light and dark moments, because no one else believes in her. Partly because she's female. Except Elody and D'artagnan hate each other from the beginning, and she doesn't know if she can trust him."

"That sounds bleak."

"I know!" I squealed. "I love it. It's called the enemies-to-lovers plotline, and it's my favorite. There's drama and tension built in. I mean, you can't ask for any better challenge than dragging two people who hate each other into the depths of love, right?"

"Disagree."

"Then what's your favorite challenge?"

"Free-climbing El Capitan."

I laughed as the movie started. "Fair enough."

"You know they get together in the end, though," he whispered as the lights dimmed. He'd leaned in closer, the sweet and salty smell of kettle corn on his breath. "How can you really enjoy it if you already know the ending?"

"It's precisely *why* I love it. I know it'll happen, but I don't know how. I don't know what moments will bring them together. What tension will build? It's really all about *how* they connect, not *if* they connect. The enjoyment is in the imagining."

He made a noise in his throat as the camera panned over a view of a castle, and I silenced another internal squeal. I'd been waiting *forever* to watch this movie. Having him, of all people, right next to me couldn't have been any better.

Or so I hoped.

If he tried to ruin this for me, I'd throw popcorn on him and take the Zombie Mobile so he could hitchhike home.

Thankfully, he fell into it as quickly as I did. The biggest challenge was focusing on the screen, and not on the way his arm pressed against mine because neither of us lifted the armrest. Or on the occasional hint of forest that lingered in the air when he shifted. Halfway through the movie, an old man behind us coughed.

I leaned closer to JJ. "We should invite him to sit with us."

He sent me a confused look.

"He's all by himself," I whispered.

"Yeah, probably because he wants to be."

"Maybe not?"

"It'll distract from the movie."

I'd mostly been teasing, so I sent him a rueful smile and turned my attention back to the screen, but he remained leaning closer to me than ever. I almost missed the epic first-kiss scene inside a waterfall.

"It's so *Last of the Mohicans*," I whispered in delight. "Well done, screenwriter."

JJ outright laughed.

When the movie ended and I blinked back tears from an utterly perfect proposal, JJ let out a long breath. The lights slowly brightened, flooding the room. Behind us, the old man trundled to the end of his row to quietly head down the stairs. I didn't want to leave.

"Well?" I asked. "You had so little to say."

"Surprisingly." JJ blinked. "It's . . . interesting. I see why you like it."

Then why did he look so confused?

I'd already given up hope that JJ would see romance the way I did. Now, I just wanted his acknowledgment that romance was real. *I better earn a point of concession out of this date,* I thought.

"Rate it out of ten," I said. "With *one* being you hated it and will never give romance another chance and *ten* being it's the best movie you've ever seen."

"A five."

"Respectable!" I cried. "And far better than I thought."

He offered a relaxed grin. His gaze had softened through the movie, losing its edge of intensity. My heart beat like a drum under my rib cage when he reached back, pulled his hair out of its bun, and let it fall to his shoulders. He normally wore it up, but now it rested around his face and cast shadows on the hollows of his cheeks. I could only stare at his sculpted face as something warm ignited in my belly.

His arms flexed as he ran his fingers through his hair, then pulled it back out of his face and turned to me again. When he looked at me, his expression had reverted to his usual careful amusement.

I swallowed hard.

But I thought that he, too, had some sort of uncertainty in his gaze. An uncertainty that, like mine, could mean he had some feelings for me. That my obsession wasn't totally one-sided.

Maybe.

"Thank you for coming with me," I whispered instead of shouting, *Holy palm trees, kiss me right now!* "I've been waiting for the movie to come out so I could rent it and watch with Bethie."

His gaze dropped to my lips for half a second before they returned to mine. "Was this better?" he asked.

"Definitely."

"My pleasure." He smiled softly. "Really. Are you interested in some lunch before we head back?"

"Yes, please."

He held out his hand. It was warm as it clasped mine, tugging me to my feet.

It was no first kiss.

But his hand in mine sure felt good.

Chapter Twenty-Two

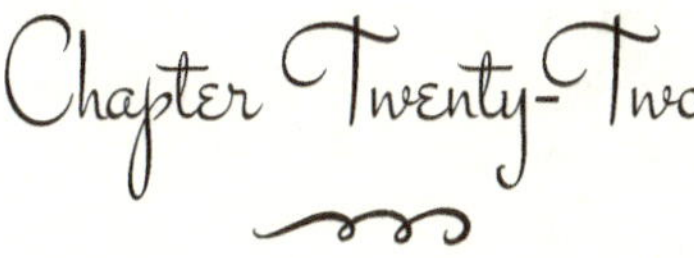

JJ

I imagined what one of Lizbeth's romance books might say about our impromptu date. I'd only read five of them so far—all of them different romance subgenres—but they all seemed somewhat the same.

For a date like this, I could imagine the books describing a rush of giddiness with butterflies. Or a feeling of some caution from one of us, likely her. Instead, she appeared to be an open book. Made eye contact. Smiled. Revealed no wariness or uncertainty.

Meanwhile, *I* felt a slice of euphoria and a deep sense of *finally* as I stared at her across the table. And I had no idea why.

"I suck at this, Lizbeth," I said, just to make my thoughts clear. "I haven't been on a date in a long time."

Her head tilted to the side. "Why don't you go on dates?"

"What does the gossip around town say?"

A sly smile twitched on her lips. "That's for me to know. Let's face it, Mark is too in love with his career to date and—"

"He wants to."

"Really?"

I nodded. "Very much. Mark could almost be called a romantic, but all of his relationships fail to land. Just when they seem to be going somewhere, they die."

"Why?"

"He's had a hard time finding a girl who can handle his energy, I think. He's erratic and so full of ideas it's annoying. A lot of women find it . . ."

"Unstable?" she ventured.

I laughed. "Definitely that."

"Well, gossip around the town speaks highly of both of you, if you must know. Of the two of you, you're the more mysterious."

At that, I laughed harder. Pineville had always been *very* small. But then, we'd always given reasons for people to talk about us. "Good, I'm glad. And there are a lot of reasons I haven't dated, but Stacey is the main one. And my parents' divorce," I tacked on with a grimace. "That hasn't felt good."

Lizbeth leaned back a little. "Oh. I hadn't thought of that. If it's easier for you, we can just call this lunch. Doesn't have to be a date."

"It's a date," I said immediately.

Lizbeth's lips twitched. The bunched-up muscles in my neck relaxed. A waitress handed us plastic-covered menus, rattled off specials, and disappeared. I skimmed the menu, grateful for a few moments to recover my wits.

"Their butternut ravioli is amazing," I said. "I've tried to mimic it, but I can't."

When I glanced up, she was cautiously eyeing her menu.

"Something wrong?" I asked.

"No." She waved a hand. "I just . . . had a weird experience with a date recently when we went to order."

"Tyler?" I asked. She fought off a smile when I muttered, "Idiot," under my breath.

"Anything else you recommend?" she asked.

We tossed favorites back and forth, unable to decide, until I set my menu down and said, "Let's share. I'll get the butternut ravioli, you get the chicken parm. I hear it's breathtaking."

Her gaze tapered. "But you're vegetarian."

Taken aback, I stared at her for a moment. "How did you know that?"

She shrugged. "I don't know. Must have come up in conversation at some point at the coffee shop, or something. I'll get something we can really share."

"You don't have to do that. I can have some of the pasta. Mark says it's the sauce that really makes it legendary."

She smiled at me over her menu. "I want to."

Stunned, I simply leaned back. When was the last time anyone had made a concession to my belief systems? Almost never. Point for Lizbeth, because that could almost be called romantic. After we ordered, she leaned forward. Strands of glimmering red hair tumbled onto her shoulders. I wondered how soft it felt.

"Tell me about your day," she said.

"My day? Oh. Ah . . . I think Mark spoke with the contractors today. It's official that he's accepted—"

"No. Not about Mark. About *your* day."

Stupidly, I had to pause for a second. Unzipping myself from Mark wasn't a natural process, but I appreciated her calling it out so gently. "Right. Well . . . I'm trying out a new recipe."

She brightened. "Oh?"

"Madeleines. They're finicky, but delicious."

"Have you always loved baking?" she asked.

Her question forced me to think. Did I enjoy baking? Yes. I enjoyed the challenge and precision of it, just like climbing. Not to mention a delicious and tangible end result. Most of all, I liked that it enabled me to live at Adventura and climb as much as I wanted. Climbing was the real queen here.

"I like baking."

"Like." Her eyebrows rose. "Not love?"

Ah, perceptive.

"There's not much I truly love. I don't apply the word as liberally as you," I said with a quick wink. She smiled, but I sensed deep thought behind it. "I've only really concentrated on baking lately, though. Once I stopped traveling in a van and lived in one place long enough to focus."

"You should sell everything you bake."

I almost choked on my water. "Yeah." I coughed. "Maybe one day."

The conversation turned to her thoughts on working with Mark. My only regret was that I couldn't hold her hand from across the table.

"Has it been weird for you to have me there all the time?" she asked.

"Not at all," I said.

There was a lot I left out. That it felt nice to have someone else around. That I didn't mind having a grateful person to pamper a little bit, because Mark was like a black hole. We'd been together our whole lives and had fallen into our patterns, like rivets in rock. Water flowed easiest downhill. I couldn't stop watching out for him, simply because it's what I had always done.

But it felt nice to see a far more beautiful face at home.

The waitress set a plate of black bean enchiladas in front of Lizbeth and handed the butternut ravioli with a sage and brown butter sauce to me. As soon as the waitress disappeared, we swapped half of our portions.

"Thanks." Her eyes twinkled. "I've never shared on a date before."

"A travesty."

"Can we swap something else?" she asked as she sliced into a piece of ravioli with the edge of her fork.

"Depends."

"If I tell you what I think is romantic, will you tell me what happened with Stacey?"

Hearing Stacey's name from Lizbeth's lips sent a shudder through me. Did I want to revisit that day?

Definitely not.

But did I want to know what Lizbeth found romantic—since she obviously didn't like rich guys who overflowed with all the stereotypical trappings of romance?

Definitely yes.

Full of thoughts I didn't quite understand, I turned back to my ravioli. She gave me a little space to think. To weigh out whether I wanted to dredge this back up. I hadn't spoken about Stacey in eight years.

But I had a feeling it would be worth it.

Finally, I looked at her and nodded. "Exchange accepted."

Lizbeth grinned. "I'll go first," she said. "With a caveat. I don't know if any of this is real."

My eyes almost bugged out of my head. She didn't know if romance was real?

Before I could clarify, she continued, "I mean, if I *really* find these things romantic. There have been a few times lately that should have been wildly romantic, but they weren't. At least . . . maybe they were in hindsight, but . . ."

She trailed off for a second, shook her head, and started again. "These are the things I find romantic when I read books or watch movies," she said. "Sometimes when I have a hard time sleeping, I get on YouTube and watch compilations of the most romantic scenes in movies. And the moments I love the most are almost always the little things."

"Like what?"

"Like . . . a hand on the small of the back. A look across the room. Maybe someone doing or saying something small to show they're paying attention."

Interesting.

"So it's not always about the grand gestures?" I asked. Which would be nice because that took some pressure off.

She shrugged. "Those are good, too, but without the little stuff, it doesn't mean as much. Or it's not quite as exciting. Snuggling on the couch always seemed more romantic than anything else, frankly. I wouldn't honestly know."

"A real travesty," I said softly.

She smiled. "My friend Leslie says the most romantic thing in her world is when someone else makes dinner."

The impossible intricacy of romance never ceased to amaze me. While there seemed to be standards in movies and books, real-life romance appeared to be far more . . . subdued. Making dinner was romantic? Cleaning a cabin was romantic?

How could I ever figure it out?

"What situations were supposed to be romantic but weren't?" I asked, hazarding my true burning question.

She hesitated, and it was then that I realized those situations might have involved me. And a car plunging off a cliff. And the fact that her entire world had burned down and she still wouldn't talk about it.

Were *those* romantic?

Lizbeth stared hard at me. She didn't fill the silence or change the subject like Mark would have. Instead, she said, "Well, you saved my life, and then we were stuck in a wintry cabin together for days."

"Let me guess." I leaned forward. "There are books about that situation?"

She grinned and nodded. Unable to help myself, I glanced at her lips, then back at her eyes. Man, did I want to kiss her.

"Did you want that to be romantic?" I asked quietly.

She nodded.

"And it wasn't?"

She hesitated again. So there must have been some romance,

but when? What? What had I done then so I could do more of it now?

"There was," she said with a little smile. It seemed like an attempt to play this off as something small when, in reality, it was big. "I mean . . . the whole almost-dying thing was only terrifying."

"Of course."

She let out a long breath and then chuckled. "I feel like I'm making this totally awkward. I didn't mean to imply that you did something wrong, just that . . . maybe you're partially right about romance."

"What?" I cried, acting scandalized.

"Only partially!"

"Of course. Because what man is ever fully right compared to a woman?"

Her laugh lightened the air, but her voice remained sober.

"I haven't actually fallen in love or been in a relationship, so I may have idealized romance too much. Now that I'm experiencing it in different ways, I can't help but wonder why. What does it mean?"

"Something worth exploring?"

She pressed her lips together and nodded. Something lurked beneath her expression.

Although the last thing I wanted to do was talk about Stacey, I took the moment to save her. "Now I think it's my turn."

Visibly relieved, she nodded and turned back to her food. I braced myself for the inevitable rush of feels, but none came. Instead of pain, I felt something like resignation, maybe distance.

"Stacey and I dated my senior year of college." I played with my fork to have something to do. It had been years since I'd sussed out the details. "She was bright, enigmatic, and popular. I was quiet, focused on my studies. We were total opposites."

Like us, I thought.

"How did you meet her?"

"Through Mark, the way I meet most people. Stacey and I were friends for a while. Our relationship moved slowly at first, but then seemed to happen all at once. One minute I was admiring her work ethic—she wanted to be a veterinarian—and then I was head-over-heels for her. I thought it was the same way for her."

Lizbeth's eyebrows rose. "You thought?"

I laughed, but it was bitter. "Oh, yeah. Stacey was all about the romance. Flowers. Chocolates. Bracelets. The grand gestures."

Was Lizbeth paling a bit?

"What happened?" she asked.

"We kept dating. I thought we were drawing closer together, but I can see now that I was enraptured and she was in love with attention. After a while, Stacey was my whole world. I couldn't live or breathe without her. Metaphorically speaking, of course."

Lizbeth chortled, but her face remained empathetic.

"After graduation, shortly before she was going to move on to vet school, I planned the perfect date. Picnic on the beach. Candles. Romantic music in the background. An isolated location—just the two of us beneath the stars."

"Oh no," she murmured.

"Stacey loved it. At least she seemed to. Then I started talking about what I really wanted—commitment. Marriage. I'd go with her to her next place and support her as she pursued her dreams."

Lizbeth swallowed, her food long since abandoned.

"She said no?"

"Worse. She said, 'Where is this coming from, JJ? I thought we were just friends.'"

Lizbeth's mouth dropped. "No!"

"Yes."

"She friend-zoned you in the worst way."

The pain tugged at me again, but it wasn't so bad this time. Instead, it hovered in the background, a reminder of how romance really ends.

"What did you do?" she asked.

"Not sure." My brow wrinkled. "There's a sense of shock that makes everything foggy. I think we argued. I remember rehashing everything that had happened between us in my mind. I had no idea how she could think we weren't . . . *something*. Later, I realized she was just a manipulative person who hated commitment. She never finished her vet degree and has disappeared into the world somewhere." I waved a hand. "Regardless, it was a good thing I didn't marry her, but it hurt like hell then."

Lizbeth blinked. "Wow. No wonder you have a thing against romance."

"It's not so much *a thing* as experience. Romance leads to a broken heart."

"That wasn't romance's fault," she said. "Your romantic gestures were a sincere reflection of your effort and the way you felt. The fallout? That was Stacey. She used you and manipulated you. A person broke your heart, JJ. Not love."

Her words hit me like a punch to the gut. She was right, and I felt it in my bones. Perhaps I'd held a vendetta against romance all these years because I assumed Stacey was in love with love. But really, Stacey had been in love with herself.

Romance had nothing to do with it.

With a sigh that dropped my shoulders an inch, I nodded. "You're right. Point to you, Lizbeth. Romance often gets blamed for people's problems, and I've been guilty of that for the last eight years."

No sense of victory lit up her gaze, and I knew the feeling well.

She set down her fork. "Are you going to hold my hand again when we leave?"

"Yes. Do you want me to?"

She nodded, and I offered her a soft smile as we dug back into our food.

Chapter Twenty-Three

LIZBETH

The next day, I sat in the office and stared at the rest of the papers.

Only one small pile remained. One stupid, ridiculous group of papers left and I could move on to developing the online interface for the investors and working on the websites.

Still, I wanted to stick a fork in my eyes at the thought of scanning one more page. When I finished the paperwork, half my work here would be done. The online stuff would move easily and quickly.

Except, I wasn't entirely sure I wanted to finish.

Now that I'd Pinnable'd this place out, it wasn't half-bad here at the office. Living in the warmth of Adventura had felt so . . . easy. Uncomplicated.

Did I want to leave?

There was also the matter of JJ and whatever was budding between us. I thought for far too long of the way it felt to sit next to him in the Zombie Mobile, his hand in mine.

Was this real?

Then again, how could it not be?

To make the day bearable while JJ tortured me by working in

the main kitchen for far too long, I uploaded files and puttered around the office. Shelved books by topic and height. Placed a blanket that I'd found in the spare bedroom over the back of the couch for a splash of color. A little organization had a profound effect.

Though the Bailey boys hadn't said anything, the way they stopped and stared as if they couldn't figure out what had happened always made me giggle.

While I waited for the latest batch of pictures to upload, I leaned back in the chair and grabbed my newest read, *The King's Desire*. An otherworld, Regency-esque romance with said castles and dresses. So far, it hadn't disappointed, though it had been a bit . . . rote. Since when did I predict *so much* of the plot?

Annoyed, I set it aside, grabbed the love binder, and updated my observations. His confession about Stacey had been a big one. The fact that he'd conceded a point to me should have thrilled me, but it didn't. I recorded it, but didn't like the way it had happened. So far, we were even.

Romance still had a chance.

And maybe *we* did too.

Something definitive had shifted between us yesterday. My mind kept wandering to the movie. Then lunch. Now I wanted more. More of him. More confessions. More JJ in his element.

The rustle of JJ's parka and snow pants drew me out of my reverie. He shuffled in through the main door with a smile. My stomach flipped.

"Hey," he said.

"Hi."

He set a plate on the table. The smell of sugar and butter drew me closer. Pastries! A glaze had crisped along the edges. I broke a piece off, and it crumbled on my fingertips.

"Oddballs," he said as he tossed his coat onto a peg on the wall. "They look a little funny, but taste delicious."

In truth, I thought their gleaming brown tops graced with

fruit compotes were gorgeous. I snatched one with a grin. Where was he taking the non-oddballs? And why all the secrecy around the baked goods?

With a wink, he pressed a quick kiss to my cheek, then grabbed a coffee mug. My heart raced like a hummingbird when he leaned against the table and just looked at me. "You look beautiful today," he finally said. "Like always."

"Oh." Heat rushed to my cheeks. "Thanks."

"Mark and Justin plan to offer their tribute of fire to the gods of paper and snow tonight, if you want to come." He poured himself a fresh cup of coffee. "I plan on making home-made hot chocolate."

"I'll be there."

Images of chanting, fire, and snow flashed through my mind. I had little doubt Mark would make it dramatic—probably with copious amounts of lighter fluid. It fit his rampant energy.

Regardless, it was the perfect culmination to finishing all the paperwork.

JJ lounged back against the sink. "That was a huge project, Lizbeth. Well done."

"Thanks."

The end of the *huge project* left a sizeable gap in my plans for the week. Further grilling of Mark had given me no guidance on what to do next. I'd probably start with the website. He'd been using social media and one web page that looked like a dinosaur had created it.

While I was excited to work with design again, I couldn't wait to revisit my Pinnable corkboard. Not only because I'd been trying to ignore the fact that I hadn't heard back on the job despite emailing them to ask for an update, but because there was something steadying about making plans.

"I started a new romance book after our date last night," he said. "One that came on my mom's recommendation."

"Oh?"

My curiosity was piqued even as I relished the words *our date*. Romance was one thing. Plot structure was another. Every dissection of a romance novel gave me a physical thrill.

"It's about pirates," he continued.

I gasped. "Please tell me it's *His Pirate Princess*."

"Yes."

"With Johanna?"

"Yes."

I faked a swoon. "So good, JJ! What do you think?"

His chuckle was a low, cavernous rumble. He hadn't shaved, so glints of stubble illuminated his cheeks in the right light, like a fractured diamond. I wanted to run my fingers across it.

"I think it's oddly suspicious that the same woman keeps getting mixed up in situations where she needs saving."

I burst out laughing.

"How does the hero always happen to be there?" He looked at me. "Seriously? How do you explain that?"

"It's great plotting, that's what."

He rolled his eyes, then kept going. "And how do these women get into these dramatic situations? I mean, Johanna was kidnapped by one pirate. Okay, I can get behind that. But that was the bad pirate. Then a supposedly good pirate—which isn't a thing—rescues her from the first one. In the meantime, the military guy who's a good guy and genuinely wants to help her not live a life of crime is kind of the loser. It's a love square!"

My laughter deepened.

"Then what about all these first kisses?" he continued without stopping. "What does toe-curling even mean? I—"

"It's supposed to be that way!" I said as I stopped to catch my breath. He did the same. I could *feel* his skepticism.

"What?" he asked.

"It's what every reader wants to happen. The woman is supposed to be in trouble and is supposed to be saved. That's when the romance happens. Otherwise it's just a really boring exposition on life as a pirate."

He stared at the wall across from us. "Oh."

"This isn't about reality, JJ. This is about the experience of romance. It doesn't matter if what happens is closely aligned with reality. In fact, the less real, the better."

"So you agree that romance isn't realistic?"

I opened my mouth to protest, then shut it again. He grinned a little too roguishly for my liking. In fact, I couldn't turn away even though I wanted to. Because he'd trapped me. Really and truly trapped me.

"Uh-huh," he sang. "Point for JJ."

With an annoyed sigh, I muttered, "Point for JJ."

I'd never live that one down. Now we were uneven again.

"Mark left this morning to meet with the bank early." JJ half-yawned and ran a hand through his hair. "Apparently the City of Pineville is putting up a stink about the spa. Anyway, he told me I had strict instructions to take you into Jackson City and buy you books."

I blinked. "What?"

"Your books were all burned, right?"

"I think so. I haven't gone back yet." I cleared my throat. "Maverick said most of the attic was unsalvageable."

"Right. So Mark, as a thank-you for your work so far, wants me to buy you more books."

"But he's paying me a ridiculous amount per hour."

JJ shrugged. "Mark may not be great with details, but he appreciates people. I think you should take the offer."

Several seconds passed before I recognized this for what it was: a gift from a friend. The Bailey boys might be the two most frustrating men on the planet, for different reasons, but they were my friends now.

I nodded slowly. "Well, that sounds great."

JJ held out a hand. "Good. I know just the place."

* * *

Bells clanged in my head as we drove up the canyon.

The twists and turns made me sick to my stomach, even on a beautiful, clear day like this. At least I hadn't had to drive it alone yet. That would happen in the summer, with no ice and safe roads.

JJ distracted me with a story about a time he and Mark had cruised around South America and Mark got in a fight at a bar—which led to them meeting the mysterious and infamous Justin. All the while, my mind spun.

Did Mark really come up with this idea?

Was JJ letting him have the credit?

Mark did have a thoughtful side that often surprised me, but this kind of specificity had JJ written all over it.

So why did I feel so hesitant?

With great effort, I forced those thoughts to the back of my mind and just enjoyed the time with him. He'd grabbed my arm and pulled me close the moment I climbed into the Zombie Mobile. Even if we didn't speak, I liked being close to him. Romance books had that right—point for romance.

Twenty minutes later, JJ announced, "Here it is."

We pulled into the parking lot of a used bookstore I'd frequented so many times I knew most of the workers by name. Inside, the smell of old paper and ink overwhelmed me. Books rested on every available surface. A spot on the counter had been cleared so customers could pay, but towers of books ringed either side.

The curator, a middle-aged man named Leroy, waved. "Haven't seen you in a while!" he called to me.

"Been a bit busy."

"Heard about the car." He grimaced. "Glad you're okay. Got lots of new romance titles in. You know where they are!"

With another wave, I strode farther into the shop. Instinct

took me to the back-left corner, where women in busty dresses and men with half-lidded eyes populated almost every cover. JJ trailed behind.

Halfway there, I stopped. For some reason, my feet wouldn't move. My throat felt itchy, and a rush of heat spread through my body. My palms turned sweaty. Books awaited me back there. Romance books. Books that were once my best friends. Books that had filled my entire room to a ridiculous degree.

Books that were now completely gone.

"Oh!" I cried. "A new fantasy book. Check this one out." I snatched a book with a goblin on the cover that made me queasy.

"Fantasy?" JJ asked, looking puzzled. "What about—"

"Yeah, in just a second."

He followed as I moved to a different shelf and perused the back of a book about elf maidens. My mind didn't catch the words even as I cruised through the first chapter. I was too busy trying not to think about all the romance books in the corner. Of flames, and cinders, and ashes—and of Mama, for some reason.

Other books caught my attention, but I couldn't remember what they were about five seconds after I read the backs. I reshelved them, lost. All the while, the romance books sang to me from the corner of the store.

"What about this?" JJ handed me a cozy mystery that showed a teakettle sitting on a lace doily.

I skimmed the first chapter, then slid it back. "Looks nice."

"Nice? Lizbeth, are you all right?"

"Yep."

He studied me, but I quickly moved on to the middle-grade section. I'd read a decent number of those in elementary school. After half-heartedly giving him a brief tour of the best titles, we turned down horror lane.

"You like horror?" he asked. He studied a cover with a demon and its spawn crawling out of a dark hole.

"Not particularly."

"Did you want to go check out the new romance titles?" He hooked a thumb back that way.

I waved a hand airily. "In a moment."

"Lizbeth . . ."

"Oooh, new cookbooks!"

That would distract him and buy time for my heart to stop pounding. For my breath to catch up with my body.

My plan worked. He eagerly perused a few titles, mumbling about *patisserie* and *choux pastry.* In the cookbook aisle, I took a few deep breaths.

I could do this.

I could go back there and face those books without thinking of the Frolicking Moose. Without thinking of everything I'd lost that, until this point, I'd avoided thinking about. But now it slammed into me all at once.

All those books.

By sheer force of will, I swallowed my tears. Sweet baby pineapple, this place smelled like my attic room. Like books. Like paper and safety and home. Like I'd stepped *into* a story and wrapped myself in its pages. The attic room that would never be the same.

The books. My room. Even my laptop, clothes, phone with the sparkly cover. It was all *gone.* Not only had I lost my books, I'd lost my friends. Those books had gotten me through Mama's death. Dad's drinking. The escalation of his abuse.

Now they were ash.

Like a vengeful ghost, another memory of Mama whispered through my mind. *"The books have it right, Lizbeth. If you can find a man in real life that's just like the ones in the books you and I read, you snatch him up. He'll keep you safe forever."*

"Lizbeth?"

I jerked, startled by the sound of JJ's voice. He peered at me, a French pastry cookbook in his hands. He set it aside and closed the space between us in two strides. All of a sudden, he was there, hands on my shoulders to ground me.

"You all right?"

"I can't go back there," I whispered.

"Why?"

"Because . . . I can't see all those books. They remind me of home. Of . . ." A sob peeped out of my throat. He reached up, fingers threaded into my hair as his hand pressed against my cheek.

"Of all you lost in the fire?"

"So many books, JJ."

"Nine hundred fifty-seven," he said softly.

Tears filled my eyes, and I nodded. How did he remember that number? How was that the most perfect response?

"Books I can never replace." I still couldn't raise my voice above a whisper. "They're worn in the right places so I can quickly find the best scenes. They were with me in the worst times of my life. Now they're just *gone*. Along with everything else. Just . . . not there. They were . . . they were my friends."

JJ looked over at the shelves and back to me. His hands tightened, giving me a comforting squeeze. "Then don't go back there. Stay here with me."

My heart stumbled over itself. Why did it feel like he meant more than that?

"Okay."

He smiled and tucked a strand of hair behind my ear. "Grief waits, you know. You can ignore it until you gather your strength. Instead of buying books, let's look at delicious pictures of food that we can make together."

"Really?"

He nodded. His hair swayed gently around his cheeks. "If

you're not ready, then you're not ready. You don't have to go back yet, anyway. I still get you."

His face was a breath away from mine. My gaze dropped to his lips, half-parted, for a mere second.

"What if I'm never ready to face it?" I whispered.

"You will be, because that's the kind of person you are. But it doesn't matter if you're ready now. The books will be here when that time comes. While you're figuring that out, let's find something to make for dinner tonight. Together."

His hand dropped to my neck. The other one found mine and braided our fingers together. I wanted to pull myself into him and stay there.

"Sound okay?" he asked.

Relief flooded me at the thought of more time with him. Less time with ghosts. I nodded and stuffed the image of Mama away. If I was with him, I could do anything. Even forget all I'd lost.

Because if I hadn't lost it, would I have ever found him?

"Okay," I managed.

He smiled, pulled me close, and turned us back to the cookbooks. "Okay. Let's check out what they've got. I, for one, am always craving Indian food."

Chapter Twenty-Four

JJ

My ice cleats dug into the snow.

Breath puffed out in front of me in a fog as I ascended a particularly steep section of trail. I'd broken through thigh-high snow for an hour, and my heart was pounding so hard it shook my torso. Adventura lay at nine thousand feet elevation, but I pressed higher. Close to ten thousand. Shifting through sand-like snow for this long meant my heart would be bruised.

Felt so good.

For a moment, I stopped to scan the mountains. This high, I had a new view. A different perspective. The canyon lay to the south. Ahead of me rose a mountain so high I couldn't see the top. Last summer, I'd climbed it with Mark while Justin spotted.

Being with the rocks again felt like a cool kiss on frazzled nerves. Mark was feuding with the city council, so he'd slipped into full brooding mode, sitting in his pajamas and staring at the ceiling. It's where his magic always happened, so I left him to it, but Lizbeth was checking on him every five seconds.

My mind drifted back to our perfect evening last night. We'd found a recipe for spinach lentil dahl in an Indian cookbook, shopped at the grocery store, and fixed it together. She brightened when we discussed her favorite romance plots, then listened intently while I talked about climbing.

The whole night could have been ripped right from a book. Particularly the part where I desperately wanted to kiss her.

But I didn't, because . . . I didn't know. Maybe the expectation of the first kiss? Did she have massive dreams for this?

This morning, she'd started into the website project with her usual organized gusto. She'd rattled off a whole bunch of information about landing pages, CSS coding, and professional photographs of the campground. The checklists and spreadsheets she could muster at a moment's notice were impressive, to say the least.

But now things had changed between us. Nothing was the same. We'd shown a level of interest beyond friendship. I had no idea what to do next. Let this ride? Enjoy the time with her while I had it?

Kiss her already?

Definitely.

Why does it matter? The answer came easily enough. It mattered because Lizbeth mattered.

And Lizbeth mattered a lot.

Maybe too much.

On the back of a long receipt, I'd scribbled several romantic ideas pulled from the audiobook I'd been listening to. Dancing in the rain ranked at the top, apparently. Another one suggested surprising a girl with coffee and letting your fingers linger. Didn't get that, but all of this was foreign. The ones that had me most worried were *know just what to say at the right moment* and *save her from inevitable danger by being a badass at fighting.*

It all seemed so impossible. She believed in it so much. I didn't at all—at least, not really. She was twenty-one. I was thirty. Did we really have a chance?

Did I want to risk another Stacey-on-the-beach scene with a girl obsessed with romance? Or was it different this time?

No, I didn't want Stacey again, but Lizbeth was worlds different.

I shook my head, condensation from my hot breath in the cool air beading on my lower lip. A chill set into my legs where the snowbank pressed against them. I pushed forward again, nearing the top of the ridge. My thoughts moved quickly.

There was more than Lizbeth to think about today. Namely, my future career. When Mark was lounging in silence like this, he wasn't in the right frame of mind to hear my idea. He'd eat a mille-feuille—but would he understand the genius behind it?

My idea would have to wait again. Fortunately, he was the least-observant person on the planet. I could keep my baking and delivery rolling for another month, I imagined, before a decision had to be made.

Lizbeth, though, I didn't need to hesitate on anymore. I wanted to date her. I wanted Lizbeth to be mine and mine alone. Forgetting Stacey seemed effortless when I compared her against Lizbeth in my mind. There was no more space for anyone else.

Now, I just had to show her that.

Somehow.

My breath came in short, erratic bursts of frosty air that fogged up my sunglasses. Overhead, the sun beat down, but bitter cold breezed along the top of the ridge like gentle breaths. I glanced behind me at the rough seam I'd broken in the snow and sighed. My toes tingled from the thick steel reinforcement of my mountaineering boots.

Still, the cold permeated everything. Sometimes, you just couldn't fight inevitability.

I returned down the mountain as the sun sank lower in the winter sky, Lizbeth on my mind.

Chapter Twenty-Five

LIZBETH

The bustle of a small café at the edge of Jackson City flowed around me. I enjoyed the sounds and vitality of life after the absolute silence of the mountains. Ellie would stop by in a few minutes on her way back down the canyon to Pineville. I couldn't wait to see her.

At least I didn't have to stare at the burned-out shell of the Frolicking Moose. Even though I'd broken the ice on my grief at the bookstore, I still wasn't ready to face it. Then I'd have to admit how much I missed the twinkle lights around my bed. The smell of coffee. Not having to herd Mark.

Actually, that wasn't so bad. He'd come up with some amazing ideas today after sitting in a vegetative state on the couch for an hour.

Weird, but effective.

While I thought about the soft touch of JJ's hand on my knee during the ride up and the feeling of his fingertips against my back when we walked out to the truck, Ellie dropped into the seat across from me. A flurry of cold air and snow yanked me from my thoughts.

"Hey," I said.

"Sorry I'm late."

"You're not late."

Her keys jingled as she set them on the table and pulled off her parka. Beneath it she wore a fitted aquamarine athletic shirt that made her eyes bright. Two men sitting nearby perked up. She trained her cold glare on them in seconds, and they shrank away.

She wrapped her hand around a mug of hot chocolate I'd ordered for her. Snowflakes sprinkled from her hair and melted on her shoulders.

"It's good to see you," she said around a sip. "I've missed you."

"Same. Thanks for coming."

"Anytime."

"So, tell me everything I've missed," I said.

She cracked a smile. "We just talked yesterday."

"Yeah, but it's different in person! How's school? Did Mav finish the new shelves in the garage? What's going on with Devin's college admissions?" I asked. "Are the two of you still looking at State University?"

Her forehead wrinkled. "Not sure. He hasn't said much about them, which is weird because he seemed all excited for a while. Then he spoke to some recruiters, and now he's quiet."

"Think he'll go into the military?"

She shook her head. "No way. He promised me State University so we can go together. I'm graduating early next year so I can get in sooner. He's going to work, save up, and wait for me. There's no way Mac and Millie can afford to send him anywhere else, anyway. He needs the money in the worst way."

"Where is he now?"

Ellie glanced outside, as if her answers lay there. The grooves between her eyes deepened. "Dunno. We were going to do homework earlier and he had to leave all of a sudden."

For any other pair of humans, that would seem totally

normal. For Ellie and Devin? Strange. Something was brewing, but I could tell she didn't want to talk about it.

Ellie eyed me. "You have something on your mind, don't you?"

With a half laugh and a shrug, I said, "I think Mama's haunting me."

One fine black eyebrow quirked. I nodded. What other explanation could there be for the memories that were always surfacing? The whisper of Mama's voice in my mind at the weirdest times? She seemed everywhere to me now.

"Do tell," she murmured.

A thousand pictures played back through my head, racing on the heels of the others, Mama's voice in the background.

"There's always one man out there who will love you, understand you, and keep you safe. Make sure you settle with that one. You'll know it if he brings the romance, Lizzy."

"If the romance isn't there, then neither is the ring. That's all I'm saying."

"Make him swoon you a bit, sweetheart."

Her advice had been in direct opposition to the way she'd lived her life. Mama had met Dad, sensed that he wouldn't let her go but also wouldn't ask her to stay, and held on.

Then she'd sought love elsewhere.

She wouldn't let Dad go, but she wouldn't love him, either.

Like she despised him for being the person she relied on the most.

Meanwhile, she wove magic around romance every time she gave me advice.

"You know who your father is, don't you?" I asked instead of diving back into Mama.

First, I needed answers.

Ellie froze, then reluctantly nodded.

"How did you find out?"

"Watched Mama. Followed her over to his house a few times in the middle of the night when I was six or seven." She set her mug down. "Most of the time she stayed until just before Jim returned from . . . wherever he went at night."

"The bar, probably."

Ellie nodded.

"How old were you when you found out he was your father?"

"Six."

"How?" I asked with a shake of my head. "How did you know?"

"Mama caught me following her over there one day. I dug into a hay bale to stay warm and waited until she came back early in the morning. Mama told me everything then. Besides, she hated Jim and I looked nothing like him. Then I saw Trevor and it confirmed it for me. I have his eyes." Her expression softened slightly.

Trevor. She'd never told me his name before, and Mama had never said it. Ellie knew our neighbors and land better than anyone else. She often slept outside in the summer to be closer to the cats and horses. Something about animals reassured her. She always had one in her arms, even now.

"Does Trevor know the truth about you?" I asked.

"Mama never told him."

"Why?"

"She said it would ruin the romance."

My heart sank all the way into my nauseated stomach. What kind of a mama said that to her daughter? A mama totally obsessed with something that wasn't real. For the first time, I began to notice a sense of familiarity around Mama's love of romance. A familiarity that made me want to vomit.

I shoved that aside.

"Did you ever talk to Trevor?"

"Only once."

I waited for more, but Ellie stopped talking. She'd already given more than I'd expected. It didn't feel right to push her farther.

"Thanks," I said. "All that information, it . . . it helps."

Her gaze tapered. "What's going on?"

My fingers fidgeted with my cloth napkin in an unsuccessful attempt to smooth out nonexistent wrinkles. The past couple of days with JJ had been . . . lovely. Perfect. A balance between surreality and hope.

Days that I wouldn't give away or change for anything.

Yet Mama plagued me.

I'd asked Ellie here because I needed validation. Did I remember Mama correctly? The memories hovered on the surface of my mind in bright flashes, almost as if she were standing right in front of me. Obsessed with a specific vision of love that she'd chased her whole life and never found. Had I made some of this up? It seemed too wild to be real.

Would I end up just like her?

"What do you remember about her?" I asked instead of answering her question.

Ellie frowned. "That's not a fair question. I was so little."

"You loved her more than anyone. Maybe you remember something different than me or Bethie."

She growled, "I'm not doing a walk down memory lane unless you tell me what's going on."

"How about I tell you what I remember?" I said quickly. "I remember makeup. Tight dresses. Big heels. I remember her smiling most of the time, unless she wasn't. There wasn't neutral on Mama, just . . . happy or angry. I remember Dad being jealous when he was drunk and Mama slapping him for it seconds before she took his paycheck to the bank."

Ellie's expression soured, but she hadn't left, so I knew she'd stick with it. After a long pause, she said, "I remember love songs."

"Love songs?"

"Mama always played love songs. Cheesy ones. Ridiculous ones." She rolled her eyes. "The kind you could buy off of a commercial for $9.99. She'd sing them at the top of her lungs while she danced around the house."

That stirred vague memories. Ellie twiddled her fingers, as if to flick it away.

"She did it mostly when you were at school. Said she didn't want it to distract you from studying. That your mind was going to take you places. That you wouldn't need a man to save you like she did."

My nostrils flared. "She never said that to me."

"I know."

Ellie's calm expression sent a bolt of fire through me, but it faded.

"What else didn't she say to me?" I asked.

"A lot of things." Ellie looked down at her hands. "Mostly about Trevor."

"Did she love him?"

"She said she did." Ellie's brow rose halfway to her hairline. "Could Mama really love anyone but herself?"

"Maybe."

"Then why didn't she leave Jim?" Ellie countered. "Why torture him and us? No, Mama didn't know anything about love. Didn't understand love. What she thought was love was addiction. Desperation."

I had no answer to that. Ellie and I had gone to therapy for over a year after Bethany got custody of us. I'd continued intermittently through college. Ellie had stopped the moment Bethany let her, but her insights always impressed me anyway.

"What else did Mama say?" I asked.

Her expression darkened. "Nothing."

"She—"

"What's going on?" Ellie demanded. "Tell me, Lizbeth. You have me all freaked out. We haven't talked about Mama in years."

The reply stalled in my throat. *Because I'm afraid I'll end up just like her.*

"I care about JJ," I whispered.

Ellie didn't seem fazed, and that frightened me. Was I so transparent? Did he see it? He must—why else would he show me such lovely affection?

Would it be a bad thing if he knew?

The waitress handed me another warm mug of tea and turned to Ellie, who shook her head and waved her off. It bought me a few seconds to pull my scattered heartstrings back together.

"And?" Ellie asked.

"And I . . . I don't want to end up like Mama."

"You're afraid that if you commit to someone you'll end up like her?"

"Yes."

"Why?"

"JJ doesn't believe in romance."

She stared at me in puzzlement, then her eyes grew wide and her mouth dropped open.

Before she could argue, I held up a hand. "Hold on. Don't jump to conclusions. I wouldn't say no to JJ just because he doesn't believe in romance like I do. I know that romance isn't everything, it's just . . ."

Unsure of how to finish that thought, I let it trail away.

Ellie leaned back, the pad of her thumb running over the top of her mug. She regarded me, then asked, "And has it been romantic with JJ?"

"Well . . . no. And definitely yes."

Her brow furrowed. "What?"

I threw my hands in the air. "I don't know, Ellie! I'm so confused. All the things that were supposed to be romantic didn't really feel that romantic. There are moments I care so much about him I could choke, but they're never the times I expect."

"So?"

"So?" I cried. "So what if I fall for him even harder? What if we get into a relationship and the romance fades and it all falls apart and I turn into Mama? Or worse—what if I turn JJ into Dad?"

Ellie blinked twice. "Just because Mama was a mess over romance doesn't mean you're going to live her life."

"*I'm* a mess over romance, Ellie! I remember her obsession with romance. She read books as fast as I did. Watched the movies with me. Convinced me that romance was the only way to be safe."

"And it's not?"

"No! Maybe. I don't know. Real life is different. It's not what she told me it would be. While parts of my time with him are wonderful, some of it isn't. It frightens me because I'm not sure what to believe anymore. What's real?"

"Your feelings for him must be real."

"They are, and I care for him." *Maybe love him.* I tucked the traitorous thought away for later. "Maybe Mama felt that way about Dad at first. About Bethany's father. About Trevor. When it comes to romance, Mama and I . . . we're practically the same person. That side of Mama lives on in me."

And it may have been her darkest legacy, I silently added.

To that, Ellie had nothing to say. Finally, she reached a hand across the table and grabbed mine. Uncertainty—even fear—lurked in the depths of her bright, glacial eyes.

"I don't know what to say, Lizbeth. I'm sorry. I'm not great at this. But I just don't think you're doomed to be like Mama because you love romance. You're not Mama."

"Maybe not," I whispered. "But what if I'm enough like her that I destroy everyone who's important to me? What if *romance* is what drove her to make all the decisions she did? I'm not . . . I'm not even sure romance is real anymore." I looked away. "Not the way I imagined it. Maybe it's just been a crutch. A place to hide."

Until I said the words, I didn't realize how deeply they'd bothered me. Pricking thorns on my soul. Festering wounds. The devastation in my heart left me breathless. Romance in real life was breathtaking and exciting, but also treacherous. Although the books described anguish and heartbreak, it never felt real to me until now.

Romance was more than just hope—it was agony. Duality. A double-edged sword. As dark as it was bright, as bloody as it was holy. As menacing as it was comforting.

How had I been this naive? How had I come this far in life, lauded for my intelligence, but still holding on to such a ridiculous farce? Books. Movies. Stories I'd relished to the depths of my bones. Had the music, the costumes, the ideas in my head somehow hidden the truth?

That love broke as much as it restored?

"I'm sorry that I don't know what to say," Ellie whispered.

With warmth, I gripped her hand and mustered a smile that seemed to appease her a little. "Thank you. I just needed to know that I hadn't made this up. That this side of Mama was real. You said all the right things."

"Mama was lovesick, Lizzy," she whispered. "And she let it rule her. Don't do that, and you'll be fine. I love you."

"I love you, too."

"Do you need a ride back to Adventura?"

I shook my head. "JJ was doing something somewhere. He'll text me when he's done and take me back with him."

Ellie hesitated as if to say something, then decided against it and gave me a little smile. "Then I better go. I have class tomorrow and homework to finish. Keep me updated, okay?"

I nodded. With that, she squeezed my hand, grabbed her car keys, dropped five dollars on the table, flipped the bird to the two men still staring at her, and slipped outside.

I gazed at the door through which she'd left, my mind whirling.

JJ

An order of fifty éclairs of many colors and flavors accompanied me into Le Grand Boulangerie in the middle of Jackson City. The warm smell of yeast and sugar filled my nose.

Two men stood behind the counter of the eclectic shop decorated with lights, mason jars, and pastries. One of them let out a cry when he saw me.

"Those must be the éclairs!" Grant squealed with a flap of his hand. "Our final test. Get over here, J-man. Let's see them."

I gently slid the box toward them.

"The conquering hero returns," Immanuel drawled.

Immanuel and Grant, newlywed owners of the bakery, opened the éclairs. Of the two, Immanuel was the pickiest. He had a sharp nose, a broad face, and a constant five o'clock shadow. His personality was as prickly as his appearance, but he reminded me so much of my dad that we'd ended up friends.

Grant was sunshine to Immanuel's sharpness. He smiled constantly, and his moonbeam-blond hair only heightened the effect.

Immanuel inspected the éclairs visually first. He twisted the box to the left, then right. Peered up close, then stepped back.

Grant tried to reach for one, and Immanuel slapped his hand away.

"Uniform," Immanuel said with a quick glance at me. "Impressively so. Choux pastry is hard to predict and get right. Particularly at altitude."

The two batches in the garbage back at Adventura proved him right. Not that I was going to volunteer that detail.

"I like the color and the frosting," Immanuel continued. "Your piping skills have come a long way. Sufficiently so, I think."

"Buttercream and I have become good friends," I said.

A ghost of a smile appeared on Immanuel's face. He gestured to Grant, who snatched the first éclair he could reach and took a bite. A raspberry vanilla-bean curd lay thick inside, with a subtle layer of chocolate frosting piped on the top. Grant chewed, hesitated, then melted to the floor.

"Well," Immanuel drawled, "I think you pass."

From the ground, Grant mumbled something dramatically unintelligible. I agreed with him, if I did say so myself. They were delicious éclairs.

Immanuel waved a hand over the box. His gluten intolerance prevented him from tasting them. "Perfect, as always. It was our final recipe for you to try."

"And what updates do you have on the build-out?"

Immanuel tilted his head toward the back wall, which was made of old brick and crumbling in the right places. Behind it lay their normal baking area. Ovens. Rolling counters. Barrels of flour. They had enough space to keep their store stocked, but not much else. They often sold out of their most popular desserts—éclairs among them.

"The city rejected our plans for expansion in the back," Immanuel said. "We're looking with a realtor to find other options. The warehouse on the other side of town is more than we could afford . . . right now."

His gaze met mine with a subtle hint of challenge.

I knew exactly why.

"Then expanding into catering with my help will be a good stepping stone," I said.

He nodded. Immanuel was never really enthused about anything. Grant, on the other hand, popped up again with a bright smile.

"I'm confident that we can move on to the first phase of our plan," Immanuel said, "which means we're officially ready to hire you—starting today."

"Today?"

He nodded. "We'll notify our customers interested in catering that we're offering bulk orders and wedding catering for baked goods only. We'll provide shipments of supplies to Adventura, since your health inspection document is already on file from the summer."

Well, no putting this off anymore, I thought. Mark had to know about my idea. Immanuel studied me as Grant reached for the éclairs with a piece of tissue paper and arranged them in the display case.

"Everything okay?" Immanuel drawled. "You've received your brother's approval to use the kitchen at your summer camp to fulfill catering orders for us, correct?"

"It'll be fine."

Immanuel eyed me. "Because if not, we have a backup. Darlene down in Territory is ready anytime. We'd prefer you, of course, because there's less travel time for the pastries but—"

"Not necessary. I'll sign right now to prove it."

He hesitated, then shrugged. "Very well. I had my attorney draw up the contract last week, just in case. Let me grab it. It details compensation based on order price and lasts for a year."

While Immanuel went to the back, Grant took his place with a broad smile. We chatted for a few minutes about ski traffic and what was selling the most. Before I'd really recovered my composure, Immanuel returned, slid the contract across the table, and handed me a pen.

For a full five seconds, I stared at the words on the page without comprehending them.

This was not what I'd expected from this trip. A signed contract today?

Of course, why not?

In their eyes, it was all ready to go. I'd successfully baked and transported all their recipes to their satisfaction. Both of us were confident in my work, and they stood to benefit as much as I did.

Except Mark knew nothing about it.

"Everything good?" Immanuel asked as I fiddled with the pen cap.

My eyes scoured the words, moving quickly. Everything was as simple and straightforward as we'd discussed. It basically guaranteed my availability for the next year, that I'd keep the kitchen up to all health code standards or assume liability myself, and never share their recipes. They'd have supplies delivered so I wouldn't have to keep running to the grocery store on their behalf.

How this would work in the summer at Adventura, I had no idea. There were a lot of things I didn't know. But if I didn't do it, the opportunity would go to their backup person. This was too perfectly convenient to my climbing lifestyle to give up.

So I signed it.

Once I finished, Immanuel pulled the contract back. Then he gave me a check for compensation for the tests and the last five desserts I'd brought in. He also handed me a book with a copy of all their super-secret recipes created in the years before his gluten issue developed.

A half smile crossed Immanuel's face. "Welcome to the team, JJ. You're our first official overflow baker. We've already had an order of croissants and pain au chocolat come in for a local business meeting with realtors. Information is in the email I'll send after you leave."

"Thanks, guys."

"Expect delivery tomorrow afternoon!" Immanuel called as I headed out the door. I waved to acknowledge it, but my mind was already spinning. How would Mark feel about me signing a contract on behalf of Adventura? He was the official owner. While I'd helped, the camp was in his name.

He'd certainly had plenty of crazy ideas of his own that I'd gone along with.

He probably wouldn't care.

I hoped.

* * *

"Everything go okay with your sister?"

Lizbeth nodded with a tight smile as she climbed into the truck. I almost invited her to sit next to me again, but she quickly put her seat belt on and looked straight ahead, her hands under her thighs and her lips pressed together in a thin line.

Something hadn't gone well.

"Good," I said for lack of anything else.

The engine roared as I pulled away from the café and headed down the highway and into the canyon. My concern over the café deal faded in the uncomfortable silence. My inability to read Lizbeth was a heady reminder that, for all my happy feelings about her, we still didn't know each other that well.

"Were you glad to see her?" I asked just to break the ice.

She cleared her throat. "Yeah. It's always good to catch up. I've missed her."

"You're close."

She nodded.

Quiet fell over us again. I let it ride this time, unsure of what to say or how to ask what it meant. I'd forgotten how awkward relationships could be. Forgotten about the battle between what I wanted to say and what was probably safe to say. Then again, I could always channel my inner Mark and just say whatever the hell I wanted.

Sometimes that actually worked out for him, but I blamed ninety percent of his relationship failures on his mouth.

Instead, I let the silence accompany us back to Adventura.

We pulled in, and Lizbeth didn't look at me when she said, "I'm pretty tired. I think I'll go to bed. Thanks for the ride, JJ. I appreciate the chance to talk to Ellie."

Before I could tell her to sleep well, she shut the door and walked around the outside of the office to head to her cabin. I stared at the dark spot where she'd disappeared. A heavy feeling told me something wasn't right.

Shaking my head, I pushed that off. Mark and I had unfinished business to deal with now. I'd focus on that first.

* * *

Mark was sitting behind his desk, a perplexed expression on his face, when I stepped inside.

"Seriously, JJ, when did the office start to *smell* good?" he asked.

No papers or office supplies were scattered across his workspace. Not even three different pens and four colors of highlighters. He looked totally out of place in the clean landscape. The wood of the desk, which had been hidden beneath the layers of dust he'd allowed to collect, had turned out to be cherry. Now, it gleamed a gorgeous red.

"When Lizbeth started." I peeled my coat off. "She lights a candle thing all the time."

Mark glanced at my jacket as I hung it on a peg—a whittled bear—that had appeared on the wall one day after lunch. It had kept our chairs blessedly unburdened. They didn't topple over quite as much.

"Oh," he said as if he'd also just noticed that peg. "Where is she?"

"Just went to bed."

The Zombie Mobile keys clattered when I tossed them into a multicolored clay bowl on the makeshift table. *Himalayan,* Lizbeth had said, claiming she'd found it under some junk in the spare room. I seriously doubted that, but loved the aesthetic all the same.

"I'm a little worried." Mark peered at the desk as if it held the answers to the universe. "I'm running out of work for her. She's been getting the website and investor dashboard up like a crazy person. She has a website for a spa that hasn't even been approved yet. How wild is that? And it looks freaking *good.*"

"Oh?"

"Yeah." He frowned. "I don't really want her to go, do you? But if I can't drum up something else, she'll be gone soon."

"How soon?"

"Dunno. By the end of the week at the latest."

I almost choked on my tongue. "The end of the week? What?"

He nodded, his face a picture of concern. "Yeah. She's been pretty great to have, don't you think? Like, I actually have a desk now and someone who doesn't put up with all my crap. What am I going to do? Just bulldoze over people again?"

"Probably."

He sighed. "I'll try to come up with something. Maybe I need to create a new business for her to run. Think she'd take the spa? Because that would be awesome. Wait, doesn't she have a job coming up?"

"Not sure if she's heard back yet."

He eyed me. "Huh. How *are* things between you?"

Actually, I didn't know. They'd been magical. Even romantic. But after our drive back tonight, I wasn't sure where she stood. Lizbeth always had a sense of hesitation about her, but now it was amplified.

The couch groaned when I collapsed onto it.

"Honestly? I have no idea. I think they're good."

"Good, as in dating?" His grin lit up the office.

"Not necessarily."

"So you're not dating?"

"Well, not that, either."

"You're a friggin' mess, JJ. Why did you wait so long to get over Stacey? Now you're going to be all awkward with Lizbeth."

I threw a pillow at him. He chucked it back, but I blocked it.

"Oh, I forgot to mention that I had an interesting offer come our way yesterday." Mark stacked his hands behind his head. "Wanted to see what you thought, because they're waiting on me to call back after I reach out to the board."

My mouth closed. The board?

"What is it?"

"A company wants to contract to use our kitchen in the off-season. Weird, right? Never thought about that before."

Several moments passed before I could assemble that in my head.

"Wait. What?"

He shrugged. "Apparently kitchen space is at a premium, and we have that paperwork filed with the state. Companies will rent out kitchens to do bulk orders. Anyway, it's a health-food granola company starting out of Jackson City. You've been on me for a while to use Adventura in different ways, right? They'll pay us to use the kitchen."

What were the odds?

Was this a coincidence?

"Also," Mark continued as he tossed a wad of paper into the air, "I had an idea about horses, but ask me about that later."

My throat felt sticky as I tried to form the words. Mark

wouldn't be angry about my idea to do basically the same thing, but he *might* be upset that I'd not mentioned it to him before. Or that I'd signed that contract without his permission.

The whole we-live-each-other's-lives thing always got in the way.

"So, about that idea." I cleared my throat. "It's a great idea, actually. Ah . . . I sort of just signed a contract on behalf of Adventura's kitchen and have a proposal for you that's similar."

He paused mid-throw.

"What?"

With a deep breath, I said, "I . . . I've been experimenting for the past few months with some bakery recipes. Patisserie stuff. Petit fours, croissants, that sort of thing. One day while in Jackson City, I stopped at Le Grand Boulangerie and tried a few things. The owners and I started to talk. Eventually they mentioned that they wanted to start catering but didn't have the space."

Mark stared at me with a glass expression, which was the first red flag. Mark's face *always* showed emotion. The absence of it was reason enough to run.

Second, his jaw was ticking.

Deciding that getting it over with was best, I pushed through the worst part.

"I told them I'd like to try making some of their recipes to see if I could help them out, so they sent some with me. As you said, we have paperwork filed with the state health department for our kitchen that allows us to make commercial food, so I tried a few things—tarts, cakes, cupcakes—and took it back to them." I shrugged. "They liked what they saw. So they asked if I'd like to partner with them."

His other eyebrow rose. "Partner with them?" he repeated dully.

"Just in catering. They've wanted to open up to big catering orders but don't have the space. You know how cramped downtown Jackson City is. So they're looking into a build-out or buying space somewhere else. But they'd like to test the process and build their revenue. They liked the way I baked—"

"—so they want you to cater from Adventura."

I hated it when he connected the dots ahead of me. His toneless voice sounded so much like Dad's did when we got busted for doing something stupid.

"Yes. I thought I'd give Adventura a cut of each order. That way I can work and climb and still help out here but actually make some money. Eventually, I have to figure out my own life. This may be the path to that."

Mark frowned. "How long has this been going on?"

"Two months?"

His eyes widened. "And you didn't tell me?"

"You've been so focused on everything else. I didn't know if this would go anywhere. I mean, c'mon, Mark. You've eaten a little of everything that I fixed. It's not like I hid it."

"But you did. For two months you've been sneaking behind my back with plans you never shared with me."

He stood, hands planted on the desk. The defensive posture wasn't unexpected. Mark had anger, but not aggression. He had the weight and strength advantage, but not speed or stamina. For brothers, we're strangely well matched in a fight. This could definitely come to fists.

Stupider things had in the past.

"I haven't been *hiding* it," I said. "I just haven't been discussing it. I've tried to bring it up a few times, but the best I was able to do was mention doing something else with Adventura. Then something always came up to distract you."

He shook his head and took a step back, raising his hands. "I'm done, bro. This is insulting. First of all, it's not yours to contract out."

"I know that, and I'm sorry. They sort of sprung the contract on me and I didn't want to lose the chance. I hate the idea of not having a job all winter, and Adventura is largely your idea. I love helping with it, but it's your baby."

"Well, now you may be in breach of contract with the bakery. Hope there's no fine associated with that. Also, screw you for not claiming Adventura. This was for both of us. The board has to approve your contract, by the way. What are you going to do in the summer when we need the kitchen to feed the staff and the campers?"

"I haven't worked through that yet."

"And are you giving up your position as a counselor?"

I ran a hand through my hair. "No, of course not."

"So how's that going to work?"

"I-I don't know yet."

"But you signed a contract anyway." His eyes flashed. "After going behind my back to partner with someone else. Douchebag move, brother."

With a growl, he stormed out the back door.

The screen slammed against the wall with a *crack*, then whipped shut.

I winced, stung at the betrayal in his expression.

Chapter Twenty-Seven

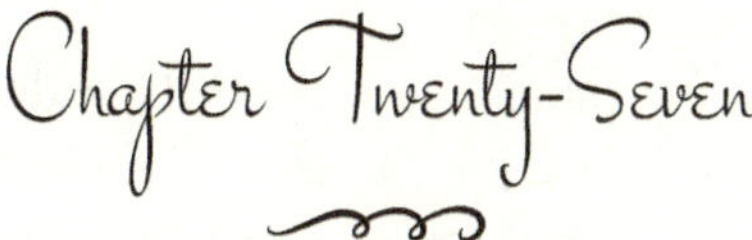

LIZBETH

The fire crackled the next morning as I sat on my bed and stared at the ceiling. My conversation with Ellie had played through my mind all night. Finally, at four thirty, I'd built up the fire and mentally thanked Justin for restocking my woodpile. Then I'd sat in a ball of blankets and tried to disappear into a romance novel.

JJ intruded on my thoughts too much.

He seemed close enough to touch, but so far away at the same time. I'd been so distant yesterday and hadn't explained myself. Guilt flooded my chest. Then regret. He'd been startled. Confused. I could see it in his eyes when I didn't sit next to him, then didn't speak.

How could I explain what I hadn't even sorted through myself?

The uncertain side of romance really sucked. I'd always waved it off when the heroines experienced it in the novels. Said it was necessary for character development and made the story better. Now? I only felt miserable, confused, and terribly uncertain.

A ding from my phone pulled me from my thoughts. Ten

o'clock. I'd lounged all morning in my cozy little cabin with frost on the windows, but now I had another ugly reality to face. With great effort, I shoved JJ to the back of my head, pulled in a deep breath, and let it all out in one great *whoosh*.

Time for my call with Dad.

The door to my cabin was locked, the radio turned off. I pulled the curtains, too, just in case. Couldn't imagine how horrified I'd feel if JJ or Mark came to ask me something and saw an inmate in a bright orange jumpsuit who happened to be my father. The whole situation was embarrassing.

"I can talk to Dad and not be confused," I chanted as I navigated to the appropriate web page. "I can talk to Dad and not be confused."

For fifteen or so minutes every December, we met on a videochat. I gave him updates, and the call ended. Every time I sent him a letter or joined our yearly call, two parts of my heart spoke to me. *Are you crazy?* one half of me said. *That man would have killed you if you hadn't gotten out of there. You're lucky he didn't do worse.*

That part was totally true.

The other half said, *But there were good times,* and that was also totally true.

Something in me couldn't let go of those good times. They'd been few and far between. Fleeting, like glimpses of sunshine in a rainstorm. But he was my father.

Ellie didn't know I'd kept up an erratic correspondence. At least, I didn't think she did. At first, my therapist had suggested I reach out. For some reason, I felt better after talking to him. Like I didn't have to erase a part of me or pretend it hadn't happened. I was already trying so hard to erase Mama.

The prison had an online system that allowed me to videochat him for a small fee. I never really looked forward to it, but felt obligated all the same. The calls were mostly dry and stilted, but they satisfied the part of me that couldn't pretend like he didn't exist.

Today, however, our talk might actually be helpful.

The call rang, and my stomach gave a nervous flip before I answered it. Only a few seconds passed before the picture cleared, bringing Dad into focus with his usual orange jumpsuit, buzzed hair, and pale expression. While he was offered outdoors time every day, it didn't seem like he took it.

In the five years since he'd been sentenced, he'd grown gaunt. Hollows had appeared in his cheeks and dark lines under his eyes. He'd never really been conversational while I was growing up, but was even less so now.

I conjured a smile.

"Hey."

He cleared his throat. "Hi. Good to see you."

Is it? I wanted to ask. He remained classically stoic and unreadable.

"How are things?" I asked instead.

"Good."

"Any word on your sentencing?"

"Still on good behavior," he said. "There's a chance for parole in a year or two."

My eyes widened. That was news. "Really?"

He nodded a little.

Resisting the urge to text Ellie a warning was hard.

Somehow, my dad occupied three spots in my mind. The drunk, the dad figure, and the jailbird. Right now, I couldn't picture this sedate, boring guy as the one who'd stormed into the Frolicking Moose and almost shot Bethany in a drunken rage.

But I could never forget it, either.

"Any news from there?" I asked, then almost winced. How awkward. What could possibly be news in his world?

He just shook his head, lips puffed in a closed line.

"I, uh . . . it's been eventful here," I said. "Almost drove my car off a cliff the other day."

"Oh?"

"Yeah, but . . . it worked out okay. Car is totaled, but I'm alive."

"Good. Insurance cover it?"

"Not sure. We're waiting to hear back."

"Glad you're safe."

"Me too."

Another painful silence. Moments like this reminded me why it seemed so easy for Ellie to cut him from her life without a thought. She hadn't even spoken his name since that awful day in the coffee shop.

"Listen, Dad, can we talk about Mama?"

His features darkened. He shifted a little in his seat but didn't stop me.

I pressed on. "I'm . . . I'm trying to remember her. Remember our life together. It seems so long ago, and . . . I'm not sure I'm remembering what was real or who I *think* she was."

He scoffed. "Whoever you thought she was was probably wrong. There wasn't a person on this planet who could peg Kat down."

I frowned. "Okay, but . . . was she a romantic?"

"She claimed to be a hopeless romantic."

My heart sped up. "Was she?"

He shrugged. "What does that even mean?"

"You know . . . the kind of person who really believes in love. In the safety and power of romance as a force for good in the world."

His brow wrinkled. "That doesn't sound like her. She was an endless flirt who led men on, had sex with them, and then moved on."

I hid a wince. He wasn't wrong.

"Did you try to be romantic with her?" I asked.

"Can you fill a black hole?"

My nostrils flared with my effort to suppress my annoyance. His bitterness had only grown more concentrated over the past five years.

"Okay," I drawled. "That's fair, I guess. I just realized lately that I think I've been a little . . . naive about romance. About love. I'm afraid that I'm too much like Mama, and I'm trying to not go down the path she did."

"So what if you are?"

The question stopped me in my tracks. *Then I have to halt my life, reevaluate my plans, and change absolutely everything about myself,* I thought. *I have to make sure I never do to JJ what Mama did to you. Or me.*

I didn't answer his question.

He tilted his head back, as if in thought, for a long stretch. Eventually, he said, "She was always in love with love. It seemed like she wanted an out whenever she realized it wasn't easy."

I ran my memories of Mama through that filter, and it fit.

"Okay."

"That was Kat. Easy, fun, and spontaneous. That's what she wanted. Whirlwind romance. To be swept off her feet. Prince Charming. That load of bull. She didn't like responsibility, either," he added, "which is why we lost electricity so much. You'd think romance would dictate she pay the bills on time."

A fault the two of them had shared.

"Did she love you when you first met?"

"I don't know."

"Did you love her?"

"Sure."

A bitter edge colored his flippant response. He didn't like this conversation at all. Could I trust his responses? Was he telling me the truth?

"Why did you marry her?"

For a moment, I thought he'd end the call. His brow grew so heavy it nearly covered his eyes. Eventually, he said, "Because I think I did love her. I thought we could do anything together. At the time, it felt good."

"And then?"

He scowled. "And then you'd have to ask Trevor how things ended between me and Kat."

I blinked. "You knew about Trevor?"

"Of course I knew what was happening with Trevor," he growled. "Didn't take an idiot to figure it out. I let it go for a while because I assumed she'd get bored with him the same as she did with me. Since we had a child together, I thought she'd stay."

"She did."

"If you could call it that. The night she died? She told me she was going to leave me for him. That's what we fought about."

"I didn't know that," I murmured.

"Lovely, hopeless romantic, wasn't she? More like a tornado. Kat destroyed everyone she touched. Not even you can deny that."

More silence. Mama practically sang the ugly parts of love out of the shadows with her driving need to experience it. To *find love*. She'd escaped from reality with romance, just like me. Then she broke all our hearts. Who might Dad have been without Mama? What if she hadn't been so in love with love?

The lesson here was clear: Mama had destroyed all her relationships with her undying belief in romance.

And I would never be like her.

Cracks in my heart fractured what little strength I had left. What if I did the same thing to JJ? Would I turn him into a convict? A mess of a man who felt only bitterness? No, I'd never let that happen. Not to him. Not to me.

I couldn't endure that.

"Thank you," I croaked to Dad. "This was helpful."

Dad nodded, gaze focused off-screen. He drew in a deep breath. Then he let it out and leaned forward a little. "Listen, Lizbeth, this sentiment won't make me popular, and I'm already a jerk. But the truth is this: if I could make it so I never met Kat, I'd do that. If you ask me, that's what Kat's quest for love did. Left regret and broken hearts in its wake. You'd do well to stay as far away from it as you can."

He turned the videocall off without another word.

I closed my computer with a sob.

Chapter Twenty-Eight

JJ

Dad and I sat across from each other in a crummy diner in Pineville the day after my fight with Mark. The smell of fry oil and fake evergreen permeated the air. Bells jangled on the door every time someone walked in or out. I rubbed a hand over my bleary eyes.

Dad and I hadn't seen each other in well over a month. He sent random texts now and then, mostly pictures of fish he'd caught, questions about how we were doing, or queries about how to work his phone. I wondered if he ever felt lonely in his new little cabin by himself. The old house had sold shortly after the divorce was finalized, effectively sealing off my childhood into the realm of history.

"Your mom called me this morning," he said.

His comment puzzled me. Why would Mom call him? The fact that we were sitting in a public place together had me almost as confused. Dad hated crowds. Anything more than three people was too many for him.

Things had a weird way of tipping upside down quickly.

"What did she say?" I asked.

"I didn't answer."

I bit back a laugh. Why that was funny, I had no idea. Maybe it was a sign of my mental state when there'd been no word from Lizbeth. Mark had disappeared somewhere for the night and given me a cold reception this morning when the delivery truck arrived. He'd queried the board about it through Lizbeth's online dashboard, but I hadn't seen any responses.

"Texted her back," Dad continued, breaking my thoughts. "She responded."

I sat with my elbows on the table, my hands folded together. Two mugs of coffee cooled in front of us.

Dad watched me in his usual intense way. More of a glower, really. It had always scared rebellion out of me for a few hours when I was a young kid. Mark would usually come up with another brilliant idea shortly after any given punishment ended. Like most things, we'd accomplish the mischief together, despite the infamous Sheriff Bailey stare.

I managed to meet his gaze, and it surprised me. Today the intensity was softer.

"She said that something happened and things aren't great between you and Mark."

"It just happened last night," I muttered in exasperation. "Wait. Did Mark spend the night at her place?"

Dad shrugged. "You know Kelly," he muttered. "Always poking around. So something *did* happen?"

"Yeah."

In the briefest possible terms, I told him everything about the bakery, the contract, and Mark's response. Dad listened without changing expression.

Letting it out felt good. Having Dad's stoic mind puzzle it out was better. Like me, he tended toward facts and logic and didn't often get emotional. His responses always felt safer to me than Mom's, which is probably why Mark ended up gravitating toward her.

"I'd be pissed too," he said.

I sighed.

"You know it was wrong, don't you?" he asked.

"Yes."

"So make it right."

"How? I signed the stupid contract."

Dad waved that off. "Not that. With Mark."

"That's how I make it right."

Dad definitely glowered then. "Don't be an idiot, JJ. Mark's hurt that you didn't tell him what you were doing. He tells you everything."

"He doesn't," I replied softly.

And that's when it hit me like a punch to the sternum.

Mark hadn't told me about the escalating tensions between Mom and Dad. Or about the impending divorce. I'd been totally blindsided by my parents and siblings. This bakery job? Maybe this had been some convoluted attempt to swing back at him.

The thought robbed my breath.

"Damn," I muttered. Was I that vindictive? I didn't like that at all.

"What hasn't he told you?" Dad asked.

For five seconds, I sized Dad up.

"The divorce."

A silent question came in the form of grooves between his eyebrows. I looked away, guilty over my anger. My teeth ground into each other until my jaw started to cramp. I forced myself to take a deep breath.

"Why didn't you tell me how much you were struggling?" I asked. "Why did everyone leave me out? Megan and Mark knew everything. I had no idea."

His expression darkened like a thunderstorm. "It wasn't on purpose, JJ. I was just keeping my head above water. Plus, I didn't tell them. Your mom did."

"It made me feel like I didn't matter as much. Like you'd forgotten me."

"I'd never forget you, JJ. Your mom turned to Mark quite a bit at the time. She must have sworn him to silence, or something."

"And you turned to no one?"

"That seemed better than relying too much on the three of you," he countered. "JJ, there's no easy answer to your question. It was damned if I did, and damned if I didn't. To lean on my son as a support? That wouldn't have been fair. You had to live through this too. The pressure of helping me would have made it worse."

Certainly an angle I hadn't thought of. I wondered if Mark resented Mom's reliance on him. Maybe he hadn't wanted to know about their issues.

"I'm sorry, JJ," Dad said. "I'm sorry I wasn't more open with you. I've been an ass through the divorce, and even after. Maybe before, too, I don't know. My world's all flipped around."

I blinked, stunned. Well . . . that was something. Dad was rarely wrong in his own eyes. Not sure what to say, I let that sit there. Dad released a long sigh, then shook his head.

"Have you ever failed at something?" he asked.

"Of course."

"Failed at something that impacted you and everyone you care about?"

"Probably."

"Then maybe you know what it feels like to have your world crumble around you. To see everything you worked for your entire life just . . . fall apart the moment you thought you'd have it." He shook his head. "I thought if I just kept working, if I focused on what I *could* do versus what felt . . . impossible . . . then I'd retire, have time to do everything I wanted, and everything would be okay."

A thousand scenarios ran through my mind. Things he could be talking about. But they all vanished. Because here sat a man I'd never met: a humbled version of my father. I wiggled in my seat to find a more comfortable position. Dad's acknowledgment sobered the atmosphere. I couldn't help but admire him for it.

"What did you think felt impossible?" I asked quietly.

"Making her happy."

The haunted words cooled the fire in my body, turning my veins to ice. I stared at him, startled to see tears in his eyes. He blinked them back, his voice thick. "I have always loved your mother, JJ, and damn if I didn't know how to show it. I thought I tried, but . . . maybe I was just deluding myself."

"I didn't know you felt that way."

"I know." He met my gaze again. "Because I didn't tell you. It's not . . . it's not how I was raised. My father never spoke an emotional word in his life. Even on his deathbed, he never told me he loved me. It was always implied, just . . . never spoken."

I wanted to get outside. Dig my nails into the rocks. Feel dust crumble beneath my feet as I pushed higher, faster, and harder. *Conquer the mountain before it can conquer you.* It had always been our motto. But this metaphorical slope felt slippery, like I'd never get a foothold.

"I should have just told Kelly that I loved her. Let her know how I felt. Now I'm living in my own regrets, and it's my due." Dad leaned forward. "Whatever you do, don't make the same mistakes as me. Clear this up with Mark, all right?"

The waitress sashayed over, burdened with plates on a too-small tray. We dug into our food for a few minutes, grateful for the reprieve.

"How is retirement?" I asked.

"Quiet."

"Bet you love that."

He half-grinned. "I do. The fish don't."

I laughed. With the air cleared between us, we kept up a steady flow of conversation. Updates on Adventura. Dad's plans for retirement. Mark's new spa idea. Dad had kept up with Megan and knew about her relationship with Justin.

"He seems great. Glad she has him," Dad said as he reached for his coffee. "What about you? You ever going to settle into something?"

A few days ago, the answer would have been a firm *no*, same as always. But Lizbeth had rearranged the puzzle pieces of my future. Although I still hadn't seen her since the awkward ride home yesterday, I couldn't stop thinking about the fact that her hair was as soft as I had imagined.

"Yeah." I nodded. "Hopefully soon."

"Don't wait."

"I won't," I said, and I wouldn't. Dad was right. I needed to talk to her. Tell her how I felt. Clear the uncertainty so we could actually move forward.

This time, I wouldn't hesitate.

I'd talk now.

Dad raised an eyebrow at my response, took a sip of coffee, then nodded. "Look forward to meeting her."

"Was it worth the pain, Dad? To have loved and lost?"

Dad grabbed a fry and studied it before he nodded. "Every damn minute."

* * *

JJ: Just had a great lunch with my dad and am heading back. Missed seeing you this morning. Can we talk?

Lizbeth: Sure.

JJ: Great, I'll be home in thirty. Need me to bring you anything?

Lizbeth: I'm set, thanks.

Chapter Twenty-Nine

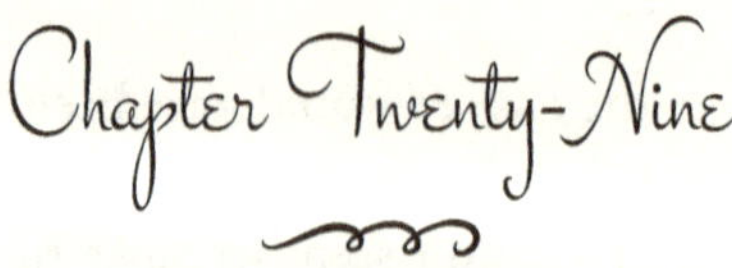

LIZBETH

With dread in my stomach, I stared at my cell phone. Although JJ's text had been innocuous, I had a feeling something was about to change.

Can we talk?

So simple, yet so terrifying.

Less than a day ago, I would have felt giddy at the thought of seeing him. Fearless. Now? Utter terror made me cold and shaky. What if JJ wanted to define this? What if he *wanted* a relationship?

I'd have to tell him no.

I wouldn't destroy his life.

A soul-deep crack had formed in my chest during my call with Dad. Now I had to do something different. Do what Mama *wouldn't* do.

I had to lean away from romance and love to save all of us.

I swallowed hard and started to pace. Two hours had passed since I'd hung up on my videocall with Dad. I still hadn't made it out of my cabin yet. My sniffles had subsided and the tears had slowed, but more were building up behind my eyes. Their pounding pressure threatened my composure.

Thankfully, no one here cared when I showed up to work, or how. Mark trusted me implicitly, which bought me some time to slowly get ready and to try not to think about Dad. Mama. And what all these revelations meant for me and JJ.

When a knock came on my door, my stomach caught painfully. I trudged over to answer it in fuzzy slippers, too-large sweats, and an old T-shirt of Bethany's. JJ waited outside, a bright expression on his face. He smiled so warmly.

"Hey," he said as he stepped inside. He shut the door behind him, then crossed the room in two steps. He touched my face with his fingertips and pulled me close. Our bodies molded against each other.

Breathless, I barely managed to whisper, "Hey."

He pulled away and cupped my face in his hands. The warmth of his breath caressed my cheek. For a moment, he just studied me. Then he smiled slowly again. His thumb rubbed my cheekbone in a gentle caress. My heart cracked.

The sheer romance of it would have broken me if my resolve to save both of us wasn't ironclad.

"It's good to see you," he said.

My voice cracked. "You too."

Lines formed between his brows. "Everything all right?"

"Yeah." I stepped away and gestured around the cabin so I didn't have to look right at him. "Just having a lazy day, I guess."

He stood there for a second, then tucked a hand into his pocket. "You seemed a bit off yesterday. Do you need to talk about anything?"

A lump solidified in my throat. I had just enough composure to smile around it. Concern filled his face, so I must have failed.

"No, thank you. I'm fine." I motioned to the bed. "Have a seat."

"Lizbeth?"

He followed me for just a step, then stopped. The cabin wasn't that big. I stopped with my back to the fire and forced myself to face him. We were only a few feet away, but it had never felt farther.

"You wanted to talk?" I asked as I rubbed one arm.

"I did." He nodded. "But now I'm not sure. What's wrong? Please don't lie to me. Don't say everything is okay when it clearly isn't."

Tears filled my eyes. I nodded and whispered, "That's fair."

"Have I done something?" He shuffled as if to move toward me again, but stopped himself. His nostrils flared as he studied me. "Did I say something?"

"No. No, this has nothing to do with you."

"Then what's wrong?"

"Me."

"You?"

"Yeah, it's . . ." I waved a hand, but the emotions built up in my throat anyway. "My obsession with romance." My voice hiccupped as I tried to hold back a sob. "I don't think this is going to work, JJ."

"What do you mean?"

His tone was carefully controlled. He'd canted his head slightly to the side in a way that was more wary than curious. My lips rolled together as I attempted to organize my jumbled thoughts.

"Mama was a hopeless romantic," I said. "She was also a lovesick mess. She chased an idealistic romance that didn't exist her whole life. Until recently, I didn't get that. I didn't understand. But now I do."

His shoulders relaxed slightly. "Oh. Well, we can talk about romance. We just need to define what you want and—"

"No, JJ. It's not that easy. I'm just like my mama, and she destroyed everything she touched. I think that if I let things continue this way with us, I'll regret it."

He drew back. "You'll regret being with me?"

"Not like that. No, not like that. I . . . I mean, what if I do to you what Mama did to me? To my dad?"

"What did she do?"

"What didn't she do?" I cried as a tear rolled down my cheek. "She broke our hearts. She broke my dad. She chased romance to her dying day and left a world of pain behind her. Mama loved romance more than anything, but the romance in her head wasn't real. Just like I think the romance in my head isn't real."

This time, he did step toward me. It was furious, controlled, anguished. "You felt something for me, Lizbeth. Don't try to deny it."

"I would never," I whispered.

He stood within arm's reach now. His presence seemed to fill up the room. My arms longed to reach out and touch his chest. Now that I'd started, I couldn't stop. I kept going, pressured to get the truth out before it broke both of us.

"Love of romance is the only trait I really share with Mama," I continued shakily. "What if I bring that here? What if I destroy you? I can't do that. I can't let myself be like her. Not even a little. I went to college because she didn't. I'm organized because she wasn't. I have plans because she didn't. I . . . I won't do what she did to the world."

Several long moments passed. Another tear fell down my cheek.

"I'm sorry, JJ. I can't do this anymore. This is beautiful and amazing and fun, but I have to stop it now."

"If it's beautiful and amazing and fun, then why do you have to stop it?"

"Because one day it won't be. One day it will be hard and difficult and maybe even scary. When that comes, I might break your heart. I might turn into Mama and leave devastation in my wake. Romance and love haven't been what I expected. For all the goodness and light I feel with you, there's the potential for as much darkness and fear. If things are good between us now, who's to say they won't be terrible later? I've been so wrong already..."

He frowned and opened his mouth, then closed it again. Tears blurred his form the longer I stared at him.

"Your parents," I whispered gently. "Aren't they a prime example?"

He sucked in a sharp breath. "That's not fair."

"Why? Because it's true? For the first time in my life, JJ, I've finally comprehended that there's a dark side to romance. That it's as much a force for bad as it is for good. I've spent years thinking love would save me. That it was only light and goodness and would sweep me off my feet into a better world, but that's not true. There's angst and pain and darkness too. I've just ignored it until now, and that's *exactly* what Mama did. So she chased it right to her grave. It's her darkest legacy, and she gave it to me."

He swallowed and stepped back. "Sounds like you've made up your mind."

"I care too much about you to do that."

"Don't do that." He shook his head. "Don't blame this on romance. You called me out on that once, and I'm doing it now to you. This isn't about me. This isn't about romance. This is about you and whatever you're afraid of."

A thousand replies surfaced, then dissipated. I couldn't keep up with all the little pieces of my broken heart. JJ ran a hand through his hair. The anguish in his eyes only fortified my resolve.

If it was this hard to bear now, wouldn't it be worse later?

"Lizbeth, I—"

"Please," I whispered. "Please don't. JJ, this is the only gift I can give you right now. Please take it. Let go of me so I don't break us later when there's so much more to lose."

He stared at me, then nodded once. "Fine."

My breath trembled when I sucked it in. "Thank you. I'm . . . I'm so sorry."

Then he was gone.

The crunch of his boots in the snow faded. I stood in the middle of my cabin until my knees gave out. It felt like someone had picked up my snow-globe world and shaken it. Disoriented, I struggled to stand in the same world, the same place, but a rapidly changing environment. The pieces would eventually settle, but not into the same spots. No, it was different now.

All the thoughts that had filled my head before vanished all at once. The vacuum they left behind allowed the pain in.

The crushing sensation of love was every bit as excruciating as I'd feared.

* * *

Somehow, I shoved JJ into a small box in the back of my mind, packed all my belongings, and forced myself back to Mark's desk in the office.

Once there, I kept my head down. The soft strains of Bocelli sang to me in the background and made my eyes hot. There was maybe an hour left of work that had to be done in the office, then everything Mark needed me to do from Adventura would be complete. The rest I'd do remotely.

Because I couldn't stand one more second of JJ's delicious smell. Not after I'd broken his heart.

JJ had disappeared, but I kept my head tucked to my chest and the chair on the shortest possible setting so the computer hid my face. I'd even thrown on a pair of old, fake glasses just to obscure my puffy eyes a little more.

Twenty minutes later, I sent Mav a text.

Lizbeth: Can you come get me? I'm all done at Adventura and can move back home. The rest of the work can be done remotely.

Maverick: Everything okay?

Lizbeth: Yep!

My entire body choked on the lie, but I sent it anyway. Things were okay between me and Mark. The erupting volcano was within *me*.

Maverick: I'm on my way home from Jackson City in a little bit. I can be there in less than an hour.

My heart clenched as I responded with trembling hands.

Lizbeth: Perfect. See you then.

One more hour, I thought as I shoved my phone into my pocket.

One more hour.

I perused a few binders I'd made for Mark. Double-checked everything in the desk. Reviewed my spreadsheet full of strikethrough font and color-coded descriptions of where each project stood. Almost all of them were done, so I updated the online interface with his business information to make sure I had it all so I could work remotely without having to call and hear their voices.

Puttering, that was it. I puttered around, trying to find something to keep me here. I would close out my life here today and be justified. Yet, my fingers wouldn't stop checking every-thing again. Maybe I'd find something to tether me to this place that felt so much like home.

Twenty minutes until JJ isn't a part of my life, I thought.

No, I almost snapped. *Stop it. Don't say his name.*

Nineteen minutes until freedom.

Eighteen minutes until that lovely, breathless feeling in the pit of my stomach never comes back.

Frustrated, I closed my eyes, drew in a deep breath, and stood up. This was the price I'd pay. Mama chased men. I wouldn't. Then I'd never be like her. In the end, it would be worth it.

Mark walked into the room, a triumphant expression on his face. Fatigue lines lay beneath his jubilance.

Interesting.

No, I thought. *NOT interesting. Not my business now, either.*

"Lizzy!" he sang, drawing out every vowel in an annoying chant. He did this every morning. I'd desperately miss it.

"Yes?"

"I may have another job for you."

My heart shriveled. "What?"

"Just an idea." He held up two hands. "We can talk details over later after J—dinner or something."

He stumbled over the words, suddenly stiff. That wasn't interesting, either. Nope. Not at all. There were other things to consider, like how was I going to close out this job? Didn't matter how, I just had to do it.

Finally, I swallowed hard and said, "Mark, I just finished everything that I need to do here."

"Great, let's look at your list. I think—"

"No, I mean *everything* is done."

He stopped, expression slack. Now it was his turn to be surprised. "Really?"

I gestured around me. "Everything is put together in your physical location. I've done what you asked me to do that requires me to be at Adventura. If you'd like me to refer to my spreadsheet—"

He impatiently waved that off. "What about the training manual for the website?"

"I'll finish that tomorrow."

"Great! We can talk about this then."

"Remotely. I'd . . . I'd like to go back to Bethany's. Tonight, if possible," I added quietly, absurdly aware of how terrible it felt to ditch them. "Maverick is on his way to get me. He'll be here any minute now."

Several long seconds passed. "You won't stay?" Mark asked.

"There's no reason to."

"There's every reason!" he cried.

"To do what, Mark?" My voice grew louder to match his. Despite my consistently professional demeanor, it felt good to let out some of the tension. "You're organized now. There's more space in this office than there has ever been. Everything is on the cloud, your data is safe, and your new Adventura website is launched." My words slowed. "You can feel justified in cutting back my pay now. I'll even continue to manage your websites if that helps."

"It was never about the money, Lizbeth. You're our friend. Practically my second little sister. Who the hell is going to give me crap now? JJ is a freaking jerk that I still don't want to talk to, but eventually will because it's what we do. You're . . . Lizbeth. You're the glue here. Lizbeth, you made this place finally smell good!"

My throat ached at the pain of holding back tears. "I know, and I appreciate that," I whispered. "But this is the right thing."

His expression softened. "Crap. This is about JJ, isn't it? What happened?"

Tears filled my eyes for the thousandth time. I just wanted to be home.

"Please, Mark. Let me go."

He must have seen something on my face. A manifestation of the terror that cradled my body. For a second, I thought he'd say something else, but he just nodded. When he ran a hand through his raven hair, it stood up on end.

"Of course. Whatever you need." He looked around the office, then back at me. With feeling, he said, "This place will completely suck without you."

Tires crunched on the snow outside, then came a quick honk. My gaze drifted to where JJ usually stood in the kitchenette smirking over my arguments with Mark.

But, of course, it lay empty.

Just like my heart.

JJ

A new cold front moved in from the west that evening, layering the office in an extra-stiff shield of ice outside. Justin tossed another thick log onto the fire, then settled back into watching a video on his phone. A stir of sparks danced up the chimney. Atticus sprawled on the floor.

A three-hour hike had worked off my initial burst of frustration. But it had done nothing to allay the soggy thoughts that remained. I'd thought so much about Lizbeth and her outburst that I was just confused now.

Mark walked in the front door. A brush of cool air came with him. He looked at me, shook his head, and shut the door with a sigh.

Seconds later, a folder full of papers landed on my lap.

"First of all, don't tell Lizbeth I printed this out, all right? She'll kill me for not using the online e-signature software stuff, but whatever. I'll get there. Those are all the signatures from the board approving your idea. We'll figure out summer later—not to mention how much rent I'm charging you for the kitchen. It'll be steep."

Relief that he wasn't still angry at me brought me out of my spiral. If I needed anyone, it was Mark. By the expression on his face, I could tell he knew that.

"Thanks, Mark."

Mark grinned, but quickly sobered. "Secondly, I'm sorry, JJ. Sorry that I flipped out and sorry that Lizbeth is gone. I don't know what happened, but Lizbeth left. She didn't look good. You all right?"

I nodded. "I'm fine."

He rolled his eyes. "Whatever. You're pissed, just own it. I would be too."

"Mark, I'm sorry about—"

He held up a hand. "Stop. You were an idiot and should have just told me."

"You're right. I should have."

"Were you afraid I'd say no?"

I shook my head and cleared my throat. "Not that. I really didn't know if it would work out, but I think I was still upset because you never told me about Mom and Dad."

He stared at me in wordless question.

"The divorce?" I said. "Their struggles? I didn't know about any of it. You and Megan both did. I've already talked to Mom and Dad about it. Although it wasn't consciously intentional, I think, deep down, I just wanted to do the same thing to you."

Mark gazed at the floor as he weighed that out, then nodded. "That's fair."

"What? No, it's not. It's stupid."

"Not stupid. Mom told me everything, JJ. Everything. I hated it. But she needed it, so I tried to be there for her. It was stupid and didn't cast Mom and Dad in a great light." He clapped a hand on my shoulder. "I guess I wanted to spare you the ugly. I'm sorry. As the oldest, greatest, strongest, and most powerful person in our family, I get a little too protective. I should have told you."

For a second, I tried to comprehend that. Dad's bitterness

toward Mom, and her reciprocation, had always driven me crazy. Bothered me more than it ever had Mark. Seeing it in that light, I realized Mark had actually done me a favor. He'd spared me pain and frustration.

"Thanks, Mark. I'm sorry. I didn't think of it that way."

He half-smiled. "I overreacted to your baking idea, and I apologize. We're in this together, bro. Whatever that looks like." Mark motioned to Justin with a nod. "You too. You'll be frosting the cupcakes."

Justin grinned. "Just don't let Megan in there. She'll do carrot or zucchini cake with coconut-sugar icing."

Mark laughed. While they drifted into a conversation about repair work that needed to be done in the pantry before summer, I let my mind slip away. Back to Lizbeth and her frightened face. The evidence of tear tracks on her cheeks.

Her romance books all had this. Heartbreak before the dramatic grand gesture at the end. But I reminded myself again that it wasn't real. This? Heartbreak? Confusion? Loneliness? This was the real end-product of romance. I should never have let myself forget. Not even Stacey had made me feel this devastated.

Although I couldn't help but wonder what Lizbeth thought of those books now.

Chapter Thirty-One

LIZBETH

A weekend at home with Shane, Bethany, Maverick, and Ellie had restored my brain to something like normal, even if I couldn't stop thinking about JJ.

All weekend I'd dreamed of Mama. Her dancing dresses. Bright lipstick. In the midst of baby time and couch snuggles, her voice whispered through my mind. I couldn't understand the words, but recognized the desperation.

Now, I sat in downtown Pineville and impatiently waited for my monthly book club meeting to start. The haunted, half-charred shell of the Frolicking Moose lurked across the street from where I sat in Carlotta's, the local Italian restaurant. I desperately tried to ignore the burned building. My thoughts came slowly, as if I were plucking at cotton fluff in a field. They gathered together in a loose ball, ready to be blown to the wind again at the first chance.

Then the warm, maternal arms of the Frolicking Moose Book Club surrounded me all at once. The women appeared out of nowhere and began to talk over and around each other. Relief at having them close filled me, salving my chapped soul.

"You've lost more weight," Stella said with a pinch to my

elbow as she pulled away. "Get some more food in you, girl. You're too skinny. Don't worry, I brought bundt cake! That'll fatten you up."

Stella was a sixty-something single woman who ran the grocery store in Pineville. She dyed her hair black every six weeks, plucked her eyebrows every Sunday, and always had a sparkling white smile for anyone. She was also as wide as she was tall and not-so-secretly envied my leaner figure.

"Leave her alone." Leslie scowled as she slipped into the booth across from me. "She's perfect the way she is." She sent me a reassuring wink, and I smiled. I'd missed her daily stop-ins at the coffee shop. In our book club, Leslie was the stable center to some pretty tumultuous book discussions. Today, she wore a bright-pink winter hat topped with a round ball. Grace, a retiree in her late seventies, had knitted it for her last month.

"Fresh lasagna from Stephanie on the menu tonight, ladies!" said Grace as she slid down the booth across from me, a bag full of knitting needles and yarn on one arm. "I called and talked to the cook myself. You know the secret is extra ricotta?" She sent me a wink.

Although Grace had a pillow of white hair on top of her head and spoke quietly while her knitting needles clacked in her arthritic hands, she had a saucy streak. All of her book recommendations ended up having naughty sex scenes. "Keeps a woman on her toes," she always said with a delicious shudder.

While the three of them settled into the booth, I tried to keep up with all their questions. They were the perfect distraction in the midst of the chaos.

Minutes later, Stephanie appeared with our lasagna. Four plates slid around the table, accompanied by silverware, the smell of basil and tomatoes, and piping hot squares of pasta I couldn't wait to eat.

"Lasagna night is my favorite." I leaned over the dish with a deep, tomatoey inhale. "You have my heart, Grace, for choosing it."

Leslie doled the rest of the lasagna and fresh bread onto each plate. Slippery pasta and ricotta cheese piled high on my fork when I took my first bite. Perfection.

Could JJ do better? Probably. He did everything so well.

Leslie slid our book forward. This month had been romance month. We swapped genres every month, repeating the cycle every six months.

"*His Hidden Secret*." She thumped the cover. "Not a bad one, if you ask me. But I think I need a break from Scottish lairds."

"Not me," Grace crooned. "I could read about those hunky men forever."

"It was good," Stella said. "But it wasn't great. The narrative was too aligned around description, and I didn't get enough back-and-forth between the characters. As a tour of Scotland, it was acceptable."

"Picky woman!" Grace cried. "Did you even notice the kissing scenes?"

"It's pretty unrealistic, as romance goes," Leslie said. "Where are the squalling children and annoyed moments? If there's not at least one scene with the wife almost slapping her husband, I'm out."

I chuckled around a bite of marinara sauce while the three ladies argued it out. The book had been a bit wordy. Of course, maybe even occasionally boring.

Somewhat repetitive.

I'd predicted every romantic scene almost to the moment.

Maybe I knew romance a little *too* well. It was hard to surprise me these days.

My phone buzzed against my thigh and caused a somersault in my stomach. Maybe it would be from JJ.

I snuck a quick glance at my screen.

A text from Bethany. I shoved it back into my pocket without opening it.

"Helloooo?" Stella crooned.

My head popped up. Three suspicious sets of eyes were locked on me. I ignored the buzz of another message.

"Sorry."

Grace lifted a thin eyebrow. "And who is more important than Laird MacLean?"

"Just a message from Bethany."

Leslie pointed a fork at me. "That aside, something is going on. You're so quiet tonight. You had no opinion on the first-kiss scene in the forest? Come on. Spill it. What happened? We're as much a gossip club as a book club."

"She's right," Grace whispered to Stella, who nodded. "We do gossip a lot."

I swallowed hard.

There was no point in lying to them. They were experienced women and could always see right through me.

Plus, I needed the help.

"Um, yes. Something did happen. With JJ Bailey and me."

"Now there's a man I'd like to see in a romance novel," Grace said with a conspiratorial gleam in her eyes.

Leslie leaned forward, lasagna dripping off her fork. "Does this have something to do with the accident?"

"Accident?" Grace cried. "What accident?"

"Tune into the local news once in a while, Grace," Stella said in exasperation. "She drove her car off a cliff, and he saved her as she was falling."

"Then her home burned to cinders," Leslie added.

"But those were two separate incidents," Stella clarified.

"It's like a romance novel," Grace muttered.

With a sigh, I related the events in full. Such drama-loving women were the perfect audience. They gasped, snorted, and sighed in all the right places.

Until I told the whole story, I didn't realize how badly I'd needed to say it all.

When I finished, the lasagna sat cold on our plates. All of them stared at me owlishly, blinking with stunned expressions.

"Well," Stella murmured. "That is *quite* the couple of weeks you've had."

"I just can't turn into Mama," I mumbled, then looked past them at the cold, dark remains of the Frolicking Moose outside. "She had it all wrong."

Grace slammed a hand on the table. "Disagree."

The rattling silverware made me jump.

Startled, I looked at her in surprise. "What?"

"*You* have it all wrong."

"How? I'm trying to save him and myself."

"You're trying to be safe," Grace countered as she picked her knitting needles back up and softly clicked them together. "You're trying to avoid the hard stuff. The lows are the things that make the highs so worth it, Lizbeth. You're afraid of something else, and you're blaming it on your mama."

Unable to comprehend that, I frowned. What else could be more frightening than being like Mama?

"Romance books are fun, but the stakes are a lot lower when it's someone else's life." Stella fiddled with a pearl necklace, her brow puckering. "I don't blame some of your disillusionment, as sad as it is."

"The books only cover a short period of time, too," Leslie pointed out gently. Her gaze slammed right into mine. "They don't show the long-term, difficult times. The boring times. The routine times. Your mama had it wrong in that she chased the giddiness of young love. But she missed the stability of sharing a life. There's something very romantic in that."

"You put too much on romance, Lizzy," Stella said as she covered my hand with hers. "You always have, ever since you started this club at sixteen. The way romance happens in books isn't always the way it happens in real life."

"I'm learning that," I whispered.

"Sounds like your mama never gave love a chance," Grace said. "She chased romance. Maybe she was afraid of something too."

I bit my thumbnail. What could have scared Mama? Aside from Jim in his drunken rages, or a life on the streets like she'd had after divorcing Bethany's father.

"It's the dark side of love," Grace said. "There's pain and loss. Sometimes there's a slow dwindling of the thing that once meant so much. When there's more to lose, it's scary. But without the ups and downs? You're not the same."

"Yes, but it's the downs that scare me," I said. "It's the downs when Mama was at her worst. The downs when Dad . . ."

My voice trailed off, thick in my throat. *When Dad was out of control and we took the blame.*

Memories hovered just this side of consciousness now, and I had a feeling *they* were what I feared the most.

Stella squeezed my cold hand with a loving smile. "You aren't your mama, Lizbeth. And JJ isn't your dad."

Tears filled my eyes. "I know."

"But do you really?" she asked.

"Why didn't you tell me?" I asked in a harsh rasp. All of them stared at me. "I broke it off with JJ but only feel pain. I can't think about anything else. I'm not sure I did the right thing. Why didn't you tell me that it hurt this much? That it was different than in the books?"

"Why ruin it for you early?" Stella murmured. "You were bound to find out one day."

"Such optimism," Grace said. "You have always been a reminder of what we had, and what we could have again, if we were brave enough to try."

"Well," I whispered, hands in my lap, "now I know. And it's absolutely devastating."

Leslie leaned over and wrapped a warm arm around me. "You're right. It is. But it's not the end, even if it feels like it."

For several moments, quiet hung over the table.

Thankfully, Grace turned the conversation back to a snowstorm moving in later that night, and then to overused tropes in romance books. My phone vibrated against my thigh, pulling me out of my inner spiral.

Numb, I answered it. Ellie's voice rocked me back to reality.

"Why aren't you answering your text messages?" she snapped. "Something is wrong with Shane. He's in the hospital in Jackson City."

* * *

My hair streamed behind me in bright, burning banners as I ran to the hospital elevator and jabbed the button three times. The hospital was a forty-five minute drive up the canyon, all the way into Jackson City. The drive had felt like a short eternity.

"Come on," I muttered. "Level three."

The speed of light wouldn't have been fast enough as I waited for the stupid elevator to arrive. The moment it opened, I rushed inside and jammed a finger into the circular three.

What felt like another eternity later, the doors chugged back open and I spilled onto the pediatric floor. Nurses and visitors whirled past me as I followed Ellie's directions, found the right door, knocked gently, and slipped inside.

Maverick stood at the end of a crib in a quietly subdued room. Bethany sat in a rocking chair holding a bundle of blankets with a clear tube trailing out the bottom. Her eyes were bloodshot and cheeks tearstained. Behind them, Ellie and Devin lurked by the window.

Tension filled the room.

"He's okay," Bethany said when she saw me. She sniffled. "Just some breathing trouble. They're doing a few tests. He's stable on oxygen right now."

Relieved, I collapsed onto a chair. "He's not going to die?"

"No." Bethany shook her head firmly. "He'll be fine."

Maverick stiffened, his nostrils flaring. He leaned over, whispered something to Bethany, then strode out of the room. At the door, he looked at Devin, jerked his head to the hallway, and disappeared. Devin filed out, leaving the three of us and Shane behind. The moment they disappeared, Bethany melted back into the chair.

"Finally," she muttered. "I thought he'd never leave."

Ellie shrugged at me when I sent her a silent question. Bethany and Maverick rarely fought. Something was clearly wrong, however.

When I looked back at Bethany, she leaned her weary head against a hand.

"Bethie, you okay?" I asked.

"Yeah, just tired and emotional and postpartum. Maverick and I . . . I'm fine."

"What's going on with Shane?"

Bethany gave me a brief update. Shane had been a little congested over the weekend, and it had been getting worse. Wasn't eating. Seemed limp and restless. Jada, Pineville's family doctor, had sent Bethany to the ER just in case. His oxygen levels were so low when he arrived that they'd admitted him immediately.

"A virus, probably," Bethany said. "He's so little he needs extra help, that's all. I think he'll be okay. Now that he's on oxygen, he's nursed better. That alone has helped because I'm not engorged. Squirted him right in the eye on accident."

She managed a pathetic attempt at a smile, but I felt only concern as I studied the two of them. They were both exhausted.

The smacking, suckling sounds that issued from the blanket every now and then reassured me.

"Why were things so tense?" I asked.

Bethany's jaw tightened. "Maverick blames me because I took Shane with me to the grocery store on Friday. He thought we should leave Shane home for the first three months of his life, but I can't deal with that. I'm going crazy at home, being cooped up all winter long. It was just the grocery store."

Ellie rolled her eyes. "Mav is being overprotective," she said. "That's all. He's stressed about a house he's working on. Renovations have been double his original estimate. Devin and Mav left to get some dinner, then Devin and I'll head back to Pineville."

The machines beeped overhead with colors and numbers I didn't understand, but Bethany's relative calm and the lack of hovering nurses helped me relax.

"Okay," I whispered.

Bethany eyed me. "How was book club?"

"Fine," I said too quickly.

Ellie folded her arms. Her gaze darted around the room uncomfortably. She'd always hated hospitals. Bethany studied me through slitted eyes, but had to readjust Shane, which bought me time to change the subject.

Within minutes, a more companionable prattle had filled the room, banishing the tension.

When Maverick returned with bags of food, Ellie and Devin took some and headed out. Shane had nursed himself to sleep, so Bethany stood up and passed him to me. I gratefully accepted the warm, sleeping bundle as she stretched her arms out and readjusted her bra.

"Stay with Shane for a bit?" she asked. I nodded. Bethany motioned Maverick out into the hall with a firm nod and pursed lips. He sighed as she followed him out.

Shane let out a little mewl as I got comfortable in the chair, then smacked his lips and settled back to sleep. My heart stirred.

Forget romantic love. Being an auntie was way better. I pressed a gentle kiss to his tiny forehead and stared at the oxygen tubing that led to his nose.

"Don't ever do this again," I whispered as I ran a finger around the shell of his ear. "Or we'll have words later."

My phone dinged with an email alert that I ignored.

When ten minutes passed and Bethany and Maverick hadn't returned, I dug my phone out of my pocket. The words *Pinnable Employment* on the preview screen made my stomach seize.

"Sweet baby pineapple," I whispered, frantically putting my password into the phone. Within seconds, I speed-read through the words.

We regret to inform you that we have not chosen you as a candidate . . .

My phone clicked as I closed it. I set it gently on the side table near the rocking chair, then leaned back.

Heat rushed into my eyes all at once. What now? What could possibly go wrong *now*?

This entire month had been nothing but obstacle after obstacle after obstacle. What next? *Anything else you want to throw at me, universe?* I almost yelled. A wordless, bubbling response surged through me. It felt like rage but tasted like bitterness, and I almost let it go. Instead, I pulled it into check. It simmered there beneath the surface.

Seconds later, Bethany stormed back into the room and collapsed against the wall.

"Bethie?"

"I don't want to talk about it." She sucked in a shuddering breath and a half sob. "I just need to cry for a minute."

Carefully, I stood. Shane stirred as I put him into the crib, and then I turned to Bethany in concern. I held out my arms. "Can you cry with me?"

She peered at me through her fingers like a lost child, then reached for me. I pulled her into my arms and held her.

"What happened?" I asked.

"I had a baby," she cried. Tears filled her eyes. "And these hormones are crazy. I feel like a psycho person that swings from one emotion to the next. I drink water all day long and it never feels like enough because I'm *so freaking thirsty* from breastfeeding, and Maverick is driving me bonkers. I'm so tired. He's tired. We're all tired from Shane being sick and work and being stressed. I just want my baby to be okay, and I want to be done breastfeeding."

She gripped my shirt in her fists.

For half a second, I expected her to let out a scream.

Then she did, right into my shoulder. It was a guttural thing, a cross between a shrill sob and a bellow of rage.

A giggle peeped out of me—I couldn't help it. I pressed my lips together in a poor attempt to hide it, but more giggles escaped me.

When she pulled away in shock, she just looked so ridiculous and exhausted and perfect.

Bethie stared at me, eyes swimming, until a half laugh, half sob burst from her. Then she really laughed.

Within seconds, both of us were belly laughing as we sank to the floor. The entire moment was so ridiculous it only made me laugh harder.

Minutes later, I sat on the floor, my sides pinching.

Bethany wiped her cheeks off with the back of her hand.

"Thanks." She sniffled. "I think I needed that more than anything."

"You sure you're okay?"

"Yeah. It's just . . . this is hard. And Maverick is trying to make it better, but he's just . . . just . . ."

"Protective?"

"Overbearing."

"Think he's scared?"

She blinked. "Why would you think that?"

I shrugged. "Just wondering. He looks overwhelmed all the time now. Like he's been staring too long at the sun and can't blink the aura away."

She giggled again. "Me, too, probably."

"I would describe you as more closely aligned with mama-zombie."

A rueful sigh escaped her. "Definitely. I'm sorry. I just needed to escape for a moment and get away from Mav. Does that make me an awful wife?"

"No. I think that makes you a real one."

Six months of intense pregnancy nausea hadn't done her any favors. She looked downright haggard now, and I wanted to fix it all for her.

Was this what Leslie, Grace, and Stella were saying at book club?

Maverick and Bethany always seemed to have the perfect romance, but it wasn't actually *perfect*. This was real-life romance at work. Bethie and Mav would pull back together—they always did.

So why wouldn't JJ and I also figure it out? came the thought. I pushed it away for now, but it hovered in the back of my mind.

When she wiped off her cheeks again, I wrapped my arms around her and pulled her close. She sagged into me for a moment, all limp and sisterly against me, until she pulled away and pressed a kiss against my cheek.

"Thank you. You're just what I needed." She scrutinized me. "Are you okay?"

"Fine," I said a little too quickly again.

"Liar."

"Not now," I whispered. "Neither of us are ready for this conversation now."

"Yes, now. Why did you refuse JJ?"

My eyes widened.

She gave me a *please* look. "Of course I know," she said before I could ask. "Ellie tells me everything. I've worked for years to get her to trust me, and now it's rock solid. She's worried about you. I'm worried about you."

"I didn't tell you because Shane—"

She cut me off by putting a hand on my arm. "It's okay, but it's time to tell me now."

Bethany had been my rock for the last five years. Not telling her about Mama and JJ and my broken heart had been eating away at me. While I was glad I could be home to help, in some ways I couldn't get away fast enough.

Home wasn't the same, because it wasn't Adventura. My homesickness for that stupidly perfect office—and JJ's smell —shook me.

"I'm afraid I'm turning into Mama," I whispered.

She reared back. "What?"

With a weary sigh, I said, "It's a long story, but I don't want to do to JJ what Mama did to Dad. I—"

The door creaked open, and a familiar woman with spiraling black hair and a warm expression peered inside. A white mask covered her face. Bethany lit up.

"Jada," she whispered. "You're here."

Bethany stood and embraced our town doctor. Jada moved to me next, warmth in her chocolate-brown eyes. The yellow gown that she wore over her clothes crinkled when I returned her hug.

"Lizbeth. So good to see you," Jada said.

"You as well."

Jada motioned to Shane with a tilt of her head. "Just here to listen and write some orders for the nurses. X-ray is concerning but not terrible. With oxygen and supportive care and time, we'll get him out of here just fine. Okay?"

Bethany nodded with a teary smile. Her hand clamped down on mine. "Thanks, Jada."

"I'll let you talk with her," I said to Bethany. "I'll be back in the morning. Let me know if I can bring anything back."

I gathered my things, murmured a quiet goodbye, and gave Shane a quick kiss. Visiting hours would end in fifteen minutes, and Bethany looked exhausted.

"You going to be okay?" I whispered to Bethany. Despite the years behind us, I still had a burning need for her to always be okay. For her to be safe, solid, and ready to bear everything, even if that wasn't fair of me to ask of her.

"Of course. I'll talk to Maverick when he gets back in here, I promise. We just . . . need to communicate our expectations better. This will all blow over. It always does. It's all normal."

"Really?"

She smiled and ran a hand down my face. "Of course."

"You and Maverick will be okay?"

"Yes!" She laughed a little. "We've weathered far worse than this, Lizzy. Of course, you were gone so soon, at seventeen, you missed a lot of it. Ask Ellie," she said wryly. "This is nothing."

"Can relationships recover from difficult times?"

The question sounded so innocent and silly coming from a twenty-one-year-old, but I couldn't help it. I didn't know. I wanted to know.

Bethany cupped her palm on my cheek. "The bad days make the good ones that much better. It's all part of the balance, Lizzy. It can never be all good."

Chapter Thirty-Two

JJ

My windshield wipers attacked the gently falling snow every ten seconds as I waited for the Zombie Mobile to warm up in the parking lot of the grocery store. A bag of groceries sat at my side. Mostly food coloring and novelties. I didn't really need them, but I couldn't handle the quiet of Adventura any longer.

After Lizbeth's departure, I'd been fortunate to land a surprising number of catering contracts, mostly for upcoming Christmas parties. When I wasn't in the kitchen, I lived on the snowy mountain. It soothed something inside me.

But riled all the rest of me up.

Every attempt to trace what had happened between me and Lizbeth failed. It had unfolded so fast I couldn't help but wonder if she was reeling in the aftermath too. Her attentiveness, zest for life, and expressive face had utterly destroyed me. My attraction to Stacey had felt nothing like this. In comparison, it was desperate. Lonely. Contrived.

But Lizbeth was real. She was hope. Light. Brightness.

Lost in my thoughts, I blinked when my ringing phone caught my attention. Megan's name flashed across the screen right before I picked it up.

"Hey," I said, relieved to talk to my sister.

"Are you brooding?"

I leaned back against the headrest and rolled my eyes. "I don't brood."

"Then you wallow. You must be wallowing. Mark said you've been an utter recluse. He's starting to get so lonely he's talking about a business idea with horses. JJ, you have to stop this. Mark on a horse? The world can't take it."

"Meg, what's the most romantic thing that Justin has ever done for you?"

If the question took her by surprise, she didn't reveal it. Instead, she responded as if she'd been waiting for me to ask. "He lifts weights with me."

"That was fast."

"It was an easy question."

I frowned. "Really? Weights?"

"Yeah."

"And you think that's romantic?"

"It's very romantic," Megan said. "It matters to me. It's . . . a connecting point. Time together. We both enjoy it, and then we get protein smoothies afterward. Health and boyfriend? The best."

"That's weird."

"You're weird."

That seemed fair. "Thanks," I said. "I was just curious. You doing all right, Meg? Justin's been gone a lot this winter. Now I know why he's all buffed out."

"I'm doing great. Debts are coming down, work is good, and Justin is better."

I scoffed. "Yeah, well, he's hogging you. We haven't gotten to see you enough."

She laughed. "I was calling to check on *you*. Mark told me about Lizbeth."

With a sigh, I said, "Don't use that tone."

"I didn't use a tone."

"*That* tone. The self-righteous one that suggests you know me better than I know myself."

"I definitely do, even if you're sort of enlightened."

"I'm not enlightened."

Megan sighed, and I felt a stab of guilt for making this hard on her. "I'm sorry about Lizbeth, JJ. It sounds like she's having a hard time. I'm sure you really miss her."

My throat worked as I swallowed. I did miss her. Like air, actually, and I hated that. Hated that segments from her stupid romance novels were coming to life in my world. Hated that something inside me had actually started to believe in her idea that *love and romance are a force for good in the world.*

Because she had been a force for good in mine. Everything I'd read about in those romance books had been utterly true. Tingles on my skin. Feeling breathless when she smiled. The desire to just be near her, even if we didn't speak.

"Yeah, I really do miss her," I said quietly.

"And I will concede that I used the tone, but it was appropriately placed," she said. "Now, spill. How are you really?"

My fist tightened around the steering wheel. "Angry."

"Good."

"Good?"

"At least you're saying it. With Stacey, you just went totally quiet. Mark said you didn't talk for almost a week. We had no idea what was going on in your brain."

"Stacey was more of an embarrassment than anything. While I was definitely sad, I can look back and see all the signs there."

"And Lizbeth broke your heart?"

"You know I hate that phrase."

"I know." She sighed. "But sometimes it's best to state the truth explicitly like that."

A gust of wind slammed into the Zombie Mobile, and I closed my eyes. "Maybe you're right."

"Sounds like she's trying to find the middle. Lizbeth has lived in both extremes. She grew up with the utter depravity of love that's used to manipulate. So she wove a different world, equally wrong but mentally safer. She used romance to feel safe. She's trying to land somewhere in the middle, I think. Her ideas on romance were a little naive, J. She's even told *me* about them when I've gotten coffee. You have to know that."

"Well, yes."

"This is her path. Let her be on it," Megan said. "Sometimes, the most romantic thing you can do is just be her friend and give her time."

"What if that's not enough?" My fingers tightened on my phone. "What if she sees this stupid plan through and doesn't ever come back? Doesn't ever date anyone?"

"She might."

"What if she's never ready?" I asked.

"That's the gamble of love. Be there for her, JJ. She's gone through a lot. I'm willing to bet she comes through."

All my hopes of Megan finding a way to fix this deflated like a bubble. She was right. I couldn't fix this for Lizbeth. But I wanted to.

"This is new for me," I said. I picked at a loose string on my pants.

"Very new for you. It's . . . surprising. I've never seen a woman unseat you from your vow of perpetual bachelorhood."

"Me neither."

"She's a good one for it."

"Love you, Meg. Good night."

After we hung up, I squinted at the sky. Talking to Megan didn't solve anything, but I felt a little better. Less cooped up in my own head, at least. I put the Zombie Mobile into gear and steered it toward the canyon before the storm blew in. My thoughts whirled like the incoming storm, and they all centered on Lizbeth.

Chapter Thirty-Three

LIZBETH

Restless, I drove away from the hospital as I headed down the canyon toward Pineville. Leslie said she didn't need her truck back until tomorrow, thankfully. It gave me time.

"You're trying to be safe," Grace had said. *"You're trying to avoid the hard stuff. The lows are the things that make the highs so worth it, Lizbeth. You're afraid of something else, and you're blaming it on your mama."*

What if she was right?

What was I *really* afraid of?

My thoughts rolled on to Shane. To Bethany's exhaustion, her annoyance with the person she loved the most. The broken expression on JJ's face when I told him to leave me. Pinnable rejecting my job application. My homesickness for the Frolicking Moose and Adventura. Mama's voice wound it all together like gossamer twine. She swam through my head in loops and forced me to ponder it all.

Love is everything, Lizzy, she'd said once. *Don't ever forget that. If you find actual love like you read about in the books, you hold onto it.*

Leslie's truck carried me to downtown Pineville just as

snowflakes started to fall. The little town was deserted in advance of the storm. Minutes later, I found myself parked behind the Frolicking Moose. Wind gusted against the truck, rocking it gently. Although the dark night swirled outside, I stared only at the harsh shadows of the burned shop.

For the longest time, I sat there. My thoughts scattered into strands that refused to gather into any semblance of order. Finally, I pushed open the car door, and a swirl of cool air revived me.

The back door of the Frolicking Moose was unlocked when I slipped inside. My footsteps echoed as I ventured into the main part of the shop. My chest felt tight as I studied the utterly changed interior. The inside had been gutted. The old cappuccino machine remained, scorched. Black marks marred the pantry. Soot and darkness climbed the walls, reaching upward.

I left all that behind and ascended the spiral stairs. Now that I'd come back, I felt lonely and overthrown. Like everything was shaking around me again.

The fire had run along the back wall, leaving the closet-sized office and stairs untouched. Ash and char filled my nose as I stepped onto the landing that led to the attic bedroom. I hadn't come before now because I'd thought I couldn't handle it. Couldn't bear to make all this loss real. My new reality.

Well, the new reality was here. Time to woman up.

Stepping into the attic stopped me cold. The mattress was a pile of ashes on the floor. The gauzy drapes around my four-poster bed were destroyed. Flames had swept across the back wall and claimed my entire bookshelf. A few titles were scattered on the floor—probably from firemen blasting them. Most were half-burned and sooty. I reached out and caressed the edge of one that had somehow survived on a shelf.

The book toppled to the ground, unseated, with a reverberating *crack*.

I stared at it and thought about the words in the book. The

romantic experiences I'd held onto so hard. Then my thoughts flittered to the night JJ had saved me from the cliff and to the date with Tyler. Two strongly romantic experiences that hadn't been anything like these books.

Had the books betrayed me, or saved me?

Maybe both, or neither.

"I'm not afraid of you," I whispered with a sudden realization. The books weren't the bad guys here. They weren't the reason I feared a life without the hope of romance or love. Without the dream of protection and security. A life without the possibility of being utterly and completely swept off my feet, breathless under the spell of someone else's affection for me.

No, it was something else.

The heroines always had this moment in the books. The moment where they struggled within themselves. When outside forces pressed on them and threatened to take away everything they'd always wanted. The love interest might break into the scene at this point and save the day.

That wouldn't happen here. I knew that. And I startled myself by not wanting it to, either.

The room felt cold as I carefully advanced further inside. The floor creaked but held firm. Only the floorboards on the far side were burned. For several minutes, I could only stare at the room, my breath puffing in front of me. Until now, it hadn't felt real. The loss was so poignant tears rose to my eyes.

I really *had* lost everything.

Another book sat on the ground, half-open. I reached for it with a trembling hand. My favorite. The one I'd tucked into my back pocket and carried with me when we'd trekked from Dad's home to the Frolicking Moose all those years ago.

Numb, I thumbed through it. Passages so familiar I could recite them verbatim swam in front of my teary eyes. Endless nights when I'd stayed up, picturing myself as the heroine. Imagining the love interest coming to find me.

Was all that wasted?

"Mama," I whispered, voice thick with emotion. "Mama, how dare you? How dare you give me false hope? How dare you make me like you?"

A tear rolled down my cheek. I shook my head, my hand falling to the side.

"You destroyed everything you touched. You're still destroying. I don't even know who I am now." My fingers fanned the smoky pages of the book, blackened along the edges. The words blurred through my tears. "I don't want to be like you, but I'm afraid I already am. That you've ruined me, even though you've been gone for so many years now."

I pressed my back against the wall and slid to the floor. Snowflakes fluttered by outside, thick as confetti pieces in the growing storm. A sob peeped out of me. I pressed my face into my knees and cried.

"I hate you, Mama! I hate you for what you did."

In a desperate move, I grabbed several pages of the book. The temptation to tear each one of them in half, throw them across the room, and scream my rage was almost overwhelming. But I couldn't. This wasn't the book's fault. This wasn't even my fault.

This was Mama's fault.

"Put it down, Lizzy."

The voice came from just behind me. My head jerked up. Bethany stood in the doorway with a concerned expression on her face.

"Bethie?"

"I followed you as soon as Maverick returned. I would have been here sooner, but I had to grab something from home."

Slowly, I stood up. She shuffled into the room, a coat hugging her torso. Her eyes were more bloodshot and determined than I'd ever seen. She wore a pair of boots she'd clearly shoved on in haste.

"Why?" I asked.

"Because you are *not* Mama, and Mama wasn't your enemy. Actually, she may have saved your life with all the romance she shoved into you. We have an hour to hash this out before I have to leave to feed Shane again, so get reading."

She threw a folder to the floor in front of me. Papers spilled across the ground, harshly white in the damaged room.

Before I could ask, she kept talking.

"I knew this moment of reckoning with Mama would come for both you and Ellie, so a few years ago, Mav and I paid a private investigator to dig up everything she could on Mama. I wanted her to build a picture of Mama's life from the very beginning."

Oh no. This didn't feel good.

Bethany nodded toward the papers. "Pick them up. She can't hurt you from here."

My hands shook as I gathered the sheaf together with soot-stained fingers. In the dim light from the window, the words were difficult to make out.

Bethany leaned against the doorframe with a weary sigh. "No need to read it," she said. "I've read it so many times I have it memorized. Kat St. Martin. Born four weeks premature in a small city in South Dakota. Her mother didn't survive the emergency C-section. She died from complications related to a drug overdose minutes after they pulled Mama out."

Ice formed inside me. A long, cylindrical, pulsing thing that spread cold through every vein in my body. I paused to listen.

"Things didn't improve from there. Mama went right into foster care. By the age of five, she'd been in three different homes. Can't imagine a five-year-old knowing three different mothers. Can you imagine Shane in anyone else's arms but ours?"

The thought made me quake from the inside. My body felt sluggish, my throat thick. "No," I whispered fiercely. I pushed off the floor, papers in my hands.

Bethany kept going. "By fifteen, she'd been in seven different homes and arrested twice for various minor charges. Petty theft. Some graffiti. That kind of attention-getting stuff. Apparently, and of no surprise to anyone in this room, she was a lot to handle.

"This is where things get interesting. Men from two of the foster homes she'd lived in—the one when she was five, and one when she was eight—were arrested on charges of sexual misconduct with minors after she was sent away. I'll let you fill in the blanks. The horrifying unknowns of her story. Can you imagine what she must have gone through at five years old?"

"Bethie," I whispered, chin trembling, "why are you telling me all this?"

Perhaps I'd always assumed Mama had no history. Or perhaps I'd just been too horrified by the possibilities to let myself think about them. I knew she'd grown up in foster care, but she'd never spoken in specifics of her time in the system. Never allowed questions about it.

Bethany watched me steadily. "Because we only knew Mama as the adult who was supposed to protect us and didn't. We saw only the survivor. The desperate one. The one so broken she broke everything else. Really, she was just a little girl looking for love. Like you. Like me. Like Ellie. Lizbeth, romance was what got *her* through. She was giving you a gift when she gave it to you. The only gift she had to give."

I sobbed. I couldn't help it. Bethany reached out and grabbed me by the shoulders. The puzzle pieces fit together a little too well.

"She broke me," I cried. "She shoved romance and love into my world and told me to believe in them. Now look at me!"

"Yes, let's look at you." She stood back, holding me at arm's length. "You are a beautiful, functioning college graduate. You can code faster than I think, and you have a successful future ahead of you. You have a family that loves you and will do anything to make sure you're fed and safe."

My lips trembled. "I didn't get the Pinnable job."

"Good."

"Good?"

"Yes. That was too far away. You'd have been miserable. I self-ishly just wanted to keep you close, too, but that wasn't why I didn't want you to get the job. You struggled with homesickness so much in college. You never wanted to be far away from us."

"That's true." I sniffled. "You're right."

"It's been quite a month. Your car is gone, so is your home and all the books you loved. That really sucks. You've lost what you thought was your dream job, and even after working at an impressive hourly wage, still have to pay down some debt. So you don't have enough money to buy some reliable indepen-dence back. Am I still on the right track?"

"Yes." Another tear trickled down my cheek. My voice cracked as I sucked in a deep breath. "I loved working for Mark. I loved Adventura. I want to go back. Bethie, what if I've messed everything up?"

"It's not too late for love. Which is fortunate, because you're in love with JJ Bailey."

I scoffed.

She glared at me, one finger raised. "Hey! Don't turn cynic on me now, Lizbeth. You didn't grow up your entire life believing in love just to let it go the first time it tests you. Don't you dare try to deny it. You love him, Lizbeth. You always have. That lovesick expression on your face has only gotten worse."

She was right. Brutally right. For all my declarations of being a romantic, I'd given up on it the moment the darkness descended. And I did love him, which made this even worse.

"You're right," I mumbled. "I do love him."

"Things have been tough for you lately, and I'm sorry that

you've lost so much. But can you see it?" she asked. "Can you see how loved and blessed you are?"

It took the rest of my courage to meet her eyes. How hadn't I seen it? How could I have been such a fool? I had so much that Mama had never had.

I nodded.

"Good." She dropped her arms back to her side. "Now, get all the ugly out. Tell me the hard stuff with JJ."

With a wobbly voice, I obeyed her command. From start to finish, we stood in the wreckage while I laid every moment out. All the time with JJ at Adventura. The small touches. His warm gaze. The sense of betrayal in his eyes when I tried unsuccessfully to explain why I wasn't good for him. My fear of being like Mama. Of turning JJ into Dad.

And finally, I heard myself say it.

"I don't want to end up alone, Bethie," I whispered. Fat, hot tears dropped down my cheeks. "If I end up like Mama, I'll be alone. I just want someone to love me. I just want to know they'll always love me." A sob broke through my words. "That's what I'm most afraid of. That's what Grace meant."

Bethie wrapped me tight in her arms, so tight I couldn't breathe, and I still tried to hold her tighter. Then I sobbed, venting all the ugly that had built up inside. She held me as I cried. Deep, cleansing sobs wrenched out from a painful place I didn't know existed. The pain, so encompassing, shook my very core. I held onto Bethany for fear I'd drown. All the fear of being Mama. All the terror of never knowing love. All the years of fearing that I'd end up alone, unloved.

Just the way Mama had entered the world. The way she'd lived most of her life. And the way she'd left it. She'd died alone in her car after revealing her plan to leave her second husband for another man. That wasn't real love.

Bethany's strength didn't falter. She held me through it all.

At the end of my emotional venting, I pulled away. Her thumbs wiped the tears off my cheeks.

"Wow, Lizbeth," she said softly. "You needed that."

A pause swelled between us. I felt thickheaded, like too much emotion had come out of me at once and left an empty shell behind.

Tears shone in her eyes. "You will never be alone," she whispered huskily. "You will never, *ever* be unloved. Not ever. So tell that frightened little girl inside you that she is safe, loved, and at home. There is nothing for her to fear again. You hear me? You. Are. Loved."

I nodded and whispered, "I love you, too, Bethie."

"Can we get something straight?" she asked, hands on my cheeks. I braced myself, because she'd switched to her sister-mama voice.

"Yes?"

"In an effort to keep from breaking JJ's heart, you decided to never give the two of you a chance to see what amazingness you could be. You left just as he was starting to do exactly what you wanted. Just as you started to feel something real."

Her explanation, stated so clearly, froze me.

"Oh no."

"Yeah. Do you see it?"

"I did it." I looked at her in horror. "I did just what Mama would have done. I ran away and broke his heart."

"When you fear something so much, Lizbeth, you end up creating it. Can you see that you're already bringing about your own destruction this way?"

The sobering reality hit like a slap.

"Yes," I whispered.

"Mama did her best, imperfect as she was. Can you see it that way? Can you see her offering for what she meant it as? Desperate love. Wild love. Love she didn't understand and had *never* experienced. When Mama gave you romance, she gave you the only gift she had—hope for a better life. She knew her best wasn't good enough, that you'd need a place to hide. That's why she gave you storybook love. She wanted better for you. If you hold onto your anger against her"—Bethany pressed her forehead to mine—"it's going to destroy you."

"What if I destroy others? What if I do to the people I love exactly what she's done to us? I could never forgive myself."

"You won't."

Tears obscured my view of her bright eyes when I pulled away. "How do you know that?"

"Because I know you, Lizbeth." She tucked a piece of hair away from my face with a soulful, loving gaze. "You have advantages Mama never had, goodness Mama never had. You're stronger than her. You're willing to go through the dark times and come out the other side. She wasn't. She didn't have anyone. You do. Even if Mama did nothing else for us, she gave us each other, didn't she?"

Bethany ran her hands through my hair with a warm, gentle smile. "Let her go, Lizbeth. Thank her for everything she gave you, then leave her in the past. Don't let her break you from the grave the same way she broke herself in real life. Can you do that?"

I nodded, unable to form the words.

"Good. Because I know you can, too. And honestly?" She sighed, a weary hand rubbing her face. "Just these past few weeks with Shane have made me realize the burden Mama really did carry. Sometimes, I think it's a miracle we're alive."

She glanced around one more time, then kissed my cheek and gave me one last hug. "Take your time here. You have lots of things to say goodbye to. Just remember that Ellie, Mav, Shane, and I are always home for you."

With that, she disappeared. I sank to the floor, Mama's paperwork still in my hand, and stared at the burned bookshelves. There was something oddly cathartic about the destruction. As I hiccuped and contemplated all those pages burning away, my thoughts turned decidedly less pessimistic.

When my thoughts turned to Mama, the darkness of her memory had ebbed slightly. In the midst of the wreckage, and with thoughts of JJ dancing in the back of my mind, I whispered, "Thank you, Mama. Thank you for giving me everything."

Outside, the lonely wind whistled in response.

* * *

An hour of quiet contemplation later, I finally stood back up. My legs felt stiff and wobbly in the cold. Outside, the howl of the storm made my bones shudder. This was a blizzard, worse than the one weeks ago. My eyes burned from all the emotion, and my cheeks stung with tears.

The attic looked different, although nothing had changed. I couldn't wait to get away. This wasn't my home anymore.

Nothing waited for me here.

Despite my stiff limbs, I hurried down the spiral stairs and into Leslie's truck. Snow fluttered everywhere, thick in the sky. It raced down my neck with an indecent tickle that set my teeth chattering. Cold air blasted into the interior of the cab as I cranked the heat all the way up. My thoughts were clear and crisp as a fresh day.

I was *not* Mama, nor would I ever be.

So I'd do what she never did: the hard thing.

Seconds later, I crept out of the parking lot and onto the main road. Wind tossed the snow with careless violence. It slammed into the truck. Ice shaped the roads into harsh white ribbons that disappeared in the storm. For two seconds, my tires skidded down Main Street. A flash of fear—and the swift memory of my car slamming to the rocks, of myself seconds away from death—caught me by surprise.

I gripped the steering wheel, grinding it in my hands as the truck came out of the skid.

JJ was worth it.

"Sweet baby pineapple," I whispered and braced myself. No one else could save me from this thing I'd been avoiding. Storm or not, I was going to Adventura to let JJ know exactly how I felt.

Love gave me wings.

* * *

My knuckles squeezed the steering wheel so hard they blanched white. An all-too-familiar mantra repeated in my head: *I won't slide off the canyon road. I won't plunge into the icy river below. I won't die tonight. I won't slide off the canyon road . . .*

Thankfully, the canyon remained open, though other cars were few and far between. The snowplows had been out, but the falling storm had quickly replaced the snow. Packed ice escorted me past the steep mountain walls.

The thought of JJ's touch on my face carried me through the storm.

Finally, what felt like an eternity later, I let out a squeak of surprise. The turnoff to Adventura loomed to the right. Though tempted, I didn't let my gaze drop to the frothing river below.

It had claimed plenty of cars by now.

With a careful foot, I pumped the brakes to test the road, then slowed.

My heart skipped a beat when the tires skidded, sliding to the left on their own.

With a smooth motion, I counter-turned and lifted off the brakes. The movement slowed.

"I've got this," I whispered.

Memories of impending doom slipped through my mind as I eased into the turn.

A snowy, dark bridge awaited.

The truck ambled onto it without a problem.

A long breath later, I'd crossed the whole thing, finding packed ground on the far side.

Shiny coconuts, but that was scary.

This road hadn't been plowed yet, and six inches had fallen in the last few hours. The truck barreled through it as I kept my attention on Adventura. The snowy conditions robbed my mind of the space to think, so I had no idea what I would say to JJ.

There was so much to explain.

Instead, I focused on getting there.

The road wound deeper into the canyon crevice until a familiar building appeared in the snowfall. The truck crunched to a stop as I parked not far from the Zombie Mobile, which was buried under inches of snow.

For five minutes, I sat there and stared at Adventura. A mixture of relief and trepidation filled me. For courage, I thought of my favorite books. The power the women showed at the end. The bravery in the face of uncertainty.

I could do this. This was real. Terrifying. Utterly unknown. My makeup was gone, eyes reddened, face blotchy, hair a mess. I smelled like lasagna and probably looked like I'd been in a car wreck. There was positively, absolutely, not a thing romantic about this day or the way I looked.

But I'd never felt more certain. More giddy. More terrified.

I could do this.

"I got this," I murmured. "I'm fine. This is fine. Everything is fine."

Then I shoved the door open.

There was no sound as I waded through the fresh snow and

up to the office door that I knew so well. My hand paused. Home waited inside. Warmth. Familiarity. Safety.

JJ.

Or maybe none of those things. This could flop, go utterly awry. He could tell me that he was never interested, that I had dreamed the whole thing up. That could happen.

And it would still be worth it.

I knocked.

Footfalls came to the door as my heart pounded, matching their rhythm. Then, all at once, it opened and JJ stared at me. He blinked once. Twice. Mark descended halfway down the ladder, stopped, saw my face, then slowly turned around and climbed back up with a goofy grin.

JJ opened the door wider. "Come in," he said.

I licked my lips but stayed rooted to the spot. The words flew out of my mouth in the midst of snow and surprise.

"No. First, I just need to say something. I'm in love with you."

JJ's expression fell. I rushed into what I had to say, because there was no other way.

Love was, or it wasn't.

"I'm the Queen of Romance, right? Read all the books. Watched all the movies. Absorbed all the possible scenarios. And I had it all wrong. I thought love was just the good stuff. The happiness. But love is that and so much more. It has a dark side. There are stretches of tough days, of heartbreak, of . . . routine. Those are the things that make the love so strong. So I was wrong. Romance and love *don't* exist the way I thought they did. It's different, but I think the real version is better."

He leaned against the door. I felt the weight of his whole attention all the way in my soul. My fingers fidgeted with the end of my sleeve as I kept going.

"I really believe that romance and love can change the world. That it makes people and things better. It . . . it got me through a lot, and I'm grateful for it. Mama, she . . . made a lot of mistakes, but the hope of love and romance wasn't one of them. I see that now. But I thought that if I let myself love you, I'd become like her and then I'd destroy you and whatever happiness we found."

His expression wrinkled, but he didn't say anything.

His silence allowed me to use up the rest of my courage and finish my very unrehearsed, anticlimactic speech with a little sniffle.

"I've loved you since the first moment I saw you walk into the Frolicking Moose. You have always been the hero in my dreams. In my books. Then you stepped into my life, and you were the hero there, too." Tears filled my eyes. "But it wasn't just saving me from going off the cliff with my car. That wasn't the most romantic thing you did for me."

"Then what was?" he asked quietly.

"Listening to me. Taking me to buy books. Putting your arms around me. Convincing Mark to hire me."

His eyes widened, and I smiled.

"Yeah, I know that this whole thing was your idea," I said. "Thanks to you, I see the truth now. You rearranged the way I look at the world until I feel almost like a new person. A better one. If that isn't love, then I don't know what love is."

We stood there, cold air whipping into the house from behind me, for a long pause. How would he respond? Was he about to thank me and then say he didn't feel the same way? Pressure built up in my chest until I thought I'd explode.

Finally, he reached out, grabbed my arm, and tugged me inside. His chest brushed against mine as he reached for the door and pulled it closed.

"C'mere," he whispered, his fingers braiding into mine. His breath was a warm caress on my cheek. "I want to show you something."

He led me through the office and out the back door. We sifted through the snow to my cabin. Although I couldn't tell what was going on, JJ was clearly on a mission. He had a determined expression in his eyes, as if he'd finally decided something. When we stepped inside, he flipped the light on. Nothing had changed except for a dozen books lying on the bed, spaced out evenly. He shut the door behind us but didn't let go of my hand.

"What is this?" I asked.

"There are twelve romance novels here." He drew in a deep breath and grabbed the closest one. "Each a different subgenre of romance. Can't believe there are *that* many, but that's a topic for another day."

"Why are they here?"

I scanned the titles. Most of them were familiar. I'd read almost all of them, but one was new. A thrill pulsed through me at the idea of having a new romance to read. JJ chewed on his bottom lip for a second.

A hint of color appeared at the top of his ridiculously perfect cheekbones.

"Because I read them," he said.

"You read them?"

He nodded. "Yeah. I read them. Not super intensely. Skimmed most of them over the past couple of days. There were others." He frowned a bit. "But I left them out."

"Why?"

"They didn't remind me of you."

"Oh."

He grabbed one. "This heroine, Kristyna something, reminded me of you because she had a lot that happened in her past, but she let go of it to become her own person." He tossed it aside to grab another. "This one? This girl reminded me of you because she stood up for herself and didn't take any crap." He ditched that with a flick of his wrist. "I couldn't put any of these down because all I pictured as I read was you. Your courage. Your tenacity. Your bravery. Then I understood what you meant.

These books are hope. When I pictured you in them, I almost felt like you were with me."

My throat clogged.

Was there anything more romantic than the acknowledgment of my beliefs? His validation that none of this was a lie? Love and romance were real. For him, they had been a force for good.

Finally.

He picked up another one. "But this one was my absolute favorite. I read every word."

My voice trembled when I whispered, "Why?"

"I saw you in this one because she didn't realize how much he loved her. How much he wanted to be with her. She was frightened that they'd destroy each other, so she left."

I swallowed. "What happened at the end?"

JJ turned to me, gaze on my lips, then back on my eyes. He yanked me into his chest. My breath caught when his hand found my jaw. His thumb lingered over my cheek, and he lowered his head until he was a breath away.

"She returned," he whispered. "And he told her that he loved her. That romance and love are real, and will be a force for good in their lives. Then he kissed her breathless until they both felt fireworks in their fingertips. They never had to part again unless they wanted to, but neither of them did."

His fingers threaded into my hair as he tilted my head back. My eyes fluttered closed the second his warm lips pressed against mine. I leaned into him. He wrapped an arm around my back to anchor me against his hard chest.

My bones melted. My body fused to his. I forgot everything but the gentle caress of that all-encompassing kiss. Everything between us was warmth and light and trust, and *this* was what a first kiss should feel like.

When he finally pulled away, his olive eyes, so murky with emotion, found mine.

"Forgive me for not coming after you?" he whispered. "For not telling you sooner that I loved you the moment I saw you staring at me from the other side of the Zombie Mobile after you almost died?"

"Always."

He kissed me senseless again until I didn't know where he started and I began. Until the velvet touch of his lips was as familiar as my own. When I pulled away, he framed my face with his hands. His thumb caressed my bottom lip.

"I didn't believe in romance, Lizbeth. Maybe not even love until you came along. But I do believe in it now. You're right. Romance is real. Sometimes it's heartbreaking. Sometimes it's sad. A lot of the time it's hard. But I also believe it's worth it. You are worth it, Lizbeth. And if you'll have me, I'll always be yours."

This moment always happened in the romance books: the turning point. The time when the love interest realized what an idiot he had been and confessed his feelings to the girl. It had made my heart thrill a thousand times.

More than once, I'd thrown the book across the room in annoyance—because, hello? Why did it take you so long to figure this out, stupid love interest?

During the long, lonely nights when Mama and Dad screamed at each other, I'd dreamt of this moment myself. The man who would come in, sweep me off my feet, and whisk me away from the hell I'd lived in so long.

And this time it felt *exactly* the way I wanted it to feel.

Like magic in my toes. Wings on my heart. Hope on my horizon. A safe place to land when all the world was dark and scary. Arms to hold me tight and promise me I'd always be loved, never alone.

"You're scared." I looked into his eyes. "Aren't you?"

He smiled softly. "Terrified."

"Me too."

JJ blinked. His expression softened. "Is it worth it to you, Lizbeth? The risk of love?"

"Yes."

JJ tightened his fingers around mine. "Then take a risk with me?"

I leaned into him and pressed my lips to his. His arms wrapped around me, his hands tangled in my hair, and I forgot to be afraid.

Chapter Thirty-Four

JJ

Mark stood in the corner of the Adventura kitchen, his cell phone pressed against his ear. He leaned back against the stainless steel refrigerator, nostrils flared, face puckered. Whatever the other person on the line said, it didn't look good from this end.

"Yeah," he muttered. "Okay. Okay. *Okaaaaay.*"

"Fine." He saw me looking at him, pointed to his phone, and rolled his eyes. "I promise I won't do anything stupid. Swear it. Okay, gotta go."

He hung up.

"My accountant," he muttered, "is the single most frustrating woman on the planet. I've never seen her face, can't remember why or how I hired her, she infuriates me almost every time we speak, and I will never, ever fire her because she is probably the only thing standing between me and utter bankruptcy."

I grinned. "Sounds like a match made in heaven."

He let out an exasperated breath. "I hope I never meet her, and I also hope she keeps telling me to stop making stupid decisions."

"She doesn't like the spa?"

"No. She thinks it's a terrible idea."

I couldn't help a smile. "But you're doing it anyway, right?"

"That depends," he drawled, then turned to Lizbeth. Just as his mouth opened to speak, she stopped him with a hand in the air.

"I already told you I'm not opening an agency," Lizbeth said from across the kitchen where she sat, her computer on her lap.

"Fine." Mark leaned against the wall and folded his arms, chewing his bottom lip in thought. "Then what if JJ opens his own catering service from Adventura, and you do the website design? We'll hire out all the back end. I do have an awesome accountant. She's irritating as all get-out but does her job well."

"That's up to JJ."

Mark groaned. "He's never going to do it. But if you have the agency and—"

"You don't know that." She fluttered a hand in a dismissive gesture. "Now, go away, Mark. JJ is making frosting next, and then we'll be back inside to start the Christmas Eve festivities. Tell Meg I'll bring some more drinks."

He scoffed. "You just want me to leave so you can make out."

"Totally," I said with a grin, the dry scent of flour in the air.

Lizbeth grinned at me and winked. Several massive cinnamon rolls cooled behind me as I slid another tray of carefully rolled balls of dough into the oven.

Mark thoughtfully drummed his fingers on the counter. "Fine, Lizbeth. Maybe you don't have an agency, just a solo venture. But my offer to back it still stands." Mark held up two hands. "I'm just saying! The board members were so impressed with the dashboard and what you did for Adventura that I don't think you'll be able to do all the work they're going to have for you all by yourself. Hence, agency. Final word. I'm out."

He backed out of the door, two hands held up in a placating gesture.

Once he was gone, Lizbeth set aside her laptop and

crooked a finger at me. Ever her obedient servant, I closed the distance between us. Her body pressed against mine as I wrapped my arms around her waist and pulled her into me. She hooked her legs around my midsection and pressed our lips softly together.

"I love it when you do that," I murmured against her lips.

Startled, she pulled back. "What?"

"Put Mark in his place." I grinned. "It's super sexy."

She tilted her head back and laughed, but didn't let me go. "I appreciate his help in starting my own company to help people with online coding problems, but it's my company. Not his."

"The flexibility you have doing an online job is amazing. Since Mark isn't charging you rent in exchange for free tech support."

"He couldn't afford me otherwise," she said with a wicked smile.

I laughed and ran my hand over her thighs, then up her back. She stared into my eyes, all warmth, light, and hope.

Snow fell outside. Christmas lights glowed from the office—put up by Justin under her strict supervision. A small Christmas tree decorated by Megan and Justin was visible through the front window. The festive mood of the season had lightened all of us.

Next to us lay a well-worn and familiar binder covered in pink hearts. She'd obnoxiously scrawled Lizbeth and JJ's Love Binder and kept daily tallies of all the most romantic things we did.

At the top of her list? "Snuggle on the couch while JJ makes me laugh" came just before "read quietly while JJ plots out new climbs."

I wholeheartedly agreed. Lizbeth was my kind of romance.

"Can you believe it's Christmas Eve?" she asked.

"No."

"Cinnamon rolls for Christmas breakfast sound perfect, by the way." She pressed her forehead to mine, nose adorably wrinkled. Her voice dropped to a whisper. "I think you have great ideas."

"You were my best idea."

She smiled. "I also agree with that."

Breathless, I could only stare at her for a moment. She wore a little Santa hat with a white shirt and red Christmas pajama pants that clashed horribly with her hair. Her slippers were obnoxiously fuzzy, and she smelled like evergreen.

Somehow, she was mine.

I stepped back and reached into my pocket.

My hand trembled as I set a box on her leg, my fingers closed around it.

"I have your Christmas present right here," I said.

Her expression brightened. "Do I get it a day early?" she squealed.

Shakily, I grinned. "If you want it. I wanted to give it to you when we were alone so I could just . . . watch you."

She sobered, and her hands came to rest on my shoulders.

"JJ?" she asked breathlessly.

I pulled her off the counter and set her gently on the ground.

Then I dropped to one knee and opened the box. My voice shook when her hands rose to her face, covering a startled gasp. Her eyes grew wide as saucers.

"Lizbeth, I love you. I love you more than I ever knew possible. I will always love you. I will always protect you. I will always be here, through the good and the bad, the fun and the scary. You'll never be alone, and you will never be unloved. Will you marry me?"

For an interminable amount of time, she simply stared at me, frozen, most of her face hidden behind her fingers.

A bolt of fear struck me.

Then her hands fell.

Tears sparkled on her cheeks.

My heart stammered.

"Yes."

She whispered it as she reached out to touch my face. The wetness of a teardrop lingered on her fingertip.

"Yes?" I repeated.

"Yes!" she cried. "JJ, yes!"

I leapt to my feet and swept her into my arms. We whirled around the kitchen, laughing, until I stopped and slid the ring onto her finger. A pink diamond, heart shaped, sat in the middle of a circle of smaller white diamonds. The simple setting looked perfect against her skin.

With tears in her eyes, she studied it, then me.

"Was this enough?" I asked with a quick glance around us at the warm kitchen. "Was it . . . romantic and . . ."

"JJ, I've never felt anything more perfect. I've never felt so loved. This was romantic perfection."

I sealed our future with a kiss. Lizbeth melted against me and I caught her.

I always would.

Runaway

A SNEAK PEEK INTO THE 3RD BOOK.

Drizzling rain pattered my windshield as I stared at a cabin built by long wooden logs stacked on top of each other. Faded white lines lay between each log, making it look ancient. Rain stained the logs a darker shade of brown, and a little wisp of smoke rose above the chimney despite the rain.

The longer I sat out here in my beater car that didn't even have a real license plate yet, the weirder this whole situation became.

And it was already *pretty* weird.

Still, there was one man that could help me, and that man both resented my existence and desperately needed it. He also proudly lived the life of a hermit in the mountains—I mean, who bragged about that?—and hated all details.

Mark Bailey.

And that alone seemed pretty ridiculous, but so was this entire situation.

A few more moments passed while I rallied my courage. In fact, I prepared myself like this every time I had to talk to Mark. I'd clutch the phone for a few minutes, think through every sentence that I *had* to say, and then hope that he didn't wander off on a list of his ideas. Eventually, he would wander. He'd talk things out, and I'd have to pull him back to reality and the main points that he'd called for anyway.

Lately, he'd called a lot more often than usual.

Today would be very different, however, because we'd be face-to-face for the first time. For half a second, I stalled this confrontation while trying to picture what he looked like. Mark and I had always spoken on the phone. He called me out of the blue one day, declared his need for an accountant, and proceeded to tell me about every business venture he'd ever started. For a man that hated details, he had a mind like a steel trap.

Plus, I'd seen his tax returns too many times. He was overly generous on charitable contributions—to the point he sabotaged any profit from his company. A bit of a bleeding heart, really.

Blonde, I'd guess. He sounded nice enough on the phone, so probably straight-laced, with short hair like a businessman and clean dress. He was single—at least his tax returns weren't filed jointly—and had no other income besides his own. Slight of frame, maybe. Like Ryan Gosling?

With a jolt, I shook my head. No, I had to stop assigning actors to everyone I met. It just . . . made people easier to approach.

With a shove, I forced myself out of my little car and into the pounding rain. It slammed into my shoulders while I shut the car door, then skirted the edges of a dirt pathway filled with water. Mud squished under my shoes as I hurried under an eave and forced myself to knock. The only thing that kept me moving was momentum. If I thought too hard about this, I'd just leave.

Ten seconds after I knocked, the door flew open. Out of sheer nerves, my heart fell all the way to the pit of my stomach.

And then I burst out laughing.

A tall, broad-shouldered bear of a man glowered at me. He had brown hair, almost black, that stuck up in odd angles from the back of his head. His beard hadn't been trimmed in days. He wore no shirt and gray sweat pants with a pair of flip flops on his feet. My glance was quick, but he certainly wasn't *slight* or *business-like* in any sense of the word.

The man had muscles.

A hibernating bear came to mind first. Hardly Ryan Gosling. Hardly what I always pictured on the other end of the phone. Somehow, though, this was better. First, who would mess with me if *that* scowl came to the door? Not many. Second, I could fit his voice with this guy.

This was a wild Mark Bailey.

Quickly, I drown my amusement in the face of his dark annoyance. Now that I thought about it, this may not even be Mark. He spoke about a brother, JJ, often enough. Behind him was a warm-appearing cabin, with a snapping fire that let out heat. A trickle of rain ran down my back, and I shivered.

"Are you lost?" he asked.

"No, I . . . I'm looking for Mark Bailey."

His eyebrows lifted. When he said nothing more, I realized that was the only response I could expect.

"Are you Mark?"

He nodded. I rolled my lips to school my laugh. No, I couldn't laugh at him again. He'd hear the wild hysteria. The tinge of desperation and fear and uncertainty that belied everything in my life now. Then he'd turn me away.

"I . . . I'm . . ."

My name hovered on the end of my tongue. *Stella Marie.* Did I dare say Marie? I'd always run my accounting business through my middle name—didn't want the world to know my first name, felt too much like an invasion—so the two names together may not clue him into who I was.

But maybe the sound of my voice *and* the name Marie would get him to thinking.

In a perfect world, I'd get through this confrontation without him knowing who I was. Mark tried to hide it, but he was always frustrated with me. Didn't like when I curbed his wild ideas with sound financial sense. If there was one thing Mark felt like he didn't have, it was time. He was in a hurry for everything even though he was what, 31? Two years older than me?

Money didn't always run at the same speed as Mark, and that galled him to no end.

"My name is Stella Marie," I finally said. Grandma had named me. *You are Stella Marie,* she always said. *Not just Stella. Be proud of your heritage.* So it felt strange to hear Stella without the Marie.

Even now.

His gaze tapered further. I swallowed a squeak of fear and the desire to ask if I could come inside. No, of course, I shouldn't ask that. I wouldn't let me inside if I were him. He hadn't let go of the door, giving me unparalleled access to his abs. By sheer willpower, I kept my gaze on his face.

"What are you doing here, Stella Marie?"

"I . . . I need some help. I heard you might have a cabin to rent."

Confusion clouded his annoyance. "Who told you that?"

No one, I thought. *Just the hope deep in my heart and what I know of your world.*

"Oh, just driving through town." I waved an airy hand in the vague direction that I *thought* Pineville would be. "I need a place to stay and I'm willing to pay cash. Maybe just for a month or so?"

His brow furrowed.

Please, I thought. *Please don't care about these details. You never have before . . .*

"Who in town told you to come here?"

Dagnabbit. Of course, he had to ask questions *now* of all times. The conversation we'd had a few months ago when he said he wanted to start a ride-a-horse operation ran through my mind. He hadn't asked how much it cost to keep a horse alive or pay vet bills or bring hay into his canyon or any of that.

No, he just found a horse he thought was handsome and wanted to try it out. Thankfully, I'd backed him out of the idea. He hadn't been happy at the time.

Now he had to know who sent money his way? Mark needed money as desperately as I needed to disappear. Why didn't he take the offer?

"$500 a month for a small cabin?" I said. Perhaps he'd be deterred away from *how* I came to know him and focus on the dollars. "I can pay in advance if you want the cash now."

The cash burned a hole in the back pocket of my jeans, but I didn't reach for it yet.

He leaned against the doorframe instead, seemingly unbothered by the misty fall air that flowed past him into the cabin. No one else had stirred inside, and I caught a vague peek of furniture and a can of something pried open with a spoon sticking out of it. Bachelor, I'd bet.

"Why do you need a place to stay?" he asked.

"Does that matter?"

His brow lifted. "It does now."

My nostrils flared. I wasn't good at this. Lying, deceptions, sneakiness. I just wanted to find a place where I could hole up and not see anyone for a while. Maybe I'd been naive to think this would be easy. To show up on his doorstep and ask if I could live with him? The man lived in the middle of a mountain canyon? *No one* drove out here unless they had to, which was perfect.

My breath was shaky when I let it out. "I just . . . I need

someplace to disappear for a while, and I've heard that you cabins to rent and no one comes out here."

He snorted. "You're hiding."

Yes, I thought.

I didn't answer him out loud, just studied his face. Beneath all that beard and wild hair, I could sense a general kindness. His gaze had an edge to it, however. He straightened up. "Look, I'd love to help. I really would. Being the nice guy used to be my favorite thing, but I'm kind of over it now. My brother just got married and moved out and I just initiated this plan to go full mountain man this winter."

I blinked. *Full mountain man?* What did that mean? The words rushed out of me before I could stop them.

"But why?"

He shrugged. "I don't know! Seems like a good idea. We'll see how it pans out. I'm full of ideas, and sometimes the ones that seem the most stupid are actually the greatest in the end. Regardless, I'm not harboring a sketchy fugitive from the law that's lying about someone in town telling her I'd rent a cabin for $500 a month on my property. Sorry. No one in town would have sent you here to rent."

My heart pattered in my chest as he reached for his door and began to close it.

"I go by Marie sometimes!"

Two inches before it shut, the door stopped. His fingers tightened around the edges, but I couldn't see his face now. A lump filled my throat and I swallowed it. My voice rang out clear despite my worry. I shivered but wasn't entirely sure it was from the cold.

"If you listen hard, you might recognize my voice. My full name is Stella Marie Lee, but I do business under Marie Lee. Mark, I know you're always annoyed with me because I stifle your ideas and I honestly have no idea why you still pay me to do your books, but I . . . I need some help."

Slowly, the door opened back up.

* * *

I hope you enjoyed the sneak peek of *Runaway*!

Go to katiecrossbooks.com or any online retailer to grab your copy.

—Katie

Acknowledgments

Good grief, how does this process surprise me every time? You'd think after writing as many books as I have, I'd be used to this.

But oh, no.

Books are like kids. They all have attitudes. Which makes the process different every time.

LOVESICK was a real terror, joy, and unfathomable mystery all wrapped into one. I had a blast writing it—when I wasn't sobbing over a wayward plotline or a character I *just couldn't figure out*.

To that end, I want to give another thank-you **to the OGs at KCW** that helped me immensely with this project.

A) for letting me think out loud and shooting down my truly awful ideas until I peeled away the sticky heart center.

B) for picking up the pieces in the company while I shut the world away to just *write it already*.

My full team at KCW: Where would I be without you? All of you mean the world to me and I'd be lost without you having my back.

My production team: McKenna, Catherine, Gemma, Darcee, Jenny, and all the others. THANK YOU so much for making my books so beautiful. Kristen, without you setting up a fake dating profile so we could do online dating research (that didn't even make it into this book, of course! XD) what would we have laughed at?

To my sisterwife, Ali: Without you to co-parent our children, this book would still be buzzing in the back of my mind.

Thanks for letting me help raise your kids while you help raise mine.

Husband, you are the JJ to my Lizbeth and I'm constantly lovesick for you. **Little Man and Warrior Princess,** you constantly infuse my life with love and adventures. My world would be empty without you. May you always use books to find your way, as I do.

And to the amazing **Claire Cain**, thank you for the phrase "sweet baby pineapple" and for letting me use it in this book! If you want to read her book where I first encountered such an AWESOME phrase, check out *Where You Go: A Sweet Military Romance* (The Rambler Battalion Series Book 1).

Finally, to **the most important people of all—my readers**. I absolutely adore you, all of this is for you, and a worthier audience could never be had.

MUAH

About the Author

Katie Cross is ALL ABOUT writing epic love stories and wild places. Creating new books is her jam.

When she's not hiking or chasing her two littles through the Montana mountains, you can find her curled up reading a book or arguing with her husband over the best kind of sushi.

Visit her at www.katiecrossbooks.com for free short stories, extra savings on all her books (and some you can't buy on the retailers), and so much more.